GIRLS
IN THE
GAME

Nikki Turner

PRESENTS

STREET CHRONICLES

GIRLS IN THE GAME

ONE WORLD

BALLANTINE BOOKS

New York

Copyright © 2007 by Nikki Turner
Street Chronicles copyright © 2006 by Nikki Turner
Introduction copyright © 2007 by Free
"Crowning Miss Baby Mama" copyright © 2007 by The People's Choice
"Power" copyright © 2007 by LaKesa Cox
"Bossy" copyright © 2007 by Tysha
"Game Face" copyright © 2007 by Meisha C. Holmes
"Beyatch!!!" copyright © 2007 by Joy
"When the Dust Settles" copyright © 2007 by Wahida Clark

All rights reserved.

Published in the United States by One World Books,
an imprint of The Random House Publishing Group, a division of
Random House, Inc., New York.

ONE WORLD is a registered trademark and the One World colophon is a
trademark of Random House, Inc.

ISBN: 978-0-7394-8619-1

Printed in the United States of America

Got our name from a woman, got our game
from a woman. . . .

—TUPAC SHAKUR

DEAR READER:

Have you ever heard the saying, "Beside every great man stands a great woman"? Well, the truth of it is behind every great man stands a great woman pushing him in the back to get him off his butt to make sure he handles his business.

When the game is referred to, it's usually the men who everyone automatically assumes are in control, running the show. Shot calling, hustling, balling, grinding, or pimping, it's the male icon that's glorified. But no one talks about his female counterpart, who more times than not, holds it all together for *her* man. For every Bishop Don "Magic" Juan, there is a Madame Marie LeVeau, and for every Clyde there is a Bonnie.

This collection of stories is not a celebration of the gangstress, pimpstress, baller chick, boss bitch, or female hustler, but a depiction of a lifestyle, the description of the unsung, and their yet untold stories. Every fable told isn't a fairy tale because every life lived doesn't have a happy ending. This is the game, from a female's perspective, penned and endorsed by some of the hottest girl writers in the game. These stories present the reality of many who lived it, and some who didn't make it through. If you can't congratulate, *don't hate,* stay in your lane and, most important, acknowledge . . . the *Girls in the Game!*

Some people may sit back, look down their noses, and judge the women in these stories from the safety and sanctity of their own world. They may call them whores, bitches, connivers, or sluts, but until they've faced their reality, they will never know what they would do if they were in these women's pumps. Others may take a look inside these chronicles and see someone they know, someone they've met, or maybe even see themselves and realize they're not alone.

Whatever you get out of these pages, don't forget that it's a dirty game and *women are usually the best players.*

I thank you from the bottom of my heart for picking up this book. It's always good to see one sister supporting another . . . and I am glad you chose me. But to you, my brothers, make no mistake about it: I love you like a fat bitch loves cake, but this one time I had to go all out for my sisters and get on some real Girl Power. I promise you, the next one's for you!

Much love,
Nikki Turner

WORD ON THE STREET

INTRODUCTION

BY FREE

Now just the title of this book alone can have your mind and thoughts all over the place, depending on who you are and where you come from. What is the game exactly? Is it like Monopoly or chess? Or both? Are you playing, or are you being played? Well, the game is what you make of it—or don't make of it. It's your choice completely.

Now being a girl in the game is as much acknowledging your power as it is being humble about it. Believe it or not, a girl can make or break a kingdom, hold up or tear down a house, make love or make war. You might ask how this is possible, when it's a man's world—or so they say.

But it's really not. Men can't have babies, so how could this be their world? Some male testosterone shmuck put that out there and it stuck. But what if they are right and it really is a man's world? Ladies, let's all just stop moving, breathing, speaking, reading, kissing, cooking, growing, treating, nurturing, and supporting and see what exactly will happen to the world.

A girl in the game must recognize early on that power is not about winning, or about cameras flashing, and that most of the time, once you get the power, you become the enemy and are looked at as having the strength of a man and will be treated like one. Watch out! Be careful what you wish for, and most of all be ready when you get it.

I read Assata Shakur's open letter to the United States. Google it ladies, and read it and weep. There's a part in her letter in which she describes a "marooned woman" as "the women of the tribe that were 'supposedly' disgraced by rape or deaths of their husbands and therefore they were pretty much ostracized from their own villages and left to fend for themselves." The idea of a marooned woman struck me. We aren't the only ones who the government "helped" become independent of our husbands in order to further the division in the race. Marooned women are also girls in the game who are stuck in catch-22's, never able to straighten out.

A girl in the game must choose her suitor well. Pick a slouch and she will be looked at as one. Pick a king and she will be treated like a queen—but only if he is a true king. But if she's a true queen, she will know that she can reign alone.

A man once told me when I was in a bad situation that you could either be the rug or the person walking on it. The truth of his words was revealed to me time and time again. This was a pearl of wisdom I wish I had lived by, but it's never too late to start. Here are a few more jewels that I've learned in my life that I'd like to share with you:

Check your emotions
Keep your own stash of condoms
Choose your suitors wisely
Remain true to your dreams
Cut and let go when shit ain't right
Be ready for power and all that comes with it
Settle for nothing
Stand proud, because you're a Girl in the Game!

Free is a singer, writer, radio and television personality, and a true girl in the game. She lives in Los Angeles.

GIRLS IN THE GAME

CROWNING MISS BABY MAMA

Definition of a "baby mama": That chick who will spite the current girlfriend or wife of the man she had a child with (aka baby daddy), and who will be connected to and able to get what she wants out of the baby daddy for life!

hoever thought a hood rat, guttersnipe young bitch like me would be rocking this nigga's world? I thought as I watched Li'l Man walk to the bathroom ass-naked. I'd just given him some of the most amazing sex of his life. The one thing that he loved about me was that I was a young thang who hadn't been passed around like some of these old chickenheads cluckin' around, so the punany was fresh. And unlike the old heads, I can be folded into any pretzel position his little heart desires.

Meeting Tyrone Simmons, known in the streets as Li'l Man,

was a once-in-a-lifetime opportunity for a nothing-ass crumb snatcher like me. I know it sounds harsh, but it is what it is. According to many psychologists, the first step to progress is acknowledging your faults. That theory alone has done the most to bring me to where I am in life. To understand me, one must study my game: the sweet roll of the dice that it took to make Li'l Man fall for me. But first, let me tell you the history behind my so brilliantly played game.

Although Li'l Man was born and raised in Tidewater Park in Norfolk, Virginia, just as I had been, he was fortunate enough to have reached extreme heights. He was no longer living in the concrete walls that kept the bullets out and the roaches in the Park. "Park" is the name Norfolk city officials have so generously given the projects to create some sort of false image. They put up white picket fences, hoping to convey the idea of a park. Unfortunately, the projects are quite different from the parks where there are happy families spending sunny days in green grassy fields flying kites and having picnics.

In the projects there are dark brick blocks that cast an everlasting shadow. The green grass is replaced with dirt paths leading through alleyways used as quick getaways from the cops and as hideouts for hos and addicts. The smiling faces have been replaced with faces of praying grandmothers who look upon unhappy families, including a cracked-out daughter, a locked-up son, and an HIV-positive grandbaby.

One thing for sure: Just like the park, the projects are full of games. But the games of the projects aren't jump rope, or hopscotch, or ring-around-the-rosy. It's more like a variation on hide-and-seek: nigga's in the cut waiting to move on the next nigga by surprise. Games of tag and dodgeball in the Park are niggas getting shot and dodging bullets. For the chicks, it's a game of chase: Everybody's after that nigga with a little bit of drug money or chasing behind that deadbeat baby daddy. So people like me and Li'l Man have been programmed to be a product of this jungle that the outsiders label as a fun-filled "park."

Generations of families living in the Park have bred a certain kind of man and woman. Conveniently, the Park has a single entrance and exit to keep *us* in and *them* out. We have our own stores and restaurants and even our own elementary schools. Until we reach our teenage years and go off to middle school, we're trapped in this box referred to as the Park.

Unaware of how the world operates outside our box, we've developed our own way of thinking according to how our world operates. Even though we're now out of the box, we operate as if we weren't, treating every situation as though we were still living in the Park. For some this outlook gets them locked up, but for others it gives them the strongest sense of survival. In Li'l Man's case, it did the latter.

He had taken his Park mentality and survival skills and developed a small drug ring, dominating the city of Norfolk. And just how did a twenty-seven-year-old dude like Li'l Man end up with a nineteen-year-old project chick like me? It's simple: Niggas always feel most comfortable with what they know, and the projects are what Li'l Man knows. A scheming bitch like me understands that. So when the opportunity knocked, I opened my legs and let him in, but not before I put a hole in the condom.

Aaaauuuuugggghhh!" I screamed nine months later as the paralyzing pains of childbirth shot through my body.

"Just take deep breaths, honey. It will be okay," the nurse calmly instructed. "Just breathe and push. Breathe and push."

Although she meant well, I'd had it with this bitch and her instructions. Besides, nothing she suggested thus far had done a

damn thang to ease the pain, so I decided to ignore her, refusing to breathe and refusing to push. As a matter of fact, I refused
to do anything, even open my damn legs, until Li'l Man got
there.

"What time is it? Where is the phone? Give me the damn
phone!" I demanded as I pushed the nurse away from me and attempted to climb out of the bed.

"Ms. Carter, you're going to have to calm down," the doctor
interjected. "Open your legs, and let's deliver this baby." I could
sense the frustration in the doctor's voice.

"I ain't got to do shit!" I retaliated, hoping he sensed the frustration in mine. "Do you know who the fuck I am? Do you know
whose baby I'm having?" My yelling silenced everyone.

Obviously these people didn't know who they were fucking
with. No one told Tiara Carter what to do, and definitely no one
told Li'l Man's wifey what to do. I lifted what seemed like my 300-
pound body out the bed and grabbed the phone. I couldn't wait
to drop this baby and this baby fat and get back to my old self. My
120-pound hourglass frame had turned into a 160-pound blown-
glass vase. My 7 Jeans and baby tees had been replaced by sweats
and oversize T-shirts.

I dialed Li'l Man's cell phone for the hundredth time. *Ring,
ring . . . ring, ring . . . ring, ring.*

I couldn't understand why the hell he wasn't picking up. I
knew damn well he got all the messages I left him on my way to
the damn hospital. He was probably with one of his bitches.

Cheating had been a regular routine of his since the first time
we officially got together. This shit was getting ridiculous. That
nigga knew I was in my ninth month and could be having this
goddamn baby of his at any time. Just then a sharp pain jolted
me. It felt as though it was electrocuting my body. It felt like my
insides were ripping in two as I returned to the bed. I knew I

couldn't keep this baby from coming, so I decided to give in. I'd just have to deal with Li'l Man's sorry ass later.

"Please, Ms. Carter. We really need you to cooperate. Your baby is in danger," the nurse begged.

"Fine. Just do whatever the hell you have to do," I said, lying back on the bed and spreading my legs. "Get this thing out of me." Just then another sharp pain ripped through me. "Damn it, Li'l Man, where the fuck are you?" The contractions were hitting my ass like lightning bolts.

The thought of having our baby without him present caused tears to roll down my face. I knew Li'l Man was seeing other women, but when it came to me, I was always top priority. After all, I am his baby mama.

The nurse examined the consistency of my contractions once more before nodding to the doctor. I knew exactly what that meant: It was time. No more fucking around; I had to push this baby out.

"Okay, Ms. Carter—" the doctor began to say as a loud ghetto voice ricocheted off the walls of the hospital hallway.

"Tee, where you at, baby girl?" The doctor's sentence was interrupted by Li'l Man's call.

"I'm in here, baby," I yelled. "Room three!" A smile managed to slip in between the pains. He'd arrived just in time.

Although I was still pissed that I'd been in labor for nearly nine hours before he'd gotten to the hospital, I was happy that he was finally here. When he came through the door, I looked at his perfect appearance.

As he walked over and kissed me on the cheek and grabbed my hand, I could smell the fresh scent of his Issey Miyake cologne. Damn, did he look good or what?

"What up, Doc? We ready. Let's have this baby, big boy," Li'l Man said, rubbing his hands together.

Both the nurse and the doctor stood speechless at Li'l Man's ghetto etiquette. He came in there as if the doctor was not going to deliver the baby until he had instructed him to do so.

"Sir, we are going to need to get you into scrubs," the nurse said.

"Scrub? Who you callin' a scrub?" Li'l Man snapped with a hard-core look on his face.

The nurse looked as though she was going to shit in her pants, and the doctor was five seconds away from calling hospital security.

"I'm just fuckin' wit'cha," Li'l Man joked. "Lace me with them hospital threads."

"Baby, you so stupid." I tried to laugh at his humor before another labor pain hit my ass.

The nurse quickly got Li'l Man into his scrubs while another nurse joined the party to assist. Twenty more torturous minutes of pushing, and the baby was out.

"It's a boy!" the doctor said as he pulled the bundle of flesh from my womb. The nurse then swept the baby off and cleaned him up.

Li'l Man followed right behind them, excited as a kid on Christmas Eve staring at the biggest box under the tree with his name on it. I was glad at least somebody was happy to have the baby here. Although I was proud to wear the title of Li'l Man's baby mama, I was not ready to be nobody's mommy. The last thing a trick like me wanted to be was all tied down and shit. The only reason that baby was here was for Li'l Man's happiness and for my security. There was no other way I would put up with his lying, cheating ass.

Although he had a nice home where he brought only me and where we spent most of our time together, I knew Li'l Man lived in the streets with chicks in each of the seven cities of VA. Still, he's the best thing that a young project chick like me could have in her life. It wasn't every day that a big drug dealer like Li'l Man wanted someone like me as his wifey. No, I didn't hit the lottery, but my long-term winnings as his baby mama were the closest thing to it. Believe you me, if it wasn't for that, my ass would have been at the first abortion clinic that would have me, knocking the doors in and climbing through windows to take my spot in the meat-chop line. But don't get it twisted. Unlike most of these broads flooding the local abortion clinics, using abortion as a form of birth control, my shit was planned . . . planned down to the muthafuckin' line that crosses the T and the muthafuckin' circle that dots the I.

Tyrone Simmons Junior is Li'l Man's firstborn, and I, Tiara Carter, am the mother. No bitch would ever have anything on me. My baby would be a guaranteed lifelong meal ticket. As long as my child is alive, I have permanent ties to Li'l Man, no matter if I am his girl or not. And so what the fuck if some other broad managed to get herself knocked up by Li'l Man as well? No bitch would ever be able to say that they mothered his firstborn. And if it were up to me, no chick would ever hold the title of his baby mama other than me. And in case a bitch did get one by on him, it still wouldn't matter, 'cause the first baby mama will always be the shit! Any other is just an unwanted burden.

Once the nurses had T.J. all cleaned up, they brought him right over to me. I guess the average mother would have been thrilled to hold her new baby, but not me. No, sirree!

"Oh, no," I said, putting my hand up and stopping the cheerful-ass nurse dead in her tracks. "Give him to his daddy. Hell, that's where he'll be spending most of his time anyway."

The nurse gave me a questioning look before handing T.J. over to Li'l Man. I must say, they looked so cute together. Maybe if Li'l Man moved me and T.J. into his home then we could raise the baby together, but just me doing it alone, I couldn't see it. Hell, no!

As Li'l Man played with our son, the nurses helped me get cleaned up and changed into my new Victoria's Secret pajamas and slippers that Li'l Man had bought especially for this occasion. I was exhausted from the long, tiring delivery and wanted to take a nap, but not before I dug into Li'l Man's ass for arriving so late. I hated to ruin the beautiful moment he was having with his child, but I had to get this shit off my heavy, overweight, milk-filled chest.

"Man, what the hell took you so long to get here?" I started. "Didn't you get my calls and my gazillion messages?"

"Damn, Tee, do you have to start this shit now?" Li'l Man said after sucking his teeth, annoyed by my questions. "We just had a baby. Can we at least enjoy this moment without you bitchin'?"

"Sure, enjoy *your* baby," I stated, pointing my finger in Li'l Man's face, then rolling my eyes before I continued my tongue-lashing. "But that's not going to stop me from saying what I have to say. Now, where were you? I was here nearly nine hours before you arrived, and you barely made it. What if T.J. would have come without you being here?"

"Look, Tee, you called me at three in the morning. I was sleeping. As soon as I got up I checked my messages, got dressed, and headed right over. Come on, you know once my head hits the pillow I'm out. You know how hard I sleep. I ain't hear that damn phone."

I looked at Li'l Man's attire as he spoke. Damn, was he fine! His New York fitted cap sat neatly over his fresh cornrows. His new white tee glowed against his chocolate skin and broad shoulders. And his sparkling diamonds added just the right touch to give his plain attire some glamour. The longer I examined him, the more shit registered. It sure didn't look like he just jumped out of bed and shot right over to me. I had to throw that shit in his face.

"Man, come on now. Do I look stupid to you? You all dressed up and shit, clothes all pressed. Hell, you even got every piece of jewelry you own on. You didn't just hop the fuck up, Man." I then sniffed the air like a K-9. "And you wasted all those squirts of Issey Miyake just to come up here to the hospital? Shit, I don't think so!"

"You know I hate the hospital smell," was Li'l Man's quick comeback. Then, just like the typical nigga, he tried to turn the tables. "See, this the shit I'm talking 'bout. Here you go with this young-ass shit again!" Li'l Man said as he stood up and handed me the baby.

Every chance Li'l Man got he would throw my age in my face. Sure, I was only nineteen and he was eight years my senior, but that's what he loved; that's what attracted him to me in the first place. He loved how tight my li'l young pussy was. He loved the fact that niggas he fucked with couldn't tell him the scent of my pussy. He loved the fact that I wasn't out in the clubs and shit, checking for the next baller. I knew this because these were the things he told me every day. These were the things he whispered in my ear right before he was about to cum. But somehow, eventually, I always ended up hearing how I was so young-acting and how it turned him off. Funny how when a nigga all up inside a broad he got all kinds of shit to say, but the minute he pull that dick out it's a whole 'notha story.

"I wasn't too young to have your damn baby, though. Now, was I?" I said sarcastically as he grabbed his keys and headed for the door.

"I'm not even gonna entertain this shit, Tee. I'm out. Kiss my baby for me," he said, opening the door.

"Fuck you! You ain't got no damn baby. This is my baby. You better hope we're still here when you return!" I yelled as he was closing the door behind him.

I knew exactly what to say to get his attention. Not even a split second later the door flew open and Li'l Man was back in the room. He ran right up to my face like a madman. I knew he had a temper, but I had never seen this look on him before, especially directed at me. He looked as though he was going to put his hands around my throat and squeeze the life out of me. I jumped and pulled my baby close to me, hoping this would prevent Li'l Man from putting his hands on me.

"What the fuck did you say?" he asked with a look of murder in his eyes.

There was no backing down. I couldn't punk out now, so I grabbed my balls and let 'em roll. "I said you better hope we are still here when you return!"

Li'l Man knew exactly what I was insinuating. Throughout my pregnancy I would threaten to leave him and tell him that he would never see the baby. Although I would never really do that, it was the one thing that I could use to keep Li'l Man in line. To my surprise, though, this time Li'l Man reacted very differently.

"Bitch!" he yelled, grabbing me by the throat. "If you ever try to take my fuckin' son away from me, or go anywhere without me knowing, I will kill your stupid ass." Li'l Man then released my neck with a hard push.

I gasped for air and the next thing I knew, Li'l Man was out the door, slamming it behind him. As I continued gasping for air, tears slowly rolled down my face, burning my cheeks as they flowed. I was in shock. Li'l Man had never reacted like that before. Before I got pregnant, sure, there were a few times here and there when he hit me. But that was always during a drunken argument, when he really didn't know what he was doing. And he would always apologize once he sobered up, and buy me something nice to make up for it. But once he found out I was pregnant, he vowed never to put his hands on me like that again. And he hadn't—that is, until now. I guess he didn't want to harm his baby, but now that T.J. was born, maybe he felt it was safe to start using me as his personal punching bag.

T he next day Li'l Man hadn't returned to the hospital to check on me or the baby; nor had he called. I was tired of being laid up in the hospital. My friends and family had come and gone. I was ready to go, too. The nurse advised me that since there were no complications and both me and the baby were doing fine, she would discuss a possible afternoon discharge with the doctor.

Damn what the doctor said—I was going home regardless. I packed everything up, anxious to get back home. Fortunately the doctor signed my discharge papers, so I didn't have any drama about checking out of the hospital. Once I had everything all together, I called Li'l Man, and, of course, he didn't answer. Still pissed at his ass from the day before, I left him a nasty message.

"This is your punching-bag baby mama. If you are interested, the doctor is releasing me and your son this afternoon. It would be nice if you were here to pick us up," I said, hanging up without saying good-bye. To my surprise, Li'l Man arrived at the hospital thirty minutes after I left the message. This time he brought a friend. Well, he said she was just a friend, but everybody knows how that song goes.

"Hi, Tee. Where's the baby?" Stacey said as she looked around the room.

"Oh, they took him for a final checkup before we leave," I responded. I then looked at Li'l Man and rolled my eyes.

What the fuck did he bring her prissy ass here for? I thought as

Stacey sat down in the chair beside me and made herself comfortable.

Li'l Man didn't say a word to me. He just sat down in the chair next to Stacey.

Stacey was Li'l Man's so-called sister, the female he had been "just friends" with since Pampers. His mom and her mom were best friends. One day Stacey's mom was coming home from a day of shopping and was hit by a drunk driver. The drunk driver hit her car so fast and hard it sent her car airborne. When it landed upside down, Stacey's mother's car burst into flames, killing her instantly.

Stacey never knew her father and was an only child. Li'l Man's mom felt it was only right to take Stacey in as her own and raise her. Although Stacey and Li'l Man both swore they were like brother and sister, I always suspected they were fucking. Hell, Stacey was beautiful and had everything a man could dream of: She was tall, slim, with a fat ass, flat stomach, perfect teeth, and skin to match. It would have been hard for a blood brother not to want to fuck her, let alone a play brother. On top of that, Stacey looked like money. Li'l Man made sure she had everything. That bitch didn't work, yet she wore every designer label known, drove only the hottest shit, and had a condo on the oceanfront. All she had to do was get up and go to school each morning and make the grade.

She'd been in college since she was fresh out of high school. Now, at almost twenty-six years old, she was just about done with her doctorate. Li'l Man always bragged how proud he was of her. Next to his newborn child, Stacey was his pride and joy.

Just then the nurse came through the door with T.J. in her arms.

"Oh, there he is," Stacey stated in her proper voice.

"Okay, who do we give him to?" the nurse asked as she looked around the room.

I guess after I refused to take T.J. in my arms when he was born, the nurse was hesitant to hand him to me again.

"Why don't we give him to his godmother?" Stacey said as she stood up and extended her arms to receive the baby. The nurse handed the baby to Stacey and advised that she'd be back with a wheelchair. Already pissed, I gave the nurse a look of death.

"I don't need a wheelchair. My legs work perfectly fine," I snapped.

"Hospital procedure," the nurse snapped back, then stepped into the hall to grab a wheelchair to wheel me out of the hospital.

I quickly turned my attention back to Stacey's previous comment.

Godmother? I know this bitch didn't say godmother, I thought, while frowning and turning up my nose. *Who the fuck said she was the godmother? I know damn well Li'l Man didn't tell this bitch she was the godmother.*

I nearly blanked out as the shit really started to register in my brain. I had to say something.

"Stacey, did I hear you say godmother?" I asked with a baffled look on my face.

"Yes, honey," she said, cooing at the baby. "Tyrone didn't tell you?" She looked over at Li'l Man for confirmation.

I hated when that proper bitch called Li'l Man Tyrone. He never allowed me to address him as anything other than Li'l Man. Nobody called him by his government name, not even his mama. Normally I wouldn't say anything, but it was time I acknowledged the fact that this bitch was overstepping her boundaries. I had officially earned the title of baby mama, and Stacey needed to take a backseat. If I didn't call him Tyrone, neither would she.

"Li'l Man, I thought you hated being called Tyrone?" I said, hoping he would straighten Stacey out immediately.

Before Li'l Man could respond, Miss Prissy was already flapping her lips.

"Tyrone is his given name, and I shall address him as such. Tyrone knows I refuse to use street names because we are not on the streets. We don't have a street relationship. What we have is real, so I call him by his *real* name."

I looked at Li'l Man for a response, but he said nothing. That shit really pissed me off. Plus, I believed the bitch was trying to say I was from the streets, since I called him Li'l Man. Trying to be respectful and not cause a scene, I decided to bite my tongue on that one. Besides, I knew Li'l Man would take her side and only upset me more or leave me feeling embarrassed.

"Oh, yeah, baby. I'm gon' let Stacey be the godmother," he added, acknowledging her statement and not mine. "I think li'l T.J. could learn a lot from her. You know, proper English, manners, and a lot of educational shit. I want to keep him away from that street life. Ya know what I mean?" Li'l Man said, changing the subject.

I couldn't believe the shit that was coming out of this nigga's mouth. Hell, he didn't even speak proper English his damn self. Like I can't give my damn child a good upbringing or something. I was insulted, but I wasn't even going to waste my breath arguing with Li'l Man.

"Yeah, whatever," I said as I got up and gathered my things. "Did you bring his car seat carrier thing?" I asked.

"Yeah, it's in the car," he answered. "Stacey bought him a brand-new Eddie Bauer one. It has the carrier, car seat, and stroller all in one. It's hot!"

"What?" I said with a puzzled look on my face. Just then the nurse pushed the wheelchair into the room. "But my sister gave us one already."

"I know, darling, but the one I purchased was rated number one as far as child safety," Stacey said as she wrapped up T.J.

I sat down in the wheelchair once the nurse rolled it over to me. Li'l Man and Stacey, with T.J. in her arms, headed for the door, and the nurse wheeled me behind them. I was fuming as I sat in the wheelchair. It took all I had not to snap off on Stacey, but nonetheless I refrained. Just how long I could refrain was the question.

Me and T.J. weren't even out of the hospital for a full week before Li'l Man started acting up. At first he was there for my every need: getting milk, Pampers, and even coming over to sit with T.J. just so I could get a little sleep. Then that all slowly started to change. I guess the time he was spending with us was starting to dip into his club and street time. He started making excuses about why he couldn't come around, and eventually started sending that bitch Stacey over to handle his business for him. At first she'd bring over whatever it was I told Li'l Man the baby needed. Then she began to just bring me the money to go get the stuff myself. Before I knew it, me and T.J. were hearing and seeing less and less of Li'l Man and more and more of Stacey.

Stacey always had an excuse for why Li'l Man couldn't come through. It even got to the point where I was leaving him messages and Stacey was calling me back. That was definitely a cue it was time to put his ass in check.

I dialed his number, almost positive he wouldn't answer. I decided in advance that I'd leave a message so grimy that he wouldn't dare have that bitch respond to the message for him.

The phone rang twice. I knew after three rings his voice mail would pick up. I was prepared to spit knives through the phone.

"Hello," a female voice answered Li'l Man's phone.

"Who the fuck is this?" I yelled, ready to attack.

"Tee, it's me. Calm down, honey," Stacey said in her best schoolteacher voice.

I hated when she talked to me in that manner. I took it as though she was talking down to me. Like she was speaking to a child.

"What are you doing with Li'l Man's phone?" I asked with a slight attitude.

"He gave it to me to hold on to just in case someone called, someone like you. He has a new phone."

That was it! This nigga had truly violated. I said nothing more and politely ended the call. That would be the last time I would dial that number ever again.

Days passed, and me and T.J. didn't see or hear from Li'l Man at all. Luckily, the last drop Stacey made for Li'l Man was enough to cover the bills and provide for T.J. for the rest of the month. I had to start planning my money hustle for the next month, because there was no way I was going to go begging to Li'l Man. Fuck him! I refused to call that number.

My phone started to ring. I rushed to answer it before it woke T.J., who I had just laid down for a nap.

"Hello?" I answered the phone with a major attitude, as if the caller knew T.J. was sleeping.

The caller ID read, WIRELESS CALLER, so I knew it could only be one person: Li'l Man.

"What up, baby girl? How's my son?" Li'l Man asked, as though everything was all good.

"Your son?" I said, sucking my teeth and rolling my eyes. "We ain't seen or heard from you in two weeks. We found a new baby daddy," I said, knowing it would burn Li'l Man up inside. But with him not being right here in my face to try to swing on me, I had mad courage.

"What the fuck you say?" Li'l Man said, infuriated.

"What, you ain't noticed? I stopped calling your ass a week ago," I said in a nonchalant tone.

"Bitch, I'm coming to get my son. Have his shit ready."

"Whateva!" I said, and hung up the phone in Li'l Man's ear.

Ten minutes hadn't even passed before Li'l Man was raging through my apartment door. In a split second he was banging on my locked bedroom door. I knew locking the bedroom door would really piss him off. The first thing he'd think was that some nigga was laid up in there with me. I picked up T.J. out of the bassinet. Li'l Man had woken him up with his banging. I took my sweet time unlocking the door and letting him in. When I opened the door, I just let it swing open, and I walked away. He followed closely behind me. I knew he was watching my ass bounce in my matching fire-red lace boy shorts and bra that I put on to entice him. I didn't say a word. I just turned around and handed him the baby, then went to lie down on my bed.

"That's it? Where his shit at? And why the fuck you got that li'l shit on?" Li'l Man asked. "Prancing around my son lookin' like some tramp."

"That's it. He ain't got shit else," I responded in reference to T.J.

I jumped off of the bed and pointed my finger at Li'l Man, but refrained from getting too close. "You ain't brought shit over here. You ain't even called to check on him. T.J. ain't got shit but a carrier. I'm sure your sister, his so-called godmother, has everything he needs. And as far as my attire, if you spent more time around here, you would know I've been wearing shit like this to bed every night," I said sarcastically.

Li'l Man didn't even put up an argument. He just turned around and headed out the door with T.J.

As soon as he left, I called up a couple of my girls to see if they wanted to go to the club. Although the club wasn't my drop, I really needed to get out and release. In the few weeks since having T.J. I'd already gotten my shape back, and I couldn't wait to flaunt it once again. Seems as though childbearing had widened my hips, and I couldn't wait to put a little twist in them.

My girls and I decided that we'd meet up at the Beach House, a club near the ocean. My sister let me borrow her car and use her ID, so I was able to get in with no problem. I didn't spot any of my girls, so I decided to go over to the bar and start the party without them. Just as I was beginning to get nice and tipsy, I spotted Li'l Man's ass at the bar hanging all over some bitch. Not only was I pissed that he was on another female, but he was here, which meant my son was someplace else. I wasted no time approaching his ass.

"Excuse me!" I said as I pushed my way between Li'l Man and the knotty-head bitch he was with. "What the fuck are you doing here?" I asked Li'l Man, grilling him in the face. My presence took him by surprise.

"What'chu mean? The question should be, What are *you* doing here!" he spit back.

"Nigga, if your ass is here then that means my damn son is wit' somebody else. Where the fuck is my son?" I snapped.

"He a'ight. What you think? I'ma leave my son wit' just anybody? He wit his godmother, so chill," Li'l Man replied, and then walked off. I watched as he walked into the VIP room.

By this time my girls had arrived and encouraged me to calm down because I was starting to make a scene. The night was still young, and they didn't want to risk getting thrown out of the club.

"Here, girl," one of my girls said, handing me a drink. "Take this Long Island iced tea. It'll make you feel betta. Don't worry 'bout that fool."

I drank the Long Island in almost one gulp. Li'l Man had me

steaming, and it was going to take more than one drink to cool me off.

"Damn, Tee, you looking better than ever, girl," a voice said from behind me.

I looked back, ready to snap on whoever that corny-ass nigga was who was breathing down my neck. To my surprise it was no corny nigga at all. It was Young Boy, one of Li'l Man's best friends. I hadn't seen him in months.

"What up, Young Boy?" I said, excited to see him as I gave him a big hug.

"Chilling, baby," he replied. "You want something to drink? I see yo' glass empty. Let me buy you one."

I readily accepted. I don't know if I was a little drunk, but Young Boy was looking damn good in his Versace outfit and smelling good with his Versace cologne. His hair was cut low, with waves flowing around his head in perfect circles. Young Boy stood an even six feet, with the perfect build. Damn, was he fine!

After I finished the Hennessy and Coke he ordered me, I was feeling real nice, almost to the point of being fucked-up! I wasted no time hitting the dance floor. The deejay was playing reggae, and I felt like I could dance all night. I moved like the dance hall queen, grabbing the attention of every nigga on the floor, and those off.

It wasn't long before cats were trying to move in on me. Of course, I turned each of them down. Well, that was until Young Boy pulled up to the bumper. I was in another world as I ground on his body. I must have really been putting some moves on him, because I could feel his manhood growing hard as I popped my ass against it. And what an awesome size it grew!

"You see what you do to me," Young Boy whispered in my ear as he grabbed my hand and placed it on his king-size penis.

I don't know if I was overwhelmed by lust or just pissy drunk, but all of a sudden the whole room started to spin.

"I don't feel very well. I have to go," I told Young Boy before rushing off the dance floor.

I headed to the club exit. I'd left just in time because as soon as I reached the door the lights were turned on and they were doing last call for alcohol. I couldn't risk the chance of anyone seeing me in such a condition. I had to get some fresh air. I didn't even tell my friends I was leaving the club. I just dipped. I planned to call them on my cell phone once I got outside and got myself together.

Once outside I decided to go sit in the car for a minute and get my head right. Ten minutes hadn't passed before I saw Li'l Man drive by with a chick sitting in the passenger side of his brand-new Range Rover. I couldn't believe he had another bitch in the truck. I hadn't even had a chance to break the leather in good on the passenger seat, and he already had another bitch in there. I was furious as I watched them pull out of the parking lot. The liquor must have had me going, because I started the car and followed behind his ass. I wasn't sure where he was headed, but it didn't seem familiar. Come to find out he was headed no place.

He pulled into a dark parking lot near a pier and parked. I passed the parking lot, swerving, and parked around the corner, nearly on top of the curb. I then stumbled back toward the area where Li'l Man was parked. I slowly approached the car. Li'l Man seemed to be very pleased with the brain he was receiving. From afar I could see the freak bitch's nappy-ass head bobbing up and down, and I could hear Li'l Man moaning. My stomach began to ache with anxiety. I couldn't take any more. I rushed to the driver side of the car and started banging on the window.

"Aaahhhhhh!" They both screamed like little bitches. I nearly scared the shit out of them both.

The girl quickly sat up, shaking in her seat. I looked directly at the bitch, paying no mind to Li'l Man. I could deal with him later.

"Stacey! You lying bitch!" I yelled as I opened the car door and jumped over Li'l Man, attempting to kill her ass.

Grabbing her by the neck with a grip of death with my left hand and punching her in the face with my right, I nearly beat her delirious before Li'l Man could get me off of her.

"Get your ghetto ass out of here," he yelled as he dragged me across the gravel parking lot by my hair. "Fuckin' hood rat." Before walking away Li'l Man gathered a wad of saliva in his mouth and spit at me. It landed on my arm.

As I lay there on the ground, exhausted and struggling to catch my breath, I attempted to piece together what had just occurred. I couldn't believe Li'l Man was treating me like this. He was actually taking up for Stacey and fighting me over her. And the ultimate . . . he had the audacity to spit on me. Li'l Man was truly treating me like I was exactly what he said—a fuckin' hood rat.

"Oh, you gon' choose the bitch over me?" I asked after catching my breath.

I struggled to get to my feet as I wiped the spit from my arm on my pants leg. "I had your damn child, Li'l Man. I'm your fucking baby mama!" I cried hysterically as I headed back to the car.

I drove back to the club in a daze. I couldn't believe what just happened. I should have gone with my instincts and the advice of my girls and just let the shit ride.

Once I got back to the club, I called my girls to let them know I was outside and ready to go. Then I turned my phone off. I didn't even want to hear the shit Li'l Man would be saying. Five minutes later my girls came out of the club with Young Boy. They all came to the car. I'd almost forgotten how crazy I looked. I was embarrassed to even look up at Young Boy. Because of the fight, I was a HAM, a hot-ass mess.

"What the fuck happened to you, ma?" Young Boy asked as he examined my bruised body and wild hair.

I explained to him and my friends the drama I had just experienced. They were all at a loss for words. Young Boy was the first to speak up.

"For real, baby girl. I don't even know what to say right now. But look," Young Boy said, taking a card out of his pocket. "Here's my number. Why don't you hit me up tomorrow?" He handed me his barbershop business card, which had three contact numbers on it.

I accepted and agreed to give him a call. Young Boy walked away, leaving my girls and me sitting there. There was complete silence, and I knew they wanted to say, *I told you so,* but none of them had the guts to do so. They knew I was drunk and pissed off, and at any moment I could lash out at either of them. After making sure I was cool to drive, they said good-bye and we went our separate ways.

When I got to my apartment door I could hear my phone ringing off the hook. I unlocked the door and walked in. I already knew who it was. I didn't even bother looking at the caller ID. I just walked up to the phone and turned the ringer off. I hopped in the bed and shortly thereafter I was sound asleep.

Bang, bang . . . bang, bang! I was awakened by the constant banging on my front door. I rolled over and looked at the clock before dragging myself out of bed. It was already twelve noon and it felt like seven a.m.

"Who is it?" I yelled as I headed toward the door.

"Wwwhhhaaa, wwwhhhaaa, wwwhhhaaa," I heard as I got to the door. T.J. was crying as though someone was killing him.

I rushed to open the door. Standing there was Brittani, Li'l Man's little sister, and she was holding a testy T.J. in her arms.

"Here, Tee," Brittani said, handing T.J. to me. "He's been crying since I got him."

"What you mean, since you got him?" I said, taking him from

her arms. "When did you get him, and where the fuck is his sorry-ass daddy?"

"I haven't talked to Li'l Man. Stacey brought T.J. over about one o'clock this morning. She said she was going to pick Li'l Man up from the club and they'd be back to get T.J. Well, they never came. Stacey's phone is off, and she's not answering her house phone. Li'l Man's phone is off, too. I don't know what's up, but T.J. has been crying for hours."

Li'l Man had really fucked up now. Disrespecting me was one thing, but neglecting our child was on a whole different level.

"Well, thank you for bringing him to me," I said, scrounging for my purse to hit her off with a couple of ends.

"Unh-unh," she said, putting her hand up and declining the money before I could even locate it. "He's my nephew." She then yawned and walked away.

I undressed T.J. to wash him up. When I felt his bare skin, he was burning up. I called his doctor's office right away. Once I spoke with the doctor, he advised me to take T.J. to the emergency room immediately. I didn't even wash my ass. I just packed T.J.'s diaper bag and headed to Children's Hospital emergency room. Once at the hospital, I cried as I watched the doctors do a number of tests on T.J.'s little weak body.

How could I let this happen to my baby? What kind of mother am I? I thought.

It wasn't until I saw my baby in this near-death state that my motherly instincts kicked in. T.J. was no longer Li'l Man's baby. He was *my* baby. I was all T.J. had. I brought him into this world. It was my responsibility to make sure he had the best care and upbringing. I swore that from this day forth I would be the best mother I could be, with or without Li'l Man. Fuck being Li'l Man's baby mama. I was *my* baby's mama, T.J.'s.

"Ms. Carter?" The doctor interrupted my thoughts.

"Yes?" I said, praying it wasn't bad news.

"It looks like Tyrone is experiencing alcohol poisoning. We've pumped his stomach, and it looks like he's going to be okay. We'd just like to keep him here for the rest of the day for observation. Also it is our policy to have a representative from Child Protective Services speak with the parents in cases such as this." Just then he opened the door to allow a social worker to enter the room.

"Alcohol poisoning?" I said in a dazed state. I was frozen in disbelief. My body became warm all over, and I felt as though I was going to faint as the doctor's words about a social worker registered in my head.

"Oh, my God! Please, no," I begged as tears began to roll down my cheeks. I knew exactly what the fuck was about to happen. They were going to take T.J. from me for neglect. I'd seen this happen one too many times in the projects, kids kicking and screaming with snot coming out their noses, and calling out to their mamas, even when their mama was the one hurting them.

"Please calm down, sweetie," the social worker said as she walked over to comfort me. "I'm Tina Morrison, and I would just like to ask you a few questions." She sat down next to me with a clipboard and paperwork like I was about to interview for a job.

"No, it's not my fault! I'm a good mother!" I paused, attempting to catch my breath and speak clearly between my hysterical cries. "He was with his father. Please don't take my child from me, ma'am. Please!" I continued to beg between tears.

"Well, it has not been determined what will be done at this point. But, Ms. Carter, your baby has alcohol poisoning." She then paused for a moment and took a deep breath. "I need to gather a little more information from you as well as the doctor. Let's start with you. How often do you drink? You've obviously been drinking. I can smell the alcohol on your breath now."

I dropped my head in my hands and began to cry uncontrollably. I knew I'd lost the battle. Yet I still answered each question Mrs. Morrison asked. After thirty minutes of interrogating, she was finally done with me.

"Thank you, Ms. Carter. We will be notifying you of our decision before Tyrone is released from the hospital," she said as she gathered her things and left me alone.

I stayed in the waiting room for hours, crying and pacing the floor as I waited for T.J.'s release. Although periodically the doctor would come and give me a positive update of his progress, it seemed like days were passing as I waited. I was glad to know that T.J. was going to be fine. But I needed to know how he got alcohol in his system in the first place. Who the fuck would give alcohol to a newborn?

I decided to start with Brittani, Li'l Man's little sister, since she was the one who had him last. I pulled my cell phone out of my purse and dialed the phone number. As it rang in my ear, I reminded myself to be as calm as possible as I spoke to her. I knew if I was too aggressive, I would get nowhere and never know who was responsible for T.J.'s sickness.

"Hello?" Brittani answered on the first ring.

"Hey, girl." I took a deep breath.

"Hey, Tee, what's wrong?" she asked.

"It's T.J. He is really sick. I need to know if you noticed anything strange when Stacey dropped him off."

"Well, T.J. was really calm, almost to the point of being spaced out when Stacey brought him. I found that kinda unusual, being that he's normally pretty active. I even asked her about it. She just said he was probably tired because she had just fed him and bathed him—"

I interrupted her midsentence. " 'Spaced out'? Could you explain exactly what you mean?"

"Well, he wasn't very attentive. He just seemed to be in his own world."

I found that pretty strange.

I asked my next question: "Did you feed him anything?"

"Yes, I did. After a while he became a little fussy, so I gave him a bottle. Stacey already had all the bottles prepared."

That, too, was strange. I continued to ask her question after question until I was sure she'd given me every detail. After speaking with her, I was sure she had no part in Stacey's evil plot to steal my crown. Now it was on to that bitch Stacey.

I knew it would be hard to get any information out of her ass, since she had just received a royal ass-whipping from me. I blocked my cell phone number from showing up on her caller ID so that I'd have a better chance of her answering the phone.

"Hello?" she answered.

"Stacey, this is Tee. I'm not calling to argue. I'm calling in reference to my son," I said calmly.

"Yes? What about him?" she said with an attitude.

"When you kept him last night, what did you feed him? Did you give him anything other than milk? Did he seem sick when you had him?" I spit out questions one after another. I was interrogating her the same way that social worker had interrogated me.

"What exactly are you insinuating, Tee?" Stacey said, obviously offended.

"I'm not insinuating anything; it's just that—"

"Look, little girl, just because you are an unfit mother, don't try to blame me for any problems you're having with your child," she interrupted. The next thing I knew there was a click in my ear and the line went dead. That bitch had hung up on me.

Now I was really pissed off. I knew that bitch was guilty of something. She was either guilty of knowing or guilty of doing.

Either way, when it came to my baby, guilty was guilty, and her ass needed to be dealt with.

I called her phone right back, ready to blast her ass just as soon as she answered, but I got her voice mail instead. She had turned her phone off. But that was okay, because I was sure to run into her ass again, and when I did it wouldn't be pretty. Premeditated revenge is the worst kind, and she had just placed her ass at the top of my "get back" list.

Just as I was getting ready to call Li'l Man and scream on him, Mrs. Morrison walked in. I already knew the verdict from the look on her face.

"I'm sorry, Ms. Carter—" she began.

"No need to go any further. Just tell me what I need to do to get him back," I said, holding in the tears, trying to be strong and just handle my business.

She explained the process to me, and as soon as she finished I walked off with tears rolling down my cheeks without saying a word. I couldn't hold them back any longer, but I wasn't going to let her see me cry.

I was all to pieces as I walked out of the hospital. I was in absolutely no shape to drive. I couldn't even see straight and would probably have driven the car off the road. I didn't even bother calling a cab. I decided to walk home. My sister would have to come to the hospital herself to get her car. I needed time and fresh air to gather my thoughts. I had to start planning how to get my son back. I knew I would need a good lawyer, so my first task was getting the money to pay for one. I factored Li'l Man in as an option, but not a reliable one. I had to think of ways I could get the loot on my own. My years in the projects made me a natural hustler, so the perfect idea came easily. Once I had my plan, all I needed to do was execute it!

Just as soon as I arrived home, I turned on the ringer on my phone and checked my voice mail.

"You have seventeen new messages," the recording said.

I wondered who in the hell would leave so many damn messages.

"Press one to listen to your messages," the recording continued.

I pressed the one to hear the first message.

"You have a collect call from an inmate at the county jail," I heard the recording say. There was a pause and then I heard a male voice: "Li'l Man."

My mouth dropped open. "Aw, hell!" I said as I threw my hands up in the air.

Each message after the first was the same. I deleted them all and hung up the phone. I wondered what the hell Li'l Man had done to get locked up. His timing was just perfect. The one time I did really need him and now he was no use. Good thing he wasn't my strongest option for getting T.J. back.

I was sure Li'l Man would be calling back, and when he did I planned to let him feel the wrath. Not only was I going to dig into his ass for the harm his little princess had done to our child, but once I was done I planned to top it all off by telling him that when he got out, he could no longer see his son unless it was in my presence. Hell, he was lucky I was even still willing to deal with his ass after that stunt he pulled last night, but the interest of my son was at heart.

I went into the bathroom to clean myself up. I had looked like a bum and screamed the scent of a wino long enough. I slipped out of my clothes and left them in a pile on the floor where they lay. I then jumped into the shower. After getting dressed I fixed myself something to eat and cleaned up my small apartment. As I was picking my clothes up off the floor, I came across Young Boy's number.

"Damn," I muttered under my breath. "With all the drama, I almost forgot about him."

I needed to call him so I could tell him about his boy, plus find out what the hell Li'l Man was doing in jail. I wasted no time hitting him up. As I dialed his number it hit me. I could use Young Boy as another option for loot!

With that in mind I was even more eager to speak to him.

Young Boy answered on the third ring.

"Yo?" he answered, as though he was sure it was one of his boys.

"Hey, Young Boy. It's Tee."

"Oh! What up, baby girl? I didn't expect you to call, on the real. I figured that was just some ol' drunken club talk you was spittin'."

"Naw. I ain't 'bout no games. And that's exactly why I'm calling. You said you was trying to hook up, so let's make this happen." I wasted no time getting to the point.

"Dat's what's up. I like a female dat's about her shit. How does tonight sound?"

Young Boy was moving just as I'd hoped. I was definitely on a mission, and I needed a dude like him on my team.

"Tonight is cool. How 'bout nine?"

"A'ight. You still in dat spot out Huntersville?" Young Boy asked, throwing me completely off.

"Yeah, and how exactly did you know that?" I asked.

"Come on, baby. I'm from the streets, you from the streets; Li'l Man from the streets . . . we all know how shit works. The easiest shit to get is information."

The words he spoke were so true. It was nothing more I could say.

"Well, I guess I'll see you at nine then."

" 'Nuff talk," Young Boy stated, putting an end to our phone conversation.

Nine o'clock rolled around quicker than I'd expected. And like clockwork, Young Boy was at my door, ringing the bell. I sprayed on a little Escada Rockin' Rio, grabbed my purse, and headed to the door.

"Hey," I said as I opened it.

"Damn, you smell good," Young Boy said.

"Thanks."

"You ready?" he asked.

I was surprised he didn't do the typical male thing and try to worm his way into my door and then into my pussy.

"I'm ready," I replied, then smiled seductively as I followed him toward his brand-new Dodge Magnum. I could see nothing but my reflection as I walked toward the gleaming black car with black-tinted windows and black rims to match. If it wasn't for the chrome lip on the rims, this car might not have been identifiable in a dark parking lot. I made myself comfortable in the front seat as I examined the black interior and scanned Young Boy's large selection of CDs. After selecting his TI CD, I quickly reached toward the CD player to insert it.

"Hold it!" Young Boy said while grabbing my wrist. "Anything from this point over," he said, drawing an imaginary line dividing the passenger side of the car from the driver's side, "you have total control over. So do as you please; but anything on the other side is my territory. So relax. I got something for us to listen to."

I rolled my eyes as he inserted Kem.

"Come on, baby girl. Kill that pouting shit. TI for da club. We gon' do grown-up things tonight. Like I said befo', relax. I got'chu."

I was kinda pissed that Young Boy was insinuating I was

young, but at the same time his thugged-out, put-me-in-my-place behavior turned me on. I didn't respond verbally. Instead I just smiled, placed my hand into his, and vibed to the relaxing sounds of Kem.

We drove to the ocean and had dinner at a busy restaurant overlooking the water. Throughout dinner I made sure that I sat and moved seductively. That was part of my plan to reel him in. At times I'd find Young Boy's eyes glued to my breasts or glancing up and down the length of my legs and thighs. Those were definite signs that my plan was working. Now that I had his attention and knew he'd do anything for the kitty cat, it was time to put in the hustle. I started gazing off at the ocean and picking at my food, trying to give signs of distraction and frustration. It wasn't long before Young Boy caught on.

"What's wrong?" he asked. "Did I say something to upset you?"

"No, I just have a lot on my mind," I said in a helpless tone.

"What is it? Maybe I can help."

Perfect response! I thought as I continued to play the game. I couldn't believe this nigga was following my lead so easily.

"No, you can't." I sighed. "Maybe we should just leave. I don't want to bring you down."

"Come on, baby girl. You know I got'cha back. What's the deal?" he asked sincerely, taking my hand in his.

"Well, it's T.J. They . . . they . . . they took him from me." I forced out the words as I broke down in tears.

No acting was needed for that. It actually hurt me to think about it. Tears began to well up in my eyes, and now I really wanted to leave the restaurant and go home.

"What! Who took him?" Young Boy asked, just as upset as if T.J. was his son.

I spent the rest of our dinner explaining to Young Boy how

T.J. was taken and how Li'l Man was not there for us like he should have been. It didn't take long for Young Boy to vow to help me get T.J. back, and all that without even giving up the pussy. My game was tighter than I thought.

Mission accomplished! I thought as we headed to the car. Young Boy was now my major option, but I still had plans to execute the others if need be.

We arrived at my house a few minutes later. I told Young Boy good night and gave him a small kiss on the cheek. I agreed to give him a call tomorrow so we could start planning to get my son back. Of course, when I walked into the house the phone was ringing off the hook.

"Hello?" I said in an annoyed tone as I answered the phone. Just as I figured, it was Li'l Man. As soon as I heard the operator informing me that I had a collect call from an inmate, I knew what was up. I accepted the call, and immediately Li'l Man started spitting shit.

"Why the fuck you ain't been answering the damn phone?" he yelled.

Click! I hung the phone right up in his ear without saying one word. I was not in the mood for his shit. If anyone should be yelling, it was me. Two seconds later the phone was ringing again.

"Hello?" I said, just as annoyed as before, and then pressed one to accept the call. I knew it was costing me, accepting these collect calls, but I enjoyed the tingle in my clit that slamming the phone down in Li'l Man's ear provided.

"What's up with you?" Li'l Man said, now a little calmer than before.

"What the fuck do you want, Li'l Man? Why don't you call your damn girl, your sister, your son's godmother, or whoever the fuck she is to you?" I yelled into the phone.

"Man, I ain't fucking wit' dat bitch!" he responded.

There was no way in hell I was going to believe that shit. He had to think I was a damn fool. I know jail talk when I hear it. Stacey was just sucking his dick last night, and now he was yelling he don't fuck with her. The words *project chick* might have been stamped all over my forehead, but *dumb-ass project chick* surely wasn't!

"Whateva, nigga," I responded, sucking my teeth and picking at my fingernails. "Yo' ass just ain't got nobody else to holler at right now, so you saying whatever you can to get me on your side."

"I don't need shit. I was just calling to see how my son is doing."

Little did he know he'd just said the wrong damn thing.

"First of all, he is no longer *your* son. That shit you did last night was the ultimate . . . just foul. If you're lucky, I might let you see him every once in a while, and that's only if I am around to supervise the visits. Second, right now I don't know how T.J. is, because Child Protective Services took him from me. And third, you can thank your little college, proper English-speaking princess for all of this shit!"

"Stacey told me you were going to use T.J. to pull me in whateva direction you wanted me to go. I should have listened to her a long time ago and made your ass get an abortion in the first damn place."

Click! I hung up on Li'l Man's ass again. And again he called right back. This was my final time accepting his call. One more outburst and there would be a block on the phone. Just as soon as I pressed one to accept the call, Li'l Man began speaking.

"Why you let them take my damn son anyway? What the fuck did you do? I knew yo' ass was unfit!" Li'l Man went off on a tantrum.

"Look, muthafucka, if you blaming anybody it should be that bitch of yours. Don't you worry, though; I'm going to handle things with my son."

"What did she do, Tee? Since you want to switch the blame,

tell me, what exactly did Stacey do to make them take my son from you?" Li'l Man demanded to know.

I told him just as I had explained to the lady from social services and Young Boy. By the time I was finished with my spiel, his whole attitude had changed.

For a minute, Li'l Man was silent. He sighed, then began to speak. "I'm sorry, Tee. It's my fault. I shouldn't have left him with her. I'll hit you back. I'm 'bout to call her and see what's really going on," Li'l Man said before hanging up the phone.

I could tell he was confused and didn't know what to believe. But he had to know that I would never do anything to hurt my own baby. He had to know that Brittani wouldn't do anything to hurt the baby either. It had to be Stacey. Although Li'l Man had apologized to me, there was one thing he said that stuck in my head and made my blood boil.

Stacey told me you were going to use T.J. to pull me in whateva direction you wanted me to go. I should have listened to her a long time ago and made your ass get an abortion in the first damn place.

The words pierced my heart. I always knew that bitch was jealous that I had Li'l Man's son.

While I waited for Li'l Man to call me back, I got undressed and called up my girl Coco, who worked at a strip club and brought in all kinds of loot. She'd been trying to bring me in since she started, but I always refused. Hell, I figured you only did that kind of shit if you were desperate for money. And I had never been that desperate—that was, until now.

O nce I got Coco on the phone I told her my deal and plan to get T.J. back. She sounded glad to know I was ready to enter the strip scene. She was probably thrilled because misery loved company, and it had to be miserable keeping company with some of the grimy niggas that frequented the strip clubs. Although some strippers had anything-goes-to-make-a-buck standards, I did have a few restrictions. I told her that I could not participate with her during the week because she danced locally, but on the weekend she traveled to North Carolina and sometimes Washington, D.C. Those would be the times I would participate. She understood. Fuck dat. I was still Li'l Man's baby mama, and I had a reputation to uphold, and it was not that of a stripper.

My phone beeped just as Coco and I were wrapping up our conversation. Assuming it was Li'l Man, I answered right away without even looking at caller ID.

"Hello?" I said.

"Where the fuck do you get off blaming me for T.J.'s sickness?" a voice yelled on the other end of the line.

It was Stacey, and I was glad it was her, because—fuck the dumb bitch—I needed to give her a piece of my mind for real. I was tired of playing games with her, trying to be calm when I was finding out what the hell happened with my son.

"Bitch, I got some for yo' ass," I snapped back. "I can't believe you even called my muthafuckin' house! If you knew what was good—"

"Are you threatening me?" she asked.

"Nope! I promising yo' ass. Fucking my man, then lying to my face is one thing, but fucking with my child is another. All I can say is, you betta stay in the house and never show yourself!" I stated before hanging up the phone.

A few minutes later the phone rang again. This time I glanced at the caller ID to see who it was. If it was Stacey, I was going to ride around the streets of Virginia Beach until I ran into her ass and then beat the fuck out of her. Lucky for her she'd decided not to call back; it was Li'l Man instead.

"Hey," I said, after accepting the call.

"What up, Tee?" Li'l Man said, sounding exasperated. "I don't know what's up with that chick. She call her ass snapping on me for blaming her and shit. I put my foot down, though. I'm going to give her the benefit of the doubt, because we don't really know what the hell went on. It could have been my little sister. I told her y'all are going to have to squash that beef shit, because my son is at stake right now. She's got the key to my safe, so you're going to have to holla at her for a minute. She's supposed to hit you off with a grand tomorrow and, like, five hundred each week after that until I get out of here and can handle things on my own. I don't know when I'll be home, 'cause these niggas talking some bullshit. They got me in here on some probation violation shit. But just try to deal wit' Stacey until I can get out of here," Li'l Man pleaded.

I was pissed at the fact that Li'l Man gave that bitch a break, because I knew she did it. I knew she was jealous of the bond me and Li'l Man had because of T.J. But for my son's sake, I'd have to deal with her.

"Okay, Li'l Man," I replied. "But I'm only tolerating her ass for my son's sake."

I agreed to let things ride without an argument. I didn't even bother telling Li'l Man about the earlier conversation I had with Stacey. I promised him that I was going to chill, so I would; but I still had plans to get her ass. Once things were said and done and I had my son back, I would definitely get that bitch. After I promised Li'l Man that I'd be on my best behavior, we got off the phone.

As the weeks passed I got my hustle on in a major way. I was thrilled all my hustles had turned out as planned. Young Boy had started putting out the loot, and, surprisingly, I still didn't have to put out the ass. All this nigga wanted was a little time and teasing. My strip hustle was coming along better than I had originally expected, too. I know I ain't no ugly chick, but I never knew I could pull in as much money as I was pulling in just from shaking a little ass in some pervert's face.

Dancing wasn't that bad, after all. Guys were excited to see a new face, some fresh meat on display. It didn't take long before I began to build a little clientele. Each weekend I knew there would be at least three guys I could depend on for major loot, and there was one guy in particular I actually looked forward to seeing each weekend—Roc.

Luckily, I was able to get him on the team. Of course, I put in a little work, but it wasn't nearly as hard as I'd expected. It started off with a simple dance; then it turned into dances with a little extra seduction, caressing, and sweet nothings in the ear. Then I pretended to be interested in things about him other than his money. Before long we'd become pretty close—close enough for me to tell him a little about my situation and for him to vow to help, and the good thing was, he agreed to do a little more than just hit me off with loot. He was my MVP.

It was getting closer and closer to T.J.'s date in family court. With the money Stacey was hitting me off on Li'l Man's behalf, the money Young Boy was giving, and the money I was making dancing, I was stacking major loot. I hired the best attorney that I could find. Shit was definitely coming together! The only problem and unfinished business I had was Stacey. Although we both agreed to chill for the moment, neither of us was really feeling the other. And recently the bitch hadn't been bringing my money over as directed. I had some ill feelings toward her from jump, but I had really been building up even more of them for her conniving ass.

After Stacey brought me the first one thousand dollars, as Li'l Man had instructed her to do—and it took her ass two weeks to

nickel and dime me that—I ain't heard from or seen the bitch. At
first I was complaining to Li'l Man left and right. He would call
her to see what was up, and she was always supposed to be on her
way. But after the first few days Stacey didn't show, I knew what
the deal was. Li'l Man was sure he could straighten her ass out and
she would be bringing me the money, but he was in for a big surprise.

After a week of him constantly calling Stacey and her making
false promises, that bitch eventually put a block on her phone.
That put an end to all contact. We tried calling her on a three-way
a couple of times, but that bitch was obviously hip to that shit,
too, because she would never pick up. Of course, Li'l Man was
boiling inside, but it was quite comical to me. I was happy Li'l
Man finally got a chance to see Stacey's true colors. I couldn't help
but tell him, "I told you so."

"I told you the bitch was shiesty!" I would constantly remind
Li'l Man. It didn't take long before my words got in his head, and
he began to curse the ground Stacey walked on.

"Man, I should have known what was up with that bitch from
the jump!" Li'l Man said, frustrated that Stacey didn't answer another one of our three-way-call attempts.

"Li'l Man, I don't even know why you tripping. I told you from
the start that bitch was a hater! But you were so sure she had no
reason to hate on me that you wouldn't listen. I read her from
the jump. I knew after she gave up the first bit of dough that I
wouldn't see her again. That bitch had no intention of bringing
me shit else. That wasn't nothing but hush money."

"You right, baby girl," Li'l Man finally admitted. "Now that I
think back, there was a lot of little shit she used to say that I
should have caught on to. She never wanted you to have the baby.
Every day she had a reason why I should make you have an abortion, and believe it or not, the shit she was saying was really con-

vincing. Then once she knew there was no changing my mind about you having the baby, she turned to convincing me that you were going to use T.J. against me to get whatever you wanted from me. At first I was like, 'Nah,' but then she started pointing out how often you called and little shit like that. I eventually fell sucka to that shit, too. I don't know what I was thinking. I fucked up, Tee. You were right. I don't know what else to say."

Li'l Man had finally seen the light. I never thought I would see the day when he realized his little princess was really the devil's daughter. Now that Stacey had broken the truce, it was time for me to get my revenge, and I knew just how I would go about getting it.

Timing was everything as I prepared to execute my plan. I reviewed it over and over in my head as I got dressed for court. Constantly watching the clock, I wanted everything to be perfect. It all had to be executed on point to be sure I would never be a suspect in the shit that was about to go down.

Stacey had made the ultimate mistake, and it was time for her to pay. I actually thought about what I might wear to her funeral as I scrolled though my closet to pick out the perfect outfit for court.

What a day, what a day! I thought, taking a navy blue dress from the rack. I placed it up against me and turned to the full-length mirror on the closet door. I smiled at my reflection as I thought about the joy I'd feel when I got T.J. back and revenge on Stacey. Just then my doorbell rang. I looked over at the clock. It read 8:30 a.m. It was Young Boy, and he was on time, as usual.

He'd been by my side since the first day I told him about losing T.J. He had promised to take me to the court and stand by me before and after T.J. was home. I was actually thinking of making

Young Boy T.J.'s godfather. He'd been the closest thing to a god-parent that T.J. had. Hell, he was the closet thing T.J. had to a fa-ther. Young Boy was the one putting up most of the money for the lawyer, taking me to see T.J., paying bills, and doing all the things Li'l Man was supposed to be doing. He even paid the damn phone bill Li'l Man ran up with all those collect calls. So in my eyes, Young Boy was more than worthy to be T.J.'s godfather. Shit, I figured Li'l Man didn't bother asking me about that shiesty bitch Stacey being the godmother, so I didn't owe him the respect of asking if Young Boy could be the godfather.

After letting Young Boy in, I went back to my bedroom and slipped on my navy blue dress. I called my people up real quick and gave them the okay before leaving my apartment and hop-ping in the car with Young Boy. As we drove to the courthouse I constantly checked my watch. The sweet smell of revenge was in the air. At nine o'clock I would be sitting in the courtroom, and that's when the shit would hit the fan. My stomach bubbled with fear as the reality of the events that were about to occur set in. But there was no turning back now. The ball was already in motion.

For the past few days I had watched to see when Stacey arrived and left school. This day she wouldn't arrive. Nine o'clock came and passed. Court began and was adjourned, and as expected, T.J. was returned to me. Thanks to money and people Young Boy knew, I was presented as the world's fittest mother. He arranged for everyone from pastors to doctors to testify on my behalf.

Now it was time to see if Stacey had been dealt with. I had Young Boy stop at a convenience store to grab something to drink, and I used the pay phone there to call my people. I didn't want to use my cell just in case shit got hot somewhere down the line.

I dropped the coins in the pay phone, dialed the number, and let the phone ring. After the second ring, the phone was answered.

"How's the weather?" I asked.

"The weather is lovely," the male voice on the other end answered.

That was all I needed to hear. After his response I made arrangements to meet him later. We said as little as possible. I smiled and headed back to the car, drinking the Slurpee I had just purchased from the convenience store. I rode the entire way home with that smile on my face. My son was back with me, and Stacey had gotten what she deserved.

Once I got home I invited Young Boy inside. I figured the least I could do was cook him brunch. He'd done so much for me, all the while asking for nothing in return. Once inside my place I turned on the television for Young Boy and headed into the kitchen to cook. From the kitchen I watched Young Boy as he played with T.J. Although he had no kids of his own, it seemed so natural the way he interacted with T.J. It didn't take long before I was finished cooking and began to set the table.

"Yo, Tee!" Young Boy called in a frantic manner.

I rushed over, afraid that something was wrong with T.J. Instead I walked in to see Young Boy's eyes glued to the television. With the remote in hand, he turned up the volume. I listened as they interviewed a badly beaten woman. The reporter stated that the woman's home was burglarized, and she had been assaulted in the process. It seemed that the robbers had gotten away with a number of expensive pieces of jewelry, money, and her new BMW R X5.

"Ain't that yo' girl Stacey?" Young Boy asked.

It took all I had to keep from smiling as I answered, "Yep." I paused for a moment, staring at the television. "Oh, well, I guess what goes around carries around." I said as I walked out of the room and finished setting the table.

A smile crept across my lips as I envisioned Stacey's battered face. She was fucked-up and better off dead, if you asked me. But

I didn't feel the least bit sorry for her. That bitch had gotten what she deserved. She wasn't dead, but she was close to it. She was dead financially, though. I made sure my people stripped her of all the things that made her the prissy bitch she was: the fancy designer-label clothes, the jewelry, the car, and Li'l Man's safe. My people had followed the plan perfectly. Like clockwork, they ran up in Stacey's spot and collected everything, but not before giving her a lifelong reminder, a beating that would always haunt her. I couldn't have whipped that ass better myself. She got a blow for each day my son was away from me.

It took a minute, but I eventually put two and two together and realized that when she failed to convince Li'l Man into making me kill T.J. by having an abortion, that bitch tried to kill him by poisoning him with alcohol. That would have definitely gotten T.J. out of the picture—and me, too, for that matter, considering I probably would have had to go to jail for that shit. But none of that mattered anymore. Her plan failed and mine prevailed.

After eating, I made T.J. a bottle and began to clean up the kitchen. Young Boy offered to feed him as I cleaned. Again, things looked so natural as Young Boy took T.J. into his arms and fed him his bottle. I stood there and smiled at the sight of the two of them, but at the same time I couldn't help but think, *Why couldn't Li'l Man be here doing these things?*

Before I knew it, tears were rolling down my face. Young Boy looked up at me standing there.

"What's wrong, baby girl?" he asked.

"Nothing," I replied, sniffing and quickly wiping my tears away. "It's just that I want the best for T.J., and without a father, I don't know if he'll have it. When I look at you two together, I just think of the things he'll miss out on without an active father."

"Like I told you before, I got'cha back," he quickly responded.

Bang! Bang! Our conversation was interrupted by a knock at the door. I walked over to the door and opened it. Standing there was Roc, my dude from the strip club. He'd come through just as promised. After Roc shared a little bit about his reputation on the streets with me, I knew he was perfect for this job. It didn't take much game for him to have pity for me. So when I hit him with my plot for revenge on Stacey, he readily agreed—no questions asked!

"Merry Christmas!" Roc said before handing me a duffel bag. He winked and then walked away.

I walked into my bedroom and closed the door behind me, leaving Young Boy in the living room to finish feeding T.J. I put the bag on the bed and began to inspect the contents. I counted twenty-five stacks of ten hundred-dollar bills.

"Twenty-five thousand dollars!" I said softly. I nearly fainted. Stacey had gotten what she deserved, Li'l Man had gotten what he deserved, and I had gotten what I deserved. Now it was time for T.J. to get what he deserved.

I returned to the living room with Young Boy and T.J.

"Everything okay?" Young Boy asked, inquiring about the knock at the door.

"Yes, just perfect," I responded. "Now, what were you saying before I left?" I asked, attempting to pick up where our conversation had left off before the knock on the door interrupted us.

"I was just saying that I got you and T.J.'s backs," he replied.

I wasn't really sure what Young Boy was prepared to do for T.J. and me, but I figured this would be the perfect time to formalize his relationship with my son.

"Young Boy, you've been the closet thing me and T.J. have had to a baby father. I know you can't hold that title, but I would like to offer you the title of godfather, if you will accept."

Young Boy's face brightened as I spoke. "Fa' sho'!" he replied with excitement. "I love this li'l nigga like he my own already."

I exhaled. My struggles were finally over, and not a minute too soon. According to Li'l Man, thanks to his parole violation, he would more than likely be behind bars for the next five years. I was not about to wait around for him and continue living the life of some project chick. It took a lot of bullshit to wade through, but I realized that there wasn't shit cute about that kind of life. I wanted more for T.J. I was turning in a new direction. I had gained a motherly bond with my child that I never thought would happen. Having T.J. in my arms gave me a feeling of joy that I'd never felt before. Looking into T.J.'s big eyes made me proud to be a mom. I now looked forward to the dirty diapers, late nights, and bottles of formula. And I'd found a father figure for my son.

There was no more looking back. Everything from this point on would be for T.J. and Tee, not for Li'l Man's son and Li'l Man's baby mama. I was gladly willing to pass down that crown.

LAKESA COX

POWER

Definition of a woman with power: That corporate chick in the game who knows the power of her pussy and her mind and knows how and when to use them both.

Talk about a way to end a party! *Thump, thump, thump.* With every stroke of my manhood her head hit the bottom of the table. Hungrily, Paula sucked and licked and hit her head, sucked, licked, hit her head, all to a perfect rhythm. Paula was giving me dome like I'd never had it before, and I moaned and groaned through every lick. Good thing everybody else had left for the night; otherwise, they'd all have been getting an earful from the City of Richmond's new commonwealth's attorney, Christian Hall. Not only was I the new commonwealth's attorney, but I was also the youngest person ever to be voted into this position. At thirty-five, I was still in my prime, eager to take on the thugs and criminals who had taken over the streets of Richmond. Paula, my executive assistant, felt that this phenomenal day shouldn't end without a bang, which was just about what I was going to do in her mouth until she pulled away. I came all over the front of her blue dress. She rose from beneath my new oversize mahogany desk and sat on top of it with her legs spread open, revealing her blond pubic hair. She probably wanted me to reciprocate, but I never planned on going down on her. Not that I would have ever told her that.

"So?" she said, questioning me as if today might be her lucky day.

"Paula, you know I'm not quite ready to go there yet," I said coyly.

"Come on, Chris. When are we gonna . . . well, you know?"

"When it happens, it won't be on top of this desk, that's for sure. Be patient, sweetheart. When we take this to the next level, it's definitely going to be worth the wait."

I kissed her on the cheek as I zipped my pants. Paula sucked her teeth, grabbed her hot pink thong from my in-box, and hopped down off the desk.

"Chris, I think I've been more than patient. This is ridiculous. I want you so bad. I need to feel you inside me. Is that too much to ask?"

"No, it's not too much to ask. And yes, you have been patient. But just give me some time. It'll happen. Trust me," I replied with a sincere look in my eyes.

She flashed a smile that told me she believed me.

"Okay. I'll see you later then," she said.

"Bye, sweetheart," I said as she left my office. I made a note to go to a jewelry store to pick her up a token of my appreciation. Nothing big, just something to keep her off my back with that sex talk. See, sleeping with Paula wasn't part of my agenda. Paula was a nice girl and everything, but she was nobody I'd ever consider getting serious with. Getting blow jobs in the office is every man's fantasy, but that was about all she could offer me. Don't get me wrong—Paula gave good head, but number one, she was definitely not my type, and number two, she was dumb as dirt. Even if number one and two weren't an issue, there was still number three: my grandmother. She always said, "If she can't use your comb, you can't bring her home."

Even though I dated a white girl or two in high school, my grandmother never knew about them. Since my grandmother is my pride and joy, I always do what I know will make her proud of me. My mother was a strung-out crack addict who left when I was ten, and I haven't seen her since. My father, a two-bit hustler who introduced my mother to crack, disappeared after he found out he was wanted by the police for the rape of two thirteen-year-old girls who lived in our neighborhood. So, at the age of ten, I was forced to pack my things and move in with Grandma Lucy. My grandfather had recently died of liver cancer, so Grandma Lucy was all alone and happy to have me move in with her. She reared me the best she could, instilling in me the idea that nothing was impossible.

After watching how my mother and father lost their souls to the streets, I vowed to become a lawyer and help clean the streets of drugs and drug dealers so that other kids wouldn't have to grow up without a mother's and father's love. I made Grandma Lucy proud when I graduated from Hermitage High School in 1987 as the valedictorian with a GPA of 4.0. I went to the University of Richmond on a full scholarship, graduated, and went straight to law school at the University of Virginia. After graduating from the UVA, I took the state bar and passed it on the first try. I worked at a couple of law firms until I was given the opportunity to work as an assistant commonwealth's attorney, with a concentration on criminal felony cases. After assisting in several high-

profile cases and helping to convict some of Richmond's notorious criminals, I finally became Richmond's commonwealth's
attorney, aka HNIC (Head Nigga in Charge).

So, I had the career that I had dreamed of all my life. The only
thing missing was a woman in my corner to share my successes
with. Unfortunately, Paula wasn't that woman. By the time she'd
realize it, though, I'd have promoted her and moved her to a job
making more money, in a bigger office, and with a supervisor with
an even bigger appetite for sex. The way I saw it, she'd find a man
in the same skin she was in and would forget all about me.

I grabbed the *Richmond Times Dispatch* newspaper. Front and
center was my photo, with a headline that read, "Youngest Commonwealth's Attorney in the History of Richmond." But then,
just below my front-page article was a story about the city's most
recent homicide, which appeared to be drug related. The body of
an unidentified young black male was found over in Creighton
Court, one of Richmond's housing projects. It sickened me every
time I read a story like this. Drug dealers appeared to be running
this city, and as the commonwealth's attorney, I planned to get rid
of as many of them as possible, if for no other reason than for the
sake of my mother. As far as I knew, she could still be out there,
getting high, continuing to poison herself to death. Maybe in
some way I could get some relief, knowing that I helped get rid of
the culprits responsible for keeping my mother addicted and put
them away for a long, long time.

RENÉE

"You know what, nigga? It ain't even about you. It's about me. See,
I sent you to do a job that should've been simple and easy. But no,
you got the police coming around my restaurant asking me ques-

tions. I can't have that. I've come too far for too long to get caught up," said Tank.

I was standing outside of the two-car-garage door listening as my man, Tank, decided the fate of this dude who had double-crossed him. See, Tank was the big man around Richmond. He controlled Creighton Court, Gilpin Court, Fairfield Court, Whitcomb Court, and Mosby Court. The only housing project he didn't run was Hillside Court, which he and I were working on.

I walked to the front of Tank's colonial-style, three-story brick home, which sat on ten acres in New Kent County, right outside of Richmond, and leaned against a tall column to wait for Tank. I knew Tank wasn't going to do the dude in the garage, because it would be too messy. He was giving the dude one last opportunity to redeem himself, maybe offer up some information on the competition or something. He was definitely going to kill him, though. The only person who knew about this place was me. Then there were those who knew but wouldn't have the opportunity to tell anyone else about it. The garage door opened, and I realized this dude was taking his final walk down the green mile. He was whimpering and begging Tank to spare his life.

"Tank, man, please! My girl just had a baby and shit. She don't have nobody but me. Please, Tank, listen to me for a minute!" the dude pleaded.

"Can't do it, nigga. Just keep walkin'. I promise you, it's going to be quick and painless," Tank said without emotion.

"But, Tank, I need you to understand, the shit didn't go down the way you thinkin'. Give me a chance to explain. . . ."

Their voices drifted as they got farther away. Tank took the dude to the woods behind the house. The woods seemed to go on for miles, but Tank had certain "hot spots" where he did his dirty work. These hot spots consisted of open graves six feet deep. He forced his victims to jump down in the hole, shot them, then buried them. Only in extreme cases did Tank resort to this, since he normally had his boys handle all of his dirty work. In fact, I could count on one hand the number of situations where Tank had to take care of business himself.

I headed inside to wait for Tank, and before I could make it through the foyer I heard a single gunshot. The sound was so deafening that it startled me, and I dropped my keys. At that moment I realized the dude was dead. A chill went up my spine at the thought of someone being murdered right outside the house.

I proceeded through the minimansion to the stainless-steel kitchen. Grabbing a bottle of water, I sat on one of the bar stools, slid up to the granite counter, and waited for Tank. It's not like I didn't have any work to do. As the executive director for Richmond Redevelopment and Housing Authority (RRHA), I stayed pretty busy. But I just was not in the mood to check e-mail, approve vouchers, review proposals, or anything. I just wanted to sit and be lazy all day.

Of course, Tank would have other plans. He probably wanted to sex me all up and down this big house while he had the chance. We rarely had time to spend alone anymore. My schedule was always hectic, and Tank . . . well, his business kept him busy. There was no telling what could happen from one minute to the next, so anytime we got an opportunity to be together, we used it to the fullest. There were only a few people who even knew about our relationship, because we kept it private.

Tank and I had been together for twenty years. We'd known each other since we were five. We grew up in Gilpin Court together, went to elementary, middle, and high school together. By the time we were fifteen, we decided to take our friendship to the next level. So, one summer night, behind the Calhoun Community Center, at the bottom of a steep hill, I lost my virginity to Tank. I believe we were in love way before then, but just didn't know it. However, that night, for sure, we fell in love. To com-memorate our big night, Tank engraved, *Tank loves Renée 4 ever, 4 always* on the big tree we lay under after having sex for the very first time.

As we got older, Tank became more and more drawn to street life, while I, on the other hand, took a different path. In the evenings after school I worked for Gilpin Court's RRHA office doing menial work, filing, answering phones, etc. By the time I graduated from high school and went away to college at Old Do-minion University, Tank and I were serious. Sure, Tank had his freaks on the side, doing whatever while I was away, but I made sure that when he came to visit me on the weekends, I served him up hard enough so those freaks' jobs wouldn't be easy. I realize it was all part of his image, but I caught on quick in the bedroom and made sure Tank was and continued to be satisfied. So those tricks he dealt with while I was away were just a technicality, giv-ing Tank something to do while I was getting my education.

During summer vacations I worked at the RRHA office while Tank was in the streets making a name for himself. When I gradu-ated from ODU in 1991, RRHA offered me a job as a specialist approving Section Eight applications at their main office on Chamberlayne Parkway. I had access to all records pertaining to the different housing projects. I worked my way through several other positions with RRHA; then in 2000 I was promoted to ex-ecutive director. See, Tank had a vision. When he first mentioned it, I thought he was crazy.

"Renée, what would you do if I told you you held the key to our future?" Of course, at the time I had no idea what Tank meant.

"You approve those Section Eight applications, right?"

"Yeah, so what?"

"Look, what if I was to send some females to you that needed an application approved for a specific housing project; could you hook it up?" By now, I'm pissed, assuming Tank is talking about one of his tricks. I give him the I-can't-believe-you-parted-your-lips-to-ask-me-that look.

"It's not what you think, baby. See, all my boys, they on the come-up right now. But I hate that they have to be out there on the corners without safety. I figure if I send you some of their girlfriends, get them set up in a project nearby where they do their slinging, shit, I'll have the projects on lock in no time."

The first thing that came to mind was that I would be risking my job. But once Tank put it all in perspective, it all made sense.

"Renée, nothing illegal—all these broads need a place to stay anyway; may as well set them up where they can be the most use," Tank said.

See, Tank had a vision. He knew that he wanted to be the sole drug supplier for all of the housing projects in Richmond. With me as his eyes into each project community, I could make sure that certain Section Eight applications were filled first, and that the applicants always stayed up-to-date on inspections and so forth. By the time I was promoted, Tank's heroin business was booming; plus he'd even opened a restaurant and bar to make everything look legit, all thanks to his "plan."

So really, we had always been a team. But because of the nature of the business he was in and the nature of the business I was in, we had to keep everything private. Every now and then I might run into someone from our old neighborhood who asked what was up with Tank. Since Tank was into the street life, he was more visible on that scene. The people I came in contact with on a daily basis had no idea that I was even affiliated with someone as treacherous as Tank. So on a business level our worlds were separate, but on a personal level we shared one world. Sometimes I would feel sad because I couldn't flaunt our relationship around others. But I know how hard it is to find a good man, and Tank was always good to me. Always kept me in a nice ride—all rimmed up, of course—bought me diamonds on the regular, and the shopping sprees to Tyson's Corner . . . well, let's just say he always spent at least ten grand each time. Material things can't define love, but I knew Tank loved me because of the future we planned to have together. I was also very proud of Tank for all that he had accomplished. He was a street-savvy, intelligent brother. No, he hadn't gone to college and gotten a degree on paper, but he was able to get out of the projects and open his own business. He was equally proud of me for all I had accomplished, so together we made a great team.

When Tank came in, his cream-colored linen pants were muddy, full of blood, and his matching linen shirt was full of sweat.

"You okay, baby?" I asked, concerned.

"Yeah, I'm a'ight," he said, looking at the trail of mud he was making with his messy pants.

He walked over to the restaurant-size stainless-steel double sink and washed his hands. He had sweat all over his bronze-colored body, so much that his linen outfit clung to him. Even with sweat dripping from his bald head, he still looked sexy. He removed his shirt to display his six-pack abs. I walked over to him and wrapped my arms around him and laid my head on his back. He turned off the water, but didn't turn around to face me. Though it bothered me a little when Tank had to wipe someone out, I understood, especially when it was someone who threatened to destroy all he had built over the years.

See, I realized that one day, when Tank got tired of running the drug business, he would put all of his eggs in one basket, concentrate on legit businesses, and we would settle down and have a real family together, kids and all. Dealing with him wasn't easy, because there were so many crooks out there pretending to be his friend, yet stabbing him in the back at the same time. Not to mention the women who practically threw themselves at him. I needed to help protect him, at least until he was able to make that all-important transition from the drug game to a totally legitimate way of living.

"Hey, what's wrong?" I asked him softly, almost in a whisper.

He looked at me with his almond-shaped eyes and full, juicy lips and said, "I have a problem."

"What is it?"

He pulled away, unbuttoned his pants, and let them drop to the marble-tiled floor. Grabbing my hand, he wanted me to follow him. He was wearing nothing but his Kenneth Cole boxers. We walked through the kitchen to the family room, which was furnished with leather furniture, a plasma TV, and a custom-built pool table. He sat on the oversize sofa and pulled me onto his lap.

"I need you to do something for me," he said, looking me in the eyes.

"Of course, anything, baby," I said, rubbing my hand down his face.

"One of my connects told me the police are out to get me. They came over to the restaurant and started asking me a lot of questions about Li'l John's disappearance, but I thought that was all they wanted. Apparently they're trying to get enough information to put a murder case on me."

"But Li'l John was classified as missing, right? What makes them think he was murdered?"

"Li'l John's friend Skeet was pulled up on a conspiracy-to-distribute charge and started telling the police that he could give them info on a murder if they would reduce his charges. He started running off at the mouth, saying he saw Li'l John the same day he went missing, and Li'l John told Skeet that I was after him."

"But I thought Li'l John didn't have any idea you were onto him?" I asked.

"Yeah, me too. This shit is fucked up. I've been getting away for so long, handling my business without getting dirty. Now this!" Tank snapped.

"Well, what is it you want me to do?" I asked.

Tank took my hand into his. "Before I ask you, promise me you'll think about it first, before you give me an answer."

"Come on, Tank, what is it?"

Tank sighed heavily, then grabbed both of my hands. I had no idea what he wanted me to do, but I was willing to do whatever it took to keep my man out of trouble.

"You know that new commonwealth's attorney? That young nigga?" he said.

"Christian Hall is his name, I think. I don't know him personally, but I've been in his presence at a couple of city functions."

"I need you to get to him."

"Get to him and do what?" Now Tank had totally confused me.

"Baby, I need you to hook up with him, you know, get in his head and shit. I want you to make him want you bad enough to do anything you ask."

I jumped up. I couldn't believe he would have the nerve to ask me to do something this crazy.

"Tank, what the fuck?"

"I know it sounds crazy, but hear me out. This nigga is young, and word on the street is, he's single. I've been in the locker room at the gym with him a couple of times, and the motherfucker is cocky as shit. Niggas like him can be pussy-whipped in no time."

"Wait a minute, you want me to fuck him, too? Oh, hell, no! This shit is crazy!" I said, throwing my arms up as I began pacing back and forth.

"Baby, listen, just think about it. He's gonna think he hit the jackpot with you. You're beautiful, smart, plus you have a promi-nent position with RRHA. You two can go to different functions together, you know, start to become a couple. Throw the pussy on him and he's gonna be down for you. Get him to trust you—trust you enough that you have access to his office and his home. That's when it's gonna get grimy. We're gonna set his ass up, you know, blackmail him. Then, the only way he'll come out of it clean is to get my case thrown out."

I couldn't believe what I was hearing. Not only was he asking me to cheat on him, but he wanted me to get involved with black-mailing a city official. I didn't know if I could go through with something like that. I mean, I knew what I did at work was wrong, but there was no way to tie me to any type of illegal ac-tivity based on the information I gave to Tank. Forcing approvals on Section Eight applications is one thing, but this?

"Renée, look, I need you to do this. Can't you understand? If you don't do this for me, I could go to prison for murder. They might try to tie me to some other crimes, too." Tank rubbed his hand across his brow, wiping the sweat.

"Look at everything we've built. Think about our future that we've been working so hard to build, which is only around the corner. It's only a matter of time before I give this street shit up and we move on with our plans to get married and have us some kids. If I go to jail now over some bullshit, all that'll be ruined."

I stared at Tank and could see his eyes begin to water. I knew it was hard for him to ask me to do such a thing. Even harder for him to think about me doing it—he would probably regret hav-ing me do this later on, but right now it looked like the only way out. Tank was the only man I'd ever been with, and he had taught me well. After being together for twenty years, I'd learned a lot and done it all, but only because Tank had been my one and only.

Now he wanted me to give myself to a stranger—for a good reason, I knew, but still, I just couldn't imagine being with someone other than Tank. Even when Tank allowed those chickenheads to entice him, I always stayed true, because that was how deep my love was for him.

"Please?" he begged.

I sighed heavily.

"But, Tank, what if I can't pull this off? I mean, he might be a faggot or something," I said with doubt.

"Renée, come on now," he said in a reassuring tone.

"I'm serious. How is this shit going to work, Tank? I'll just force myself on him and he's going to go for me? Just like that?" I threw up my hands and rolled my eyes.

"You're smart and you know how to play the game. I wouldn't ask you to do this if I didn't have faith in you. Think about it, Renée. If you don't do this, they could put me under for a long, long time. No wedding, no kids—nothing for us.

"We will finally be able to put our relationship out in the open when I become legit. All them niggas and tricks will know about us, baby. Just you and me against the motherfuckin' world! Do you wanna mess all that up when you have the opportunity right now to straighten it?"

I guess he's right, I thought. Even if he wasn't right, he was not going to give up until I said I'd do it anyway.

"Okay. I'll do it," I said in surrender.

Tank planted his lips on mine, then hugged me tightly. My body language told him that I was still unsure whether I was making the right decision. He kissed me on my neck and started to tease my breasts. I turned to face him, straddling his body with mine. Now he had one hand between my legs and the other in my shirt. I moaned as he played with each nipple, while at the same time hitting my spot. His manhood was standing at attention right between us, so I pulled it through the opening of his boxers and stroked it with my hands, meeting Tank's tongue with mine. He had me feeling so wet that I got down on my knees and took him into my mouth, working it like there were no more lollipops left in the city of Richmond. His back stiffened. I began workin' it faster, making him moan. Before he had the chance to explode, I jumped on top of it and rode him, taking every inch until he came. Both of our bodies went limp and we just held each other, breathing hard. I knew at that moment, with everything in me, that no matter what, I had to do whatever it took to keep my man out of prison.

I ran out of my office on Chamberlayne Parkway and hopped into my recent birthday gift from Tank, a black 2006 C-Class Mercedes. I was trying to beat the five-o'clock rush-hour traffic and head over to American Family Fitness on Brook Road. I decided to drive through the city instead of getting on the interstate, because I knew I-95 would be bumper-to-bumper. This was the day I would make my move on Mr. Hall. I was nervous. All kinds of shit that might fuck things up kept running through my head. What if I wasn't his type? His square-looking ass was probably gay, or maybe he didn't even like sisters.

I knew I had it going on as a sistah. I worked out about four times a week, one hour a day. I had a body like Angela Bassett's in *What's Love Got to Do with It*. My caramel skin was flawless, smooth like silk, and my hair was natural, no weaves there. I never needed one, since my half–Native American father, the same one who abandoned me when I was six, blessed me with his coal-black, naturally wavy hair. I inherited everything else from my mother, who raised me and my two brothers all by herself in the projects. My mother, a thick, chocolate sister with lots of street savvy and spunk, was always weak when it came to a good-looking brotha with pretty hair. So, after knowing my father only two months, she became pregnant with me; then two years later she had my twin brothers. Soon after the twins were born she married my father. Realizing that fatherhood wasn't for him, he split. He moved to New York, leaving her a single mother of a six-year-old and two four-year-olds. So we headed to the projects.

After I pulled into the parking lot of American Family Fitness, I made my way inside the gym and headed toward the locker room to change clothes, all the while keeping my eyes open for Mr. Christian Hall, the man I planned to pussy-whip for a good cause.

Soon after changing into my red sports bra and shorts, I walked through the weight-lifting area and spotted him. I'd seen him a couple of times at recent functions, but I didn't realize the brotha was so damn fine. He had a Boris Kodjoe thing going on for sure, body and all. I hoped Tank knew what he was doing, planning this hookup with Chris.

I had to get one of the other fellas to stare at me so that Chris could follow suit. I bent over to tie my shoe, which I left untied on purpose so that I could give the guys a sneak peek at my thirty-six Ds.

"Damn, shorty!" some dude on the weight bench said. His male radar kicking in, Chris turned around and stared at me just as I stood back up from tying my shoe. I rolled my eyes and sucked my teeth at the punk on the weight bench, while trying not to notice Chris. I grabbed a couple of ten-pound barbells, then sat at an empty weight bench. I could feel Chris staring a hole through the back of my head, but I kept my composure. My cell phone rang (actually, I had set the alarm to go off). I answered it and carried on a fake conversation, knowing that there was no one on the other end.

"Hello?" I said. "No, it's no problem, Angela. What is it?"

I paused as if I were really listening to someone on the other end.

"No, I specifically told Mr. Williams that the proposal needed to be revised," I continued. "If the budget is not in compliance with the City of Richmond, then we will have to forfeit the entire agreement. Tell him I need the revision no later than nine a.m. tomorrow. Call me if you have any problems."

I closed my flip phone and laid it on the bench beside me. Before I could even begin my workout routine, Chris walked over to me.

"Excuse me, I'm Christian Hall, Richmond's newest commonwealth's attorney," he boasted. He then held out his hand. I shook it, staring at him like he was a terrible imposition.

"Okay, and . . . ?" I said, eyes wide.

"Well, when I heard you say something about being in compliance with the City of Richmond, I immediately felt obligated to jump in to assist, since I have so many connections in the city."

"Did I ask for your assistance, Mr. Hall?" I asked. Tank had warned me of his cockiness, which was being proven by the way he approached me and introduced himself. What a jerk.

"No offense, miss. I swear, I didn't mean to offend you. I just thought I could help."

"You and every guy in here, I'm sure," I said sarcastically.

"No, I'm for real. Where exactly do you work?" he asked.

"I'm the executive director for Richmond Redevelopment and Housing Authority," I replied in a laid-back tone.

He paused, squinting his eyes to observe me. "Hey, I know you. You're Denise Anderson, right?"

"Yes, but my friends call me Renée."

"Well, Renée—" he said with a huge grin on his face before I quickly cut him off.

"I said, my *friends* call me Renée," I snapped. I had to let him know right then that I wasn't some woman who needed a man with a title to identify me. I had my own title, thank you very much.

"Well, Ms. Anderson, I think we met at the Minority League's luncheon last year. You don't remember?"

"No, I don't," I said sarcastically.

"I remember you," he said matter-of-factly.

"Okay, look, Mr. Hall, I'm trying to work out. So what is it that you want?" I looked up at him. I didn't show it, but I was indeed taken by this brotha's fineness. I thought my Tank had the best lips and abs in town, but Chris was definitely strong competition.

"Ms. Anderson, I just thought . . . well, you know, I could talk to you, take you out for drink or something. I mean, damn, you really are making me look bad in front of my boy." He nodded to the dude on the weight bench.

"Maybe next time you should leave your cockiness at the door before you approach me," I said, staring at the bulge in his sweatpants. If he had gotten any harder just from staring at me, he was going to be easier than I thought.

"I apologize. I was in my work zone. I forgot where I was for a moment. Let me start over." He cleared his throat. "Hi, my name is Chris, Chris Hall. And you are?"

"Denise Anderson." I paused, turning my lips up as I looked him over. "But you can call me Renée."

From that point on, Chris and I became engrossed in city politics and discovered we had a lot in common. Neither of us got the chance to finish our workouts, because we spent so much time talking. When I finally looked down at my watch it was almost nine o'clock p.m. Chris and I exchanged business cards and agreed to meet for dinner that Friday.

After leaving the gym, I headed to my studio apartment in an exclusive Tobacco Row apartment complex in Shockoe Bottom. Before I could even reach my bedroom to unwind, the phone rang. It was Chris. Since I hadn't checked in with Tank yet, I let the call go to voice mail. I felt like I needed to let Tank know that everything was moving on as planned. I turned to walk to my bedroom and realized that Tank was standing right behind me. His sudden presence scared me to death.

"Tank, what are you doing here?" I asked, startled.

"Came to see how everything went. Based on the time and the call you just got, everything must've gone really well. I'm proud of you, Boo," he said. I could detect a bit of sarcasm in his voice.

"Listen, this was your idea. I can cut this short right now if it's going to be a problem for you."

"No problem. Just hard for a nigga to imagine his girl with somebody else, that's all. But it's cool. We gotta do this for our future." He kissed me on the forehead, then threw two stacks of money on the counter.

"I need you to put this in your account for me. I just made a big deposit in my business account, but I don't want it to look suspect."

"Tank, are you sure you're okay with this?" I said, going back to the original subject matter.

"Baby, I'm fine. Do your thing," he said nonchalantly.

"You don't give me the impression that you're fine."

"Well, I am. It's cool."

I tried to find something in Tank's face to tell me that he really wanted me to change my mind and refuse to go along with the plan, but I didn't detect a thing.

"You going up top tonight?" I asked.

"Yeah, gotta pick up a few bricks."

"I really don't want you going to New York, especially not by yourself, Tank. Not with the way things are going now," I said worriedly. "The police might be—"

"Look," he said, cutting me off, not wanting me to jinx him. "I can't trust nobody right now, so I have to go. I have to go solo."

"You can't trust *nobody*?"

"You know what I mean, them niggas. Look, I gotta head over to the restaurant and handle some business before I get on the road. Go ahead and call that nigga Chris back. Handle your business, Boo." He kissed me on the lips this time, patted me on the ass, and left. No matter what he said, I got the feeling that Tank wasn't really up for this whole deal. On top of that, he left without putting one finger on me, which made me suspicious. There were only two things that kept Tank from sexing me up—my cycle and another woman. But we'd come too far to move back to those days again. Tank's life was on the line, and I was sure that he was thinking about everything he had at stake. The reality of me being with someone else had hit him hard, too. But just like a man, he would never admit he made a mistake.

TANK

As I pulled my SUV out of the underground parking garage below Renée's apartment, I was thinking I might have made a mistake asking her to get with ol' dude. She'd never been with another man, even when she went away to college. When she found out about the li'l tricks who tried to get at me, as well as those that I hit a few times, she still never stepped out on me. She was one hundred percent wifey material, and I planned to marry her one day, just not as soon as she would like it to be. I hadn't been as good to her on the emotional end as she had been to me. But I tried to make up for it by buying her everything a girl could want—diamond tennis bracelets and solitaire earrings when her friends were still sportin' gold, a Mercedes all kitted up, even had her in Gucci long before the Asian street vendors were imitating them. I had a certain image to uphold. Renée understood that, not that she agreed with it.

I tried to remove myself from her life. Once when I thought the feds were closing in on me and my freedom was in jeopardy, I broke it off with Renée. I didn't want her to become another "prison wife," where the highlight of our relationship would be weekend visits and daily collect calls. I didn't want that for her. I promised myself if I was given another shot at freedom, I would work on going legit. Hustlin' heroin and murderin' might not have made me a bad guy in her eyes, but making her guilty by association would. I never felt bad for the things I did in the street. My pops always said, *As long as you don't become your own customer, you can survive in this game.* I always remembered that, even though he got burned back in 2000. After that he was doing twenty-five to life for two murders and conspiracy.

I just needed to make another two million dollars the wrong way, which would be enough to add to the stash, as well as front a car audio and detail store specializing in rims. The banks around here wouldn't give a brotha a break, so I had to go at it the hard way. Same as with the restaurant. I had to front all of the money to get the restaurant up and operational. I was only $200,000 short of my goal, and then I was done with this game for good. The only problem was trying to stay clean of that Li'l John murder. I been lucky to keep the po-po out my drug business. I realized they were trying to build a case against me on that, too, but I wouldn't dare tell Renée. I didn't have any other options, and so I was forced to get Renée to set this corny-ass nigga up and push him in a corner like a roach so he couldn't get out unless he helped me.

I headed over to the restaurant, which is on East Broad Street, about a block up from where the old Ivory's nightclub used to be. My spot was hot, selling the best soul food in Richmond. Since opening, I'd given the Croaker's Spot restaurant a run for their money, but there were enough black folks in Richmond that loved to eat to keep both of our businesses running. The black-and-red neon sign above the door read, KNAT'S SOUL FOOD RESTAURANT (Knat is Tank spelled backward). My man Ron was at the door, making sure we didn't get the young crowd, especially from Virginia Commonwealth University, coming in here trying to buy drinks from the bar. Downstairs I had live jazz, tables set up for dining, and a bar. Upstairs the atmosphere was different. There was a deejay and a dance floor, and those who were twenty-five and older were up there getting their party on.

"What's up, Tank?" Ron asked, letting me in. All the tables were full and the waitresses were busy, which meant this would be another stellar night for business.

"Been like this all evening?" I asked Ron, looking over his shoulder, sweeping the room with my eyes.

"All night," Ron confirmed.

"Where Chuck and them niggas at?"

"In your office upstairs."

"A'ight. Cool," I said, giving him some dap as I walked away.

I made my way through the restaurant as ballers gave me props and their women gave me looks like they wanted to give me their panties. I got to the back of the restaurant and headed up the stairs when I noticed the shadow of someone behind me.

"Tank, I've been missing you, baby," said Shelly, a pretty broad with thirty-eight DDs. Shelly was one of the bartenders at the restaurant who I could always run to for some ass when Renée was

out of town on business or attending pompous city affairs without me. Renée didn't know about Shelly and me, and very rarely
did she even come to the restaurant, which was how I wanted to
keep it, because when this was all over, Shelly was going to be a
memory.

Shelly walked up to me and ran her hand across my dick like
she owned it. She was wearing a halter top that left nothing to the
imagination, a miniskirt, and a pair of four-and-a-half-inch san-
dals. Even though red bones have never really been my style,
Shelly was fine as hell.

"What's up, Shelly?" I said, knowing that if I wanted to, I
could do her right here in the stairwell.

"You," she said, licking her lips. "When am I gonna see you
again?"

"You seeing me now," I said, shrugging my shoulders.

"You know what I mean." She came closer. "I miss you."

I was feeling her energy, but I had to shake that shit off. "Actually, I got business tonight. Maybe we can get together when I get
back."

She grabbed my hand, put it between her legs, then put my
finger in her mouth.

"Just a little reminder that this is also some business you could
be handling," she said, leaving me standing there, rock hard. I got
myself together before making it to my office, where I found
Chuck, D., and Bits. Chuck, my man from way back, was sitting
behind my desk, while D. and Bits were standing. As soon as they
saw me, they stopped what they were doing. Chuck got up and
they all walked over to me.

"What up, Tank," they said in unison.

"Nothin' much. What you niggas up to?"

"Shorty, for real, police been 'round here again today, asking questions about Li'l John," Chuck said in a serious tone.

"They even had his picture, showing it to your employees and shit, asking if they'd ever seen him in here. What's up with that shit?"

"It's cool. It's cool," I said. "I got somebody lookin' into that for me. In the meantime, can y'all get somebody to pay a visit to that nigga Skeet?"

"No doubt," Chuck quickly answered. "It's taken care of, Tank. You know I got you. So what's up? You need me to roll out with you tonight or what?"

Chuck got mad respect from me, and he had never given me any indication that he couldn't be trusted, but right now I couldn't take any chances.

"I'm not sure what time I'm rolling out," I said. "As a matter of fact, I may go next weekend. Might do a weekend trip with the old lady. I'll let you know." I knew good and well that I was rolling out early in the morning.

"A'ight, that's cool. Anything else?" Chuck asked.

"Nope. Just keep your eyes and ears open. Call me on my cell if some crazy shit comes up. Anything out of the ordinary, you call me, got it?" I said sternly. They all nodded.

Chuck was like the official spokesperson of the Three Stooges. The other two, D. and Bits, didn't ever do much talking. They were scared I might snap on them or something. They definitely knew their place with me, though.

The three men made their way out of the office, giving me some privacy. I decided to call Renée just to see if she was talking to that nigga Chris.

"Hello?" Renée's voice said through the phone receiver.

"Hey, it's me. What's up?" I said.

"Talking to Mr. Hall on the other line."

"That nigga got you callin' him Mr. Hall?" I said, turning up my mug.

"No, Tank. I mean, how else do you want me to refer to the man?"

"Call the nigga Chris. That's sufficient. Nigga don't deserve that kinda respect."

"Okay, I'm talking to Chris," she said with a sigh. "Baby, are you sure you're okay with this?"

"Renée, will you stop asking me that? I told you, handle your business. You go ahead and talk to that nigga. I'll call you when I get on the road tomorrow."

"Okay. I love you," she said.

"Me too." I hung up. I then dialed Shelly's cell phone number, hoping she had it on vibrate, because I knew she wouldn't hear it over the music in the restaurant.

"Hello?" Shelly answered.

"Yo, come up here for a minute," I ordered her in a sensual tone.

"Just one minute?"

"Take a break."

"I'm on my way."

CHRIS

It had been four months since I met Renée, and she had my nose wide open. With both of our busy schedules, we still managed to spend an enormous amount of time together. We even attended a formal fund-raising gala last month. She was perfect for me— intelligent, beautiful, spunky, and she was the first black woman I'd known who gave good head without all the fuss. We enjoyed the same music, both loved seafood, and the thing that really blew my mind was how we both drank VSOP on the rocks with Coke. I had never met a woman like her before, never. I truly believed that everything in my life was falling in place. My career was where it needed to be, so it was time to put the ball in motion for my future wife.

As I sat outside Renée's apartment, India.Arie was blaring through the speakers of my specially ordered 2006 midnight blue Chrysler 300. This was the final test. I was taking Renée to meet Grandma Lucy. I figured today would be perfect, since it was Thanksgiving and a few of my other family members would be there. Renée would pass with flying colors, but Grandma Lucy's approval would make me feel better about my decision to ask Renée to marry me. Of course, four months wasn't long enough to get to know a person completely, but Renée and I were on the same path. I wanted to get to know her better for the rest of my life. She said that she was ready to settle down and have children, and so was I. A few nights earlier I even told her I loved her, and she reciprocated.

Renée came out of her apartment building wearing a long black skirt, boots, and one of those sweaters that hang off the shoulders. She was trying to put on her coat while walking to the car. I jumped out of the car and ran to help her with her coat. She kissed me on the lips, which sent jolts through my spine. Then I opened the passenger door for her. The November air was quite nippy, even though it was sunny. We both got into the car quickly to warm up.

"You look nice, as always," I said, leaning in to kiss her.

"Don't look so bad yourself," she said, checking out my gray wool pants and black-and-gray A/X sweater. She leaned in slightly to kiss me back.

"Don't I know it," I said, smiling. Before I could pull off from in front of the apartment building, my cell phone rang.

"Christian Hall," I said in a professional voice.

"Chris, it's Bob," the caller said. "I hate to call you with business on Thanksgiving Day, but this couldn't wait. We finally got the evidence we need to hand down the indictment on Melvin Jones for the murder of John Simpson."

"What? Are you serious?" I asked excitedly. "Did they find the body?"

"No body yet," Bob said. "But we are getting a search warrant right now to go out to his house. We have an eyewitness who said he saw Jones force Simpson into his car on the day of his disappearance. The eyewitness said he also followed the car to Jones's house, where he's sure Simpson was murdered, because he heard gunshots while there."

"This is unbelievable!" I said, banging my hand on the steering wheel. "Where has this moron of a witness been all this time?" I asked.

"He said that he feared for his life, so he went away until things cooled down. Now he's willing to testify."

"This is great. Keep me posted. Try not to work too hard today. If you need me for anything, give me a call," I said, and hung up.

"I can't believe this. We are finally going to bring that thug down," I shouted, shaking my head, still not believing my ears. "He thinks he's living high on the hog with his mansion out in New Kent, and his restaurant. Thought he was going to get away with it. Not today, Mr. Jones, not today." I forgot for a minute that Renée was in the seat beside me.

"Who? What?" she asked.

"Oh, I'm sorry, baby. We promised no business today, right?"

"Yes, we did," she agreed, but she continued asking about my business. "Who is Mr. Jones?"

"Some big-time heroin dealer we've been trying to get for years but couldn't touch because he stays so clean," I answered her. "He thinks we're not onto him, but we've been on him for a long time. He has guys planted all over the city, hustling heroin for him. We want to make sure we have everything we need before taking him down. A search warrant is in the works, so now we'll be able to pin a murder on him on top of the drug case we've been building against him. His ass is going down."

Renée had no response. I looked over at her, and she looked a bit uneasy. "What's wrong? Nervous about meeting Grandma Lucy?" I teased.

"No, it's not that." Renée hesitated. "We'll talk about it later."

"No, if something's bothering you, let's talk about it now."

"Chris, right now is not the time. We'll have to talk about it later."

I shifted the car back into park, hoping not to get ticketed for being in a no-parking zone for so long.

"Baby, what is it?"

"It's nothing. I'm okay, really. Actually, I think I feel a headache coming on. Let me run into the apartment real quick to get something before it gets too bad. I'll be right back."

Renée ran back into her apartment building, looking as beautiful from the back as she did from the front. I hoped she was not having second thoughts about spending Thanksgiving with my family. That would mess up everything I had planned.

RENÉE

I ran to the elevator so fast that I almost fell. I hadn't lied to Chris—a headache was really coming on. My head was throbbing uncontrollably from what I had just heard. I needed to talk to Tank to get some clarification, because right now it seemed to me that he'd been a wanted man for a while, and not just for murder, either. By the time I reached my apartment my heart was racing and my armpits were sweating. I used my house phone to dial Tank.

"What's up?" he answered.

"Tank?" I said, almost out of breath.

"Naw, this Chuck. Who dis?"

I was a little thrown off that I hadn't recognized the voice on the other end as someone's other than Tank's. "I need to talk to Tank."

"Hold on," Chuck said.

I heard a couple of female voices in the background before Chuck hit mute. After what seemed like an eternity, Tank came to the phone.

"Hello?" he said.

"What are you doing?" I asked, my voice breaking.

"Oh, hey, baby," Tank said. "Nothing, we was just, umm, kicking it at Chuck's crib. His girl cooked Thanksgiving dinner. I thought you were gone with that nigga by now."

Thoughts of Tank's past infidelities suddenly came to mind, overriding the reason I had initially phoned him.

"Sounds like more than Thanksgiving to me," I said jealously.

"Come on, now. It's not like that."

"Where were you that you couldn't answer your own phone?"

"I was in the bathroom."

"That's bullshit, Tank. The only time you take your phone off your hip is when you're fucking. Is that what you were doing? Huh?"

"Baby, look—"

"Fuck that, Tank. I've been playing this game for four months now with Chris, and this is the thanks I get? You out there sticking your dick where it don't belong?"

"Baby, I told you, I was in the bathroom washing my hands," Tank tried to reassure me.

"Stop fucking calling me baby!" I snapped.

"Okay, look, I'm at this nigga's crib. He got people here. I don't know some of these people. I can't use your name. Somebody might overhear."

"Tank, go outside *now*. This is important."

"This can't wait?"

I sucked my teeth in disgust. "Hell, no, this can't wait. Hurry up, because Chris is downstairs waiting for me in the car, and I don't want him to come up here looking for me."

"Okay, let me grab my jacket."

I could hear Tank say something to Chuck. I assumed he was telling him that he had to step outside. I could hear his footsteps as he made his way to the door. He was probably wearing the gators I bought for him last month. He said the shoes were given to him out of guilt because I seemed to be having fun hanging out with Chris. He made the mistake of asking me who was better in bed, and because there was a slight pause in my answer, I think he assumed that my answer was Chris. Not that I would ever have told Tank, but Chris *was* better. He was more passionate, and gentler. Right about now he was more trustworthy than Tank, too, but all of that didn't matter. Chris was business. What was important was that I needed to warn Tank. Besides, I was positive that I knew the reason Tank didn't answer his phone.

"Okay, talk to me," Tank said.

"Tank, they're getting a search warrant right now as we speak to go out to your house," I said. "Chris said they have enough evidence to pin that murder on you."

"A search warrant?" Tank nervously questioned.

"Yes, and he mentioned your house out in New Kent. They know where you live, Tank."

"Fuck!" he shouted.

"That's not all. He said they've been after you for years. They know all about you dealing heroin. They've been trying to build a big case against you. It sounds like they know about your whole operation."

Tank got silent. I guess he was trying to process everything so he could plan his next step.

"You need to get out to the house and clean up," I said. "I don't know how quick they can come up with a search warrant on a holiday, but I know they're working on it. Tank, this is more serious than I thought."

"Look, go ahead to dinner and keep your ears open. I need to figure something out."

"What do you want me to do? Chris is adamant about bringing you down. I don't think I can change his mind."

"Stick to the plan. Did you leave the key like I asked?"

"Yes, I did it last night."

"Cool. I'll call you later. If something else comes up, try to call me back as soon as you can."

"Tell me you love me," I said, but he just hung up the phone in my ear. This entire situation was getting out of control. For one thing, I never thought the police were onto Tank and his drug-dealing operation. This was only supposed to be about Li'l John's disappearance. It was a whole lot bigger than I was led to believe. I wondered if Tank knew about the drug case but only told me about the murder case to get me to go along with the plan? Maybe he knew they didn't have enough evidence for a solid drug case, so if I could thwart the murder case, it would buy him enough time to get out of the drug game, as planned.

A knock at the door startled me, bringing me out of my whole train of thought. I still had my house phone in my hand, so I quickly hung it up before opening the door. When I did, Chris was standing there with a look of anxiety. He was probably worried that I had changed my mind about Thanksgiving.

"Hey, are you okay?" Chris asked.

"I'm fine, Chris. I just needed to take something for this headache. Maybe I shouldn't go to the Thanksgiving dinner after all. I'm not in a festive mood right now."

"Renée, baby, you have to. Please?" Chris begged.

Under the circumstances I didn't really want to, but I knew I had to. Otherwise, Chris would become suspicious, and Tank needed me to be his eyes and ears.

His grandmother lived in a small brick ranch-style home in an older subdivision off West Broad Street. Either we were the first ones there or this was not going to be as big a family dinner as I thought. There were only three cars in the driveway, including Chris's. Before we reached the door, a short, heavyset, light-skinned elderly woman opened the door. Chris hugged her, so I assumed she must be his grandmother.

"Grandma Lucy, this is Renée. Renée, this is Grandma Lucy," Chris said, introducing us.

"Hello," I said, filling her open arms that she had spread out to hug me. I suppose it was customary, but it felt awkward as hell.

"I'm so glad to finally meet you, Renée," Grandma Lucy said, hugging me tightly. "Chris has told me all about you. Come on in; make yourself at home."

We followed behind Grandma Lucy through a small living room as the smell of corn bread surrounded us. Her house was cozy with knickknacks and pictures all over the place. The dining room, which was adjacent to the kitchen, had an oversize oak table with eight chairs.

"Hey, Uncle Junie," Chris said to an older gentleman who was fumbling with the table leaf.

"Lucy, I believe somebody done broke dis leaf, 'cuz it don't fit," Uncle Junie said without acknowledging me or Chris.

"Hey, Uncle Junie," Chris said louder, this time causing Uncle Junie to turn around to see us.

"Oh, hey! There's my big-shot great-nephew. How you doing, boy? And who is this pretty fox you got with you?" Uncle Junie said.

"This is Renée, Uncle Junie," Chris replied.

"How are you doing?" I said, feeling more awkward by the minute. Just then I felt my cell phone vibrating in my purse.

"Where's the bathroom?" I asked anybody who could answer.

"Chris, show that pretty Indian girl to the bathroom. I can tell she Indian; look at her hair," said Uncle Junie.

"Shut up, Junie, you old fool," Grandma Lucy said. "Chris, I'll show Renée to the bathroom. Help your uncle with that table. I swear, we can't never start nothing on time. Come on here, sugar," said Grandma Lucy. I followed her through a small, stuffy kitchen to a family room. "The bathroom is over there," she said, pointing across the paneled room. Two older ladies sat on the sofa, watching a movie, and didn't move their eyes from the TV when I walked in.

"Hello," I said, but there was no response. I made it to the bathroom, sat down on the toilet, and pulled out my cell phone. I checked my missed calls. They were all from Tank. Something must be wrong, so I called him back.

"Hey, what's wrong?" I asked Tank.

"They just got to the crib, but I was able to leave a little dirt before they got here."

"Chris?" I said.

"Yeah. That nigga Chris should be getting a call real soon. I'll holla at you later." Tank hung up quickly.

I flushed the toilet and ran the water in the sink to act as if I had used the bathroom and was washing my hands. I walked into the family room, where Chris had just come in and was now hugging one of the two ladies who was watching TV. He was about to introduce them when his cell phone rang.

"Chris Hall," he answered his phone. "Tell me something good, Bob."

My heart was racing as I listened to his side of the conversation.

"Uh-huh, uh-huh," Chris said as he nodded. Then he paused. "What?!"

I watched Chris's facial expressions change. The police must have been at Tank's house now, and I was pretty sure that they'd found the fake evidence Tank had planted. Bob was probably telling him they needed to talk to him right away to discuss what they found.

"What are you talking about? Are you crazy? Okay, okay, listen, meet me at the corner of Libbie and Broad. How quickly can you get there? Okay, I'll see you then," Chris said, hanging up the phone in a panic.

"What's the matter?" I asked, trying not to appear guilty.

"I don't know, but I need to find out. Listen, I have to go. Can you stay here until I get back? I need to go and meet Bob about something he says is very important."

"But, Chris, I don't feel comfortable, I mean . . ."

"It's okay; you'll be fine. I'll be back as soon as I can. I promise."

He kissed me and then literally ran out of the house. I was left standing in the family room with the two old hags, who were now staring me up and down.

"I'm sorry, I'm Renée," I said, extending my hand. Both of them sucked their teeth and turned back toward the TV. I guess I must've offended them when I said I didn't feel comfortable stay-

ing without Chris, but I was telling the truth. I didn't know these
people. I took a seat on a slightly worn sofa and waited. Some
time went by, and then my phone vibrated again. After checking
the number and seeing the call wasn't from Chris or Tank, I let it
go to voice mail.

CHRIS

I was doing about eighty-five in a fifty-five, but I didn't care. Bob,
one of the primary detectives assigned to the Melvin Jones case,
had me a little worried. Whatever he found when they searched
Melvin's house was of some interest to me. At least, that was what
Bob said. I couldn't possibly figure out what it could be, but he
told me to meet him to find out exactly what it was. I pulled into
the parking lot of the Amoco gas station on the corner of Libbie
and Broad Streets, which was closed because of the holiday. It
would take Bob a little while longer to get over to this side of
town, since he had to come from New Kent, so I pumped up the
heat in the car and waited. I hated that I had to leave Renée at the
house with people she didn't even know, but it was better this way.
I still had no idea what this was all about. Maybe that drug dealer
was somehow affiliated with my mother. *That's it,* I thought. He
probably found some information on my mother. Maybe she'd
been arrested for buying drugs from one of his boys or something.
What a piece of crap this Melvin Jones is, I thought. When we were
finished with him and his whole crew, the projects' drug supply
was going to be hit hard.

Just as I was getting ready to change my India.Arie CD, Bob
pulled up behind me in an unmarked car. He walked over to the
passenger side, holding a brown envelope, and got in.

"Bob, what's going on? You got me nervous as hell."

"You know, Chris, we go way back, and I hate to do this to you, but—" Bob said.

"But what?" I cut him off.

"Here," he said, handing me the envelope. I opened it, pulling out about ten Polaroid pictures and a few newspaper clippings. The first picture was of a baldheaded, thick-lipped brotha with his arms around a female who looked exactly like my Renée. He was holding the camera in front of them, taking the picture himself. The next picture was the same brotha, only this time he was lying across a bed and the girl was lying under his arm, wearing nothing but a bra and panties, as he snapped the picture of the two of them. The next picture was of the girl. She was now posing, completely naked, on the same bed, and by now I realized that it was definitely Renée.

"What the fuck?" I said, now scanning through the other photos, all of which either included Renée posing naked, in lingerie, or in this dude's arms.

"Is this Melvin Jones?" I asked, holding up one of the pictures with the two of them.

"Yes. Melvin Jones, aka Tank," Bob answered. "It looks like your lady friend and Mr. Jones are very chummy."

I looked through the newspaper clippings. A couple of them were pictures of me and Renée at formal affairs we had attended together. One of the headlines read, "Has the New Commonwealth's Attorney Met His Fair Lady?"

"What does this mean?" I said, not specifically seeking an answer from Bob, more from myself. All of a sudden I felt as if someone had just hit me in the face with a cast-iron skillet. The more I stared at the pictures, the tighter my stomach got. I felt betrayed, angry, and confused, all rolled up in one.

"Listen, Chris, I didn't show the pictures to anyone. I tried to get them out of the house without anybody noticing. But there might be others."

"I know. I know. I appreciate it, Bob. I need to talk to Renée right now. Come on, tell me, as a detective, what do you think is going on?"

"Really, I thought about it on my way over here. Maybe they are trying to create a scandal of some sort and place you in the middle. 'Jealous commonwealth's attorney working to convict drug-dealing ex-boyfriend of current girlfriend.' They can make the Jones case look tainted and get it thrown out."

"Come on, Bob, I had no idea Renée had any involvement with this thug."

"I know that, but how will the defense attorney take all this?"

"Okay, okay. What is she trying to do to me? This shit is crazy! Absolutely crazy! I can't believe it! This woman told me she loved me. We talked about marriage, and she's fucking around with some thug. I don't believe this!" I slammed my hands on the steering wheel, causing the horn to blow.

"I don't know, Chris. I'm sorry, man. I need to get back to New Kent to see what else comes up. You have my number. Call me if you need me," Bob said, patting me on the shoulder. He got out of the car, leaving me there with the pictures. In one of the pictures I swear Renée was wearing one of the Victoria's Secret bra and panty sets I bought for her, which told me these pictures were recent. It didn't seem like this was an ex-boyfriend at all. But when did she find time to see him? How deep was it? Did she love him? She told me she loved me. I pulled the car onto Broad Street and headed back to Grandma Lucy's house. I dialed Renée's cell phone number.

"Hello?" she said, sounding anxious to hear my voice.

"Hey, I'm on my way. Look, we need to talk. I should be there in about fifteen minutes. Be outside in the front." I didn't even give her enough time to respond. I wanted her to tell me everything, her point of view, before I jumped to conclusions. Maybe she was forced to take these pictures so that they could be used as blackmail. Maybe he threatened to kill her if she told me. I would find out soon enough.

I pulled in front of Grandma Lucy's, and Renée was standing on the porch as requested. I didn't get out of the car. I just blew the horn so she could come and get in. Grandma Lucy was in the doorway. She had a look on her face as if she was wondering where we were off to.

"I'll be back in a few minutes, Grandma Lucy," I yelled. Renée got in the car and just sat there staring at me. She was so beautiful. I had a hard time trying to be cruel to her.

"What's going on, Chris?" she asked.

"I'll tell you in a minute." I drove away from the house and headed toward Broad Street. I pulled over in the abandoned Staples parking lot and took a deep breath before putting the car in park. "Renée, I need you to tell me everything you know about Melvin Jones." The strangest look came across her face. You would have thought that I told her I was HIV positive from her expression. She just sat there, not answering. "What did he do to you? Did he rape you? Did he force you to do something you didn't want to do?"

"Chris, calm down," she said.

"Calm down? Calm down? Here, now you tell me I should calm down." I threw the envelope of pictures to her. She took them out one by one, looking at them as if she'd never seen them before.

"What the fuck is going on? Talk to me, Renée!" I yelled.

"I don't know what to say. It wasn't supposed to happen like this," she said, continuing to look through the pictures.

"What wasn't supposed to happen like this? Tell me what is going on, now!" She appeared to be nonchalant about the whole thing.

"Chris, listen, I'm going to explain the whole thing to you, but first I need to talk to Tank. Those pictures . . . they aren't what they seem."

"You need to talk to Tank about what? You need to talk to me. Tell me what's going on. We were talking about marriage, for Christ sake! And you are going to sit here and tell me you need to talk to Tank? Fuck Tank!"

She crossed her arms and looked out the window.

"Say something!" I yelled. "Answer me, damn it!"

TANK

I couldn't believe how these motherfuckers were tearing up my house. All I could do was sit there and let them look around, trying to find something that ain't here. I never kept product in the house, never. And the bodies I had on the land, I had started moving them one by one right after Labor Day. Each day I'd take the remains, cut them up in pieces, put them in a suitcase, take a train up to Baltimore, then throw the suitcase into the Chesapeake Bay late at night. See, I knew eventually the day would come when they would come to my house trying to dig up dirt. But I dug the shit up first, literally.

The only thing they got were some pictures of me and Renée. I knew what I was doing by leaving them out. See, I couldn't let Renée know everything. If she knew everything, she probably would not have agreed to go along this far. I knew that the police had been after me for years. I knew they had been trying to build a kingpin charge on me, too, but all of that would be null and void by the time the judge saw that nigga had been trying to frame me so he could have my girl all to himself. All that needed to happen was for the police to find the fake-ass letters I planted in the kitchen drawer from that nigga Chris, threatening to set me up, all on his letterhead. On top of that, Renée left me keys to his office and his house, so I was able to plant so much evidence to incriminate that nigga, he'd wish he never even thought about meeting Renée.

I figured the original plan might've worked, but I couldn't take the chance of Renée having a change of heart. You know, she might've fallen for the nigga or something. I knew I'd done some fucked-up shit to Renée in the past. See, women get emotionally attached where men are concerned, so I had to play it safe with this whole setup. Was it right? Probably not, seeing as this put Renée in a fucked-up situation, but I needed to look out for myself. At the moment, she didn't know what cards to play. Lucky for me I knew her so well—I knew she wouldn't tell him anything until she found out what was going on. She wouldn't incriminate me in any way.

Now I had to get to Renée, tell her to tell him that we dated before, hooked up a few times since they met, but that I meant nothing to her. Plant in his head that the only reason she got with me recently was because I threatened to hurt Chris. I would tell her they found the pictures by accident, so we would have to change our stories. Everything would fall into place. I realized this scandal could possibly affect Renée's career, but she'd bounce back. She had a degree; plus she was smart, so she'd be all right. But I couldn't take the chance of going up for a kingpin charge on top of a possible murder charge, so I had to do something.

I walked outside and sat in my truck, leaving the police officers to have a field day trashing my house. I connected my voice recorder to my cell phone, then dialed Renée's cell phone.

"Hello?" Renée answered.

"Hey, baby. Where are you?" I asked her.

"Tank, you need to tell me," she said, followed by a shuffling sound. Just then, a male voice came on the line. I could only assume it was Chris.

"Look, you twisted bastard, I don't know what you're trying to do to me and my woman, but I'm going to make sure that you rot in hell. You understand me?" asked Chris.

"This must be Chris," I said, cool, calm, and collected.

"You goddamn right this is Chris. What are you trying to do, huh? You got something against me, you come to me. You don't put my woman in the middle, you sick fucker!"

"Did she tell you? Did she tell you about us? How it used to be? That's okay; she'll be back," I said.

"So that's what this is about? You crazy motherfucker. You got this woman scared to death of you, but I'm not scared. You are going to get exactly what you deserve, just wait."

"Listen, man. I need to talk to Renée. She needs to know that I still love her and I want to be with her. She needs to know that I'm a changed man."

"Are you crazy? She doesn't want you anymore. Whatever you had with her is over, okay?"

"Did you see the pictures?" I asked.

"Yeah, I saw the pictures. What did you do, threaten to kill her or threaten to kill me? She told me it wasn't what it appeared. I'll bet you threatened to kill me, huh? That's okay, because your ass is going down," Chris said.

"Tell Renée I love her," I said; then the line went dead.

RENÉE

Chris was screaming like a madman, and I was still at a loss for words. The only thing I told Chris was that the pictures were not what they seemed. I didn't know what else to say. Now he had my cell phone, yelling at Tank, and I had no idea which route to take. Chris shut my cell phone so hard that the antenna broke.

"He told me everything," Chris said, breathing heavily. "Yeah, that's a sick bastard. He confirmed everything."

"Chris, what did he say?" I asked, anxious.

"It's okay; I got his number. He confessed—not in so many words—but he confessed that he was in love with you, but you weren't with him anymore. Why didn't you tell me?"

Still a bit confused, I just played along. "I don't know. I . . . I couldn't. What exactly did Tank say?"

"He said something about still loving you and how he's a changed man. Hmph, this whole situation is foul. What I can't understand is why you never mentioned him to me. You've heard me talk about him before, but you didn't say a thing. As a matter of fact, I was talking about him this evening before you ran back into your apartment. What did you do, go and call him? This shit is not making sense to me."

"Look, that situation with Tank, it was a long time ago. He's just upset because I've moved on with my life." I leaned over and kissed Chris on the lips long and hard. "I'm with you, right? We're together, you and me. Those pictures mean nothing. They are old, before us." By now I had leaned his seat back as far as it could go. I sat on his lap, straddling him.

"But in one of them, you're wearing the set I bought you," he said.

"Shhhh," I whispered, putting my finger over his mouth. I began to chew on his ear, making him breathe hard as I ground back and forth on him, making him get bigger and bigger.

"All I want is you and only you," I said. I managed to unbuckle his pants, and before my hand reached his manhood, he was already moaning.

"Tank could never do for me what you can. You are my man, not Tank. Don't talk about the pictures. Don't even think about the pictures. This is obviously an attack on me. You let me deal with him my way, okay?" I began rubbing on his chest. I put my hand inside his sweater and played with his nipples. He seemed to get a thrill out of this.

"But . . . but . . . Renée, you were wearing the set . . . I . . . I . . . ," he stammered.

His cell phone rang, but I pushed it to the floor on the passenger side. I needed to get Chris back in sync with me and off of Tank.

"Don't talk about it. Just lean back and do me right here, right now. I need you in me. I love you," I moaned.

By this time, Chris was so aroused that I thought he was going to explode inside his pants. I took charge by pulling up my skirt, turning full circle. Then I lay on top of Chris so that he was face-to-face with my thong. I was face-to-face with his erection. I unzipped his pants and found his manhood with my tongue as he went to town licking and sucking my valley. For whatever reason, doing it in the car was something that set Chris off, so I planted my size-eight-and-a-half Ann Taylor boots on the backseat while I rotated my valley and sucked Chris, all in unison. I tried to keep my eyes out for passersby to make sure no one knew what we were doing.

"I'm coming. I'm coming. Shit, Renée, I'm coming," he moaned. His cell phone rang again, but this time we both ignored it.

"You going inside, or you want to stay outside and play?" I asked.

"Don't stop, don't stop," he said.

Then, without full warning, he just shrieked, pushing my head back, and exploded all over his pants. I moved, almost breaking the heel of my boot on the console, when his cell phone rang again. I got in his lap, facing him, and pushed my tongue into his mouth.

After kissing him, I said, "All this is yours, okay? Don't worry about that thug Tank. I can handle him just fine. Just let me take care of it, okay?"

"What if he tries to hurt you?"

"Chris, let *me* take care of this, okay?"

"Okay."

I climbed over to the passenger seat while trying to fix my clothes.

"Damn, look at my pants," he said.

"I guess we need to go to your place so you can change."

We pulled out of the parking lot and headed toward Monument Avenue. Chris's house was only about fifteen minutes away, right off of Monument, in a very prominent area. When we got to his two-story, all-brick colonial, there was a Richmond City police officer on the porch, another in a parked car.

"Now what?" Chris mumbled. "You want to come in, or are you going to stay in the car?" he asked me.

"I'll go with you," I replied. I figured that I might as well see what Tank planted, since I was the one who left the spare house key under the mat so he could get in.

"Can I help you, Officer?" Chris asked.

"Sure, Mr. Hall. Don't mean to disturb you on Thanksgiving. Just got a call from the New Kent police that we needed to check some things out over here," the officer replied.

"Check what things out?"

"Well, apparently they found some letters with your name, and I'd rather not say anything else without you having legal representation."

"Come on, Officer, I am a lawyer. You can tell me what they found. What sort of letters?"

The officer was staring at me as if I were the culprit in all of this. I wrapped my arm around Chris, giving the officer the same stare, letting him know that whatever he had to tell Chris, he could tell me, too.

"Mr. Hall, can I just come in and take a look around? Apparently this Mr. Jones character was claiming that you are out to get him, trying to set him up because of his relationship with, um, Ms. Anderson."

"What? Please tell me you're joking," said Chris.

"I wish I were. All of this sounds pretty ridiculous to me, too. But Mr. Jones said you called him, threatened him, then when the police went to his home in New Kent and found the letters . . . well, they sent me out here to check things out. Do you mind if I just take a look around? Not looking for anything in particular, just want to say I came out and did my job," said the officer.

I was hoping that my facial expressions weren't giving me away, but nervousness was starting to kick in. I had no idea what Tank planted in Chris's house, but I knew he had planted something. Not thinking with his lawyer brain, Chris agreed to let the officer in. In his mind he was totally innocent.

"Sure, come on in. Make it quick; we're on our way to Thanksgiving dinner," he said.

Chris unlocked the door. I walked in first; then he and the officer followed. I stood in the foyer, which separated the formal living room from the formal dining room. Both rooms were decorated with contemporary but very expensive Henredon furniture. The foyer had hardwood floors, as well as custom-built hard-wood stairs that led to the second floor. Chris headed upstairs while the officer motioned for his partner to come inside. I went to the living room and sat down on the oversize chocolate brown sofa. One of the officers came into the living room behind me, while the other passed by the living room and headed to the back of the house, where Chris's kitchen and home office were. My phone vibrated. I recognized the number. Tank wasn't the only one with a plan.

"Hey, I left the code under the lamp in the living room. I'll call you back later," I said, hanging up quickly.

"So, you and Mr. Hall are pretty serious, huh?" asked the pudgy white officer.

"I don't think that's any of your business, do you?" I said, staring at his pimply face.

He cleared his throat and pretended to look around the room, nervously. He obviously felt a bit uncomfortable with me in the room, so he headed over to the dining room. As Chris came back down the stairs, this time wearing a brown-and-tan sweater with brown wool slacks, the officer who'd gone to the back of the house yelled, "Hey, Peter, come here a minute!"

The pudgy officer followed the voice of his partner, who sounded as if he was probably in Chris's office. Chris had a look of curiosity on his face, so he followed. After several seconds of silence, I could hear Chris yell, "What the fuck?"

I ran to the back, full of curiosity myself.

"Have you ever seen this?" Chris asked me, showing me a manila folder with Tank's real name, and what appeared to be some very confidential documents. There appeared to be stacks of papers about Tank sprawled all across his desk, as if Chris had been investigating Tank himself. There were letters that ap-peared to have been started, then pushed to the side, that were addressed to Tank, threatening him to stay away from me. Now I could see where Tank was going with this plan—the plan he didn't fill me in on, by the way. He wanted to make it look like Chris wanted to get Tank out of the picture so that he could have me all to himself. Chris would do whatever it took, as far as the defense attorney would be concerned, maybe even helping to build a phony murder case against an innocent man. The defense attorney would have a field day painting Chris as a jealous, lovesick fool whose only plan was to remove my ex-boyfriend from the picture. Tank's case was going to appear so contaminated that the judge would have to throw it out.

"No, I haven't," I responded, now ready to play Tank's game.

"Come on, Renée, what's going on? Did you have anything to do with this?"

"What are you talking about? Why would I have anything to do with papers that are in your office, on your desk? Where would I get this type of information, anyway? I don't work for the legal system. This information looks confidential."

Chris looked at both of the police officers, pleading with them with his eyes.

"Fellas, look, really, I have no idea what's going on here, and I definitely don't know how this got here. Think about it. If I really was out to get Mr. Jones, which I'm not, why would I volunteer to let you in my house, knowing I have incriminating information all over my desk? Come on, now, does that make sense?"

Both of the officers stared at Chris, not really buying his story.

"Think about it! Think!" Chris yelled, this time, making everyone in the room a bit nervous.

"Mr. Hall, I'm going to need you to calm down. Please take a seat and don't move anything."

"Peter, you know me. Come on, tell your friend here," Chris tried to explain, but Peter just shook his head. I guess they ran across so many criminals on a day-to-day basis that they had a hard time believing anyone. Peter just paced back and forth while the other officer called the New Kent police officers, who, I assumed, were still at Tank's house. He told them his findings. They asked him some questions, and once he was finished, he turned to Chris.

"Mr. Hall, I'm sorry, but I can't let you leave right now. I have a detective who's been working on the case on his way here from New Kent. Just hold tight. We'll get this squared away."

"Peter, tell this officer—what is your name, anyway?" Chris said.

"Officer Boone," he replied.

"Officer Boone, do you know who I am? I am Christian Hall, Richmond's commonwealth's attorney. Did you know that?"

"Actually, sir, yes, I know. I'm just doing my job," said Officer Boone.

"Your job is to stand around here and harass a city official?"

"No, my job is to make sure the city official isn't committing some sort of crime, that's all."

Chris was fuming. I, on the other hand, was sitting back taking it all in. I couldn't wait to talk to Tank.

TANK

The police finally gave me permission to leave my house. Ain't that some shit? Them telling me when I can come and go on my own property. This was one of the reasons I realized I couldn't do time for nobody. I had a problem with people telling me what I could and couldn't do.

I still hadn't heard back from Renée, not since Chris snatched the phone from her and started threatening me. Lucky for me I had my recorder on, so his screaming, yelling, and threats are all caught on tape. I guess Renée threw her pussy on him to calm him down, and they were probably enjoying Thanksgiving dinner by now, not worried about a thing. In the meantime, I called Chuck back to see if Shelly was still there waiting for me.

"Yo, Chuck. Where she at?" I spoke into the phone receiver.

"She just left. Said she was heading over to the restaurant to try to set up for tonight. You straight?" asked Chuck.

"Yeah, I'm straight. They ain't get shit on me, but a waste of time. I'm clean as hell. I'm pissed, though, cause them mother-fuckers tore my crib all to pieces. Wanted to see if Shelly could come over and help me clean up and shit."

"Yeah, right, nigga. That ain't the only thing you want Shelly to do. I heard y'all in that bathroom. I'm still trying to figure out how y'all managed to do it in that small-ass bathroom."

"As long as I got enough room to put at least twelve inches between us, I'm good."

"Yeah, whatevah, nigga. I'll holla."

I made a U-turn, jumped on the interstate, and headed toward the restaurant. Since me and my moms hadn't talked in years and my pops was locked down, I normally spent holidays with Renée. I considered her my only real family, however, since she was playing wifey to this sucker, I was stuck on Thanksgiving by myself, and I couldn't have that. I dialed Shelly on her cell and she answered after the first ring.

"Hello?" she said.

"What's up?" I asked.

"Hey, baby. I just came by the restaurant, trying to make sure everything is straight for tonight's party. Where are you?"

"I'm on my way to the restaurant now. I wanted to know if you felt like doing me a favor."

"Anything for you, baby."

"The police tore my crib up today. I need some help cleaning up. I figure we can do a little cleaning, a little fucking, then a little more cleaning," I said.

"Be clear about your expectations, why don't you?" she said.

"Hey, I'm a man who knows what he wants. Can you help me out?"

"Sure. I'll be outside waiting for you."

When I pulled up to the restaurant, Shelly was standing out front wearing tall brown leather boots, a short brown leather skirt, and a tan-and-brown blouse. She was zipping up her brown leather jacket. She jumped in smelling like the new Prada perfume I had bought for her when we went shopping the other week. While Renée and Chris were out at their charity event, I took Shelly on a little shopping spree at Tyson's Corner in D.C. A nigga got needs, too, and even though I was the one who thought up the idea of Renée getting with Chris, it seemed like she was feeling him a bit more than she wanted to admit. Then, when I asked her if the nigga was better than me in bed and there was a pause in her voice, that was all I needed. I'd known Renée a long time. I probably knew her better than she knew herself. If this shit was getting to her, she'd be ready to bring it to an end right away. She didn't ask, not one time, when this gig was going to be up. So, I took that as a sign that she was enjoying herself.

Since I wasn't getting much of Renée's time, Shelly filled that void for me in every way imaginable. What I was doing with Shelly wasn't right, but I wasn't doing this to get back at Renée. I really did love her, and sometimes I did feel a little guilty because I knew if she ever found out about Shelly, she would flip the fuck out on me, probably leave me for good.

Shelly and I headed back to my house, and I felt a bit relieved that there were no police cars in sight. I pulled my truck into the garage so we could enter the house through the kitchen. I followed behind Shelly, watching that brown leather hug her ass as tight as the plastic covering on a CD. The house looked the same as when I had left it, which meant the police didn't have the decency to put anything back.

"They didn't do too bad," she said, surveying the damage. "Don't worry, baby; I'll have this place cleaned in no time."

I threw my coat on the stove and pushed Shelly up against the counter.

"Take off your clothes," I told her. She followed my instructions, stripping down to her Victoria's Secret underwear. We kissed. Then I told her to go upstairs. We needed a bed to get down like I wanted to get down. I followed behind her, peeling my clothes off all the way to my bedroom.

CHRIS

Fortunately for me, my buddy Detective Bob came over while the police were here and told the boys in blue to leave so he could take over the situation at my house. Once the officers left, I told Renée to go home so that Bob and I could talk. I was in a bad situation, and I needed it handled quickly. Bob just happened to know a couple of crooked cops on the force who'd be willing to off Tank and make it look like a drug deal gone bad, or even a robbery attempt. But if I went that route, somehow the situation could be traced back to me.

I gave Bob my word that this whole thing was a setup, and I intended to prove it, somehow, some way, in order to clear my name. I asked him to give me the address to Tank's house so that I could go out there and try to find something. He knew that I was out of my field when it came to snooping around somebody's house, so he agreed to ride out there with me. He told me that

Tank had a security system, but because he had left before the police officers, the security system was disarmed.

I called Renée before heading over to Tank's house and I got her to indirectly tell me that Tank should be at the restaurant, because he wasn't answering his home phone. Since she needed to talk to him to let him know that she was going to be with me now and that he needed to leave her alone, I gave her my blessing to go see him at the restaurant, but told her to be careful. Again, she reassured me that she could handle Tank, so I took her at her word. While Renée was at the restaurant, having a talk with Tank, Detective Bob and I would be at his house, trying to get some evidence to clear my name.

Bob and I got to New Kent in about thirty minutes. As we proceeded down a long dirt road, I noticed Renée's car in the circular driveway of Tank's enormous house. I didn't see any other cars, so I was beginning to get suspicious.

"I thought no one was here," Bob said.

"Me, too. I need to find out what's going on once and for all." Just as I was about to get out of the car, we heard a gunshot.

"Oh, shit, Bob. Something's going on in there," I said frantically.

"Come on. Follow me to the garage. Let's see if the garage door is open. Here, take this."

He handed me a .45-caliber pistol and we walked around to the side of the house. Sure enough, the garage door was open. Bob raised the garage door. I noticed Tank had a Range Rover and a Lexus GS430, just about a hundred thousand dollars' worth of cars in here. All of this from selling drugs. He was out there distributing drugs to people like my mother, who would do anything for a hit, while he lived the glamorous life. On top of it all, he was trying to ruin my life so he could keep pushing drugs on the streets of Richmond, where people were getting hooked on a daily basis. I wanted this bastard bad!

We tiptoed through the garage to the kitchen and moved slowly through the first floor of the house, trying to detect some sort of movement, but there was none. When we reached the front hall where the steps were, a male voice could be heard. It was muffled, but apparently he was the only one talking. I could only assume it was Tank. Bob motioned for us to move up the stairs, and by this time I was a little nervous. I wasn't sure if Tank had killed Renée, or if Renée had watched Tank kill somebody else. At this point anything was possible.

We followed the male voice until it got closer and closer. We passed by a couple of bedrooms and a bathroom before reaching the bedroom where the voice was coming from. Now we could hear the voice clearly, as well as a female crying softly. Maybe he didn't kill Renée after all. Bob put his finger over his lips and we listened for a moment so we could get an idea of what might be happening on the other side of the door.

"Renée, baby, please, put the gun down. Come on now, please. You don't want to do this. Just put the gun down," Tank said.

"How could you do this to me? Huh? After all I've done for you?" screamed Renée.

"Renée, look, we can't talk like this. You need to give me the gun before somebody gets hurt," Tank said.

"Bitch, get out of the bed. Get out of the bed *now!*" Renée yelled.

"Please don't kill me! Don't kill me! I didn't know! Please!" said another female voice.

"So, the joke's on me, huh? I know you so well. I call you on your cell. You don't answer. I call you at home. You don't answer. I go out to the restaurant. You're not there. I had to come all the way out here to find you in bed with another bitch. In the meantime, you change the plan and don't tell me, while at the same time you're fucking her? What did you think would happen,

Tank? Huh? Thought maybe you could pin everything on me? Huh? Do you know what you've done? Do you?" Renée yelled.

The other female in the room was whimpering, and little by little the story unfolded. Renée was telling Tank's other woman the whole plan, and I listened, feeling more and more used by the minute. Renée and Tank set me up. This whole relationship was all a setup to keep her drug-dealing boyfriend out of prison. So the joke was on me, too.

"See, bitch. You see what I've done for him, and this is how he repays me? Do you think I should let you get out of this alive? Shit, I don't have anything to lose, now, do I?" yelled Renée. Just as angry as Renée was, I was even more furious. Without any warning I pushed open the bedroom door. Tank was lying in a king-size bed, naked. There was a light-skinned woman standing beside the bed, naked, and Renée was standing a few feet away from me.

"Isn't this a nice little party?" I said. They all turned to look at me as I pointed my gun at Tank.

"Chris, what are you doing here? Get out of here! This is between me and Tank!" Renée exclaimed.

"No, the way I see it, this is between me, you, and Tank. I heard everything," I said. "All this, a setup to keep your man out of jail, and this is the thanks you get. Umm, umm, umm. Damn, they say what goes around comes around, but I never, ever thought it came around so quick."

Bob was standing beside me with his gun drawn, not sure who he should be pointing it at. The look on his face told me that he was pissed at me for barging in without giving him warning, but I didn't care. I was ready to take that punk Tank down, as well as that cunt Renée.

"Everybody, please calm down. I'm a detective," Bob said.

"Aw, damn! This motherfucker was just here! Ain't this a bitch!" said Tank.

"Renée and Chris, I need you to put your guns down. Right now, come on," Bob said. Renée seemed to be unmoved by the whole gesture as she focused her attention back on Tank and the other woman. I was watching Tank's every move, wanting to put a bullet in his chest for what he'd done to me.

RENÉE

It wasn't supposed to happen like this. Chris had no business coming here! Now my plan was ruined.

"Chris, please, can you just leave? I told you to let me handle Tank. Why did you come here?" I said.

"You need to answer that question for me. How could you do this to me, Renée? All this was just a setup? I thought you loved me," I said.

"Chris, please, just get out of here and let me handle this," I said while still aiming the gun at Tank. With Chris and the detective here, there was no way out of this mess now.

"Renée, can you just put the gun down? You almost killed me! Come on, I mean, shit. This bitch don't mean nothing to me. I just did her to pass time while you were with that nigga," Tank said.

"You're a fucking liar!" I screamed.

I pulled the trigger and fired, missing Tank as he fell to the floor to take cover while grabbing a gun from his nightstand that was blocked minutes before by the naked woman. At the same time the woman dropped to the floor and crawled over to the corner of the room beside the mahogany oak dresser. The detective tried to grab me, but Chris pushed him back with such force that he hit his head on the corner of the bedroom door and fell to the ground. Now he was out cold. I turned to face Tank, who was now pointing his gun at Chris, while Chris and I were both pointing our guns at him.

"I guess it all comes down to who gets the first shot off, huh? You feelin' this nigga or what?" Tank asked coldly.

"I need to be asking you the same thing about her," I replied.

"Renée, the ball is in your court. Tell me so I can be sure. You love that nigga?" asked Tank.

"That's right. I love him. Fuck you, Tank. Go to hell," I yelled.

All of a sudden Tank's eyes grew extremely cold, and before anybody could do anything, he aimed his gun at me and was about to shoot, but not before I fired two shots at him. Chris was still standing there with his gun aimed at Tank, which was unnecessary, since there was a hole in Tank's chest dripping blood. The bullet he took looked like it was right on the mark—his heart. Tank's limp body was sitting up against the nightstand, lifeless, gun still in hand. I walked over to him slowly to get confirmation that he was really dead. Then I looked over at the woman in the corner, who was still squatting. I was feeling a mixture of emotions, not sure if I should be sad and crying because Tank was dead, or happy and relieved because I made it out of this mess alive.

Before I realized it, Chris walked over to me and took the gun out of my hand.

"Chris?" said Bob, who was coming around. Chris went over to him and helped him up. It was obvious he was still a bit dazed, because he stumbled as soon as he tried to stand.

"It's over. Tank is dead. Renée shot him in self-defense," Chris said.

He then turned to me, and we stared at each other like we were the last two people on earth. At that moment I realized he still loved me, and when this was all over, I'd prove to him that I truly loved him, too.

"I'm going to help Bob downstairs to his car so he can get some suits out here. You two coming?" he asked.

"We're right behind you," I said as I watched the woman, who was now slipping on a T-shirt and some pajama pants. Chris wrapped Bob's arm around his neck, and they headed toward the stairs.

"So, Shelly, you okay?" I asked once Chris and Bob were gone.

"Yeah, Renée, I'm okay. This shit got real tonight, didn't it?" she said.

"I didn't think it would turn out like this. My God, I can't believe Tank is dead. I never wanted to kill him. That wasn't part of my plan. I was just trying to look out for myself like Tank was looking out for himself."

We both stared at Tank's corpse. I didn't know what Shelly was thinking, but I wished there was a way I could change the outcome of tonight. Falling in love with Chris wasn't part of the plan, but it happened. Once I found out that Tank had taken the bait with Shelly, I realized he didn't possess the type of love I needed. Therefore, I had to come up with a plan that would benefit me. I always knew Shelly had a thing for Tank and would be willing to sleep with him, if the price was right. Being the businesswoman that she is, Shelly was more than happy to take care of Tank, while at the same time ripping him off bit by bit. After tonight she would have made off with close to $100,000 of Tank's money, thanks to me providing her with the combination to the safe. I only wanted to prove to Tank that his street power couldn't touch the power of love, nor could it touch the power of revenge. For once I wanted to teach him a lesson. But now it was too late. My first love was growing colder by the minute.

"Well, it is what it is," Shelly said. "Nothing we can do to change it. I'm sorry Tank had to die, but it was self-defense. Everyone in this room knows that. Hmmph, he was really good, in more ways than one. But, you know, ballers come and ballers go. That's why I never get attached. When I'm involved, it's all about this." Shelly patted the front of her pajama pants. I guess her power was in the pussy. She picked up a leather bag that was lying in the corner.

"We make a good team, girl. Any chance of working out a similar deal with Mr. Hall? He looks like he has a few dollars," Shelly said jokingly as she glanced into her bag full of Tank's money.

"Not a chance," I told her, and headed downstairs.

BOSSY

1. GHETTO LAWS AND INNER-CITY ORDER

Kayla "Bossy" Tucker had been given the nickname Bossy by her Nana when she was just a toddler because of her take-charge personality. She was an attractive woman—and she knew it. She had a caramel complexion that turned bronze during the summer months, and her straight, long, naturally auburn-colored hair hung midway down her back. Her body alone made men fall at her feet, but there was something else about her, something not easily defined, that brought them to their knees.

Bossy sat at her cherry oak dining room table packaging freshly cooked crack cocaine with a joint balancing between her lips. She was racing against the clock to wrap up the latest shipment for Twan, a young blood who reminded her of herself during her early years in the game. He would be knocking on the door at any minute. Just when Bossy thought she would finish on time, the phone rang. She got up from the table, walked over to the counter, and removed the phone from its cradle.

"Hello," she said with an attitude, removing the joint from between her lips. She had answered the phone as if the person on the other end should have known that she had a deadline to meet and should not have been calling her.

"Bitch, stay the hell away from Twan. He got a family," a young female voice roared through the phone receiver in an attempt to sound threatening.

Because she was single and beautiful, many of Bossy's days began with petty phone calls such as this. She could usually pinpoint who the jealous, stupid broad on the other end of the phone was, and when she couldn't it was because the silly bitches would get their little girlfriends to call on their behalf. She knew the identification of this particular caller, because she had met her on an occasion or two and recognized her voice. It was Twan's main girl, LaJetia.

According to Twan, LaJetia bitched a lot about the hours he kept and had accused him and Bossy of fucking. The girl just didn't understand that hustlin' ain't got no time frame. It wasn't like hustlers, street pharmacists, pimps, and hos could clock in and out. The streets never shut down. The need for drugs, sex, and money was constant, and if you weren't available when a client wanted you to be, there was always someone ready to take your place.

Bossy removed the phone from her ear, stared at it, and laughed. *Is this shit for real?* she thought. She then placed the phone back up to her ear and spoke.

"You're just a young girl with stars in your eyes," Bossy said, snickering. "I'll give it to you, though: You must be feeling pretty strong callin' my house trying to start shit over some dick. Or you're pretty insecure and thought making this juvenile call would run me off," said Bossy in a whisper while blowing out smoke from the joint she was tokin' on.

"I'll tell you why I called—" LaJetia spit.

"That's where you fucked up," interjected Bossy, "thinking I'd give a damn why you called!"

"Aw, bitch, I'll—"

"You'll what? All you've done is shown your ho card. I care as much about that nigga as I care about you."

"I just want you to know that Twan has a woman and we got kids together," whined LaJetia.

"And what does that mean to me?" Bossy asked to piss LaJetia off even more.

"It means he ain't goin' nowhere. He stayin' wit' me!"

"Good, that's where I want him—with you. I ain't feedin', clothin', or housin' no nigga. So keep him right there with you." *Click!* Bossy couldn't hang up the phone quickly enough in order to get back to her business at hand. She felt as though it was way past time to end that conversation.

These young, insecure girls nowadays have a lot of nerve callin' another woman's house over some punk-no-good nigga, she thought. *They find a number in a pants pocket or on a cell phone call list and think they man laid up someplace. It ain't even rockin' like that at 539 Falls Avenue, Apartment B.* Bossy felt that even if she were sleeping with another woman's man, why should his chick step to her? *I ain't the one cheatin' and lyin' to her ass.*

After slamming the receiver down in LaJetia's ear, Bossy walked back over to the table to finish packaging the last of the coke. She then gathered it all from the kitchen table and placed it in a corner of her dining room. She looked at the crystal clock that was hanging on the wall and sighed, relieved that she had completed her task before Twan had arrived. As she looked down at the product on the floor, her thoughts wandered off as she began to daydream about her part in the life.

Hustlers did what had to be done in order to survive, she

thought, at the same time justifying her role. Those who came into the life and thought they could change the rules one player at a time were stupid and headed for some hard times. It didn't matter how wet a woman's pussy was or how deep her throat ran, she couldn't change the rules of the game.

Bossy knew that the streets forced you to grow up fast, and you'd better learn the rules if you wanted to survive the streets of Youngstown, Ohio. Rule number one: Trust no one. There were no friends in the game. Rule number two: A hustler must make his own retirement plan. Money should be broken down into thirds. One-third of your money should be placed aside and used to restock supply. Another one-third should be put up in case of legal trouble. And finally, the last one-third you should spend after putting away a little nest egg for your future retirement. By spend, she meant on necessities. Keep a roof over your head, clothes on your back, and food on the table. This plan required discipline and self-control.

One of the biggest misconceptions was that drug money was easy money. Wrong! You worked hard for it, so you had to use it wisely. You couldn't be a show-off. If you lived in a Section Eight house or somewhere in the heart of the ghetto, you couldn't drive a Land Rover, live in ya mama's basement, and have three plasma televisions in a house that was in dire need of a new roof and paint job. Possession of material trophies would always draw attention. Who needed it? Not a hustler, that was for damn sure.

Rule three of the game: Have a legitimate gig. Work a real job, or open some type of business. You shouldn't make it obvious how you made ya money.

Being a woman in this line of work hadn't been easy for Bossy. Many tried to take advantage of her, so she learned to be tough and ruthless. She didn't take shit from nobody. *If I put in time on your product, I want my money,* she thought. *Hell, I got bills, too. So what I was born with a moneymaker and I ain't got no kids; I still got responsibilities. Even if I didn't, so what! I want my money!*

A knock at the door interrupted Bossy's thoughts. She made her way through the living room and over to the front door. She looked through the peephole, unlocked the double bolts, and then opened the door.

"What up wit' you, boy?" Bossy asked.

Twan's muscular, lean physique walked through the door of Bossy's apartment looking good enough to eat. The throwback he wore complemented his chestnut eyes, and as usual, he was well groomed and well put together. Bossy kept herself from thinking about getting a taste of him, while she unconsciously ran her pink tongue across her thick lips. She never mixed business with pleasure, though, and anyway, Twan was only twenty-six, and Bossy never got involved with anyone younger than her. Twan came up nine years short.

"I can't call it," Twan replied. "You all right, girl?"

"You know me; I'm straight. Your shit is over there," said Bossy, pointing to the corner in her dining room. "You want a drink?"

Twan nodded his head yes, walked over to the bar in the dining room, and fixed both himself and Bossy a drink. He took a seat at the dining room table. Bossy sat across from Twan and contemplated telling him about the call she had received earlier from his little girlfriend. Since she made it a point to try to stay out of people's personal lives, she decided against it.

"It took me a minute to cut that kilo down into those twenties. Whose shit is that, anyway?" inquired Bossy.

"I'm on some new shit. Instead of puttin' a pound or two on the street hustlers, I'm placing them in my various houses during the winter months. It's easier to keep track of my money that way," explained Twan.

"I know you not still keeping track of ya money on paper. That right there will come back and fuck you."

"Naw, I got this. Don't worry about it," Twan said, sipping his drink.

Bossy shook her head. She didn't expect Twan to heed her advice. He had always been that way, since she could remember. Twan and Bossy were raised in the Westlake Housing Projects on the north side of Youngstown, Ohio. They weren't related, but their mothers came from the same stock and had mastered the same poor parenting skills.

Besides Twan, Bossy dealt with and trusted only her two best friends, Terry Benson and Aisha Woods. The three women were so close that they even had identical tattoos on their upper left arms of a dove with a ribbon in its beak, which read, KAT69. That stood for Kayla, Bossy's government name, and the year they were all born. KAT69 was also implemented in the name of their business, a hair and nail salon that was flourishing.

The fellas from the Westlake projects often told her and her girls that they were the coldest chicks on the north side. It wasn't just their looks that drew men to them; it was their attitudes. The three women would stand on a street corner, turn up a forty-ounce of Fo'-five, roll a joint, and toss dice. During the day they were just one of the fellas, but at night the woman in each of them came out. Not many women could be gangster and sexy at the same time. Bossy, Aisha, and Terry cleaned up so well it was hard to believe they were the same women who had turned up forties and shot craps out on the block.

When Bossy first moved into her apartment at 539, she threw a set every single weekend. Things were going on during the weekdays, but only a select number of hustlers were allowed. KAT69 threw parties in the early nineties that P. Diddy would be proud of. They had it so tight that no cameras were allowed. After

Teddy Bear bought the building, Aisha and Terry moved into the upstairs apartments. That way Bossy never had to worry about her neighbors calling the police on her.

Over a decade later and niggas were still talking about the sets Bossy threw at 539 Falls. Liquor flowed, weed went up in smoke, and the buffalo punch always marinated for at least seventy-two hours. If shit happened, Bossy made sure she controlled what went down, no ifs, ands, or buts about it. The sets were safe, they were fun, and what happened at Bossy's crib stayed the fuck at Bossy's crib.

Back in the day, Bossy used to pull off stick-'em-ups, burglaries, and assaults with Jalil "Big Black" Perry and Phillip "Poppy" Walters, just to pass the time. Everybody knew what was going down, but no one ever snitched or retaliated because of Bossy's relationship with Teddy Bear. She was untouchable.

2. DAMNED EITHER WAY

Winters in the Yo'—Youngstown—could be harsh and cruel to a newcomer, but Twan was a veteran, and everyone knew that the corner of Falls Avenue and Hillman Street was his claimed territory. Twan walked out of his house into the cold winter's night with one goal in mind: to replenish his stash of street candy and start making money. Hustling weed was cool, but there wasn't no real money in that. To make some real dough, Twan had recently stepped up his game and begun dealing rock. He had also been put in charge of running six drug houses on the south side by Teddy Bear.

Theodric "Teddy Bear" Sampson could be the brother of the lead singer of the old-school band The Time. He and Morris Day both had fair, high-yellow skin, a baby-soft complexion, relaxed hair, and a petite build that gave strangers a misconception about Teddy Bear when initially meeting him. Inside, demons dwelled and emerged only when provoked by deception, greed, or revenge. His reputation on the street was of being a ruthless businessman who kept his enemies six feet under and his loved ones living high on the hog. Behind closed doors, there were secrets long buried that only he and his wife knew of, and Teddy Bear chose to act as if he'd forgotten them all.

Managing the houses also required Twan to make road trips, but he continued to make time to return to his roots, the street corners. He wanted to stay connected to the people, the action, and the city.

As Twan maneuvered his three-toned hooptie toward his block, the sight of police cars and medics parked one block away sent a chill down his spine. Police car number seventy-three was occupied by two of the Yo's worst. Officers Powell and Meeks were as crooked as any public servants could be. They were notorious for kicking in the doors of drug houses, robbing the occupants of all their money and drugs, and then leaving out the same doorway they'd entered, making no arrests.

There was no reason for Twan to suspect that the officers were burglarizing one of the houses he managed. Teddy Bear Sampson kept the boys in blue taken care of when he started paying them to leave his associates alone after the first time they had hijacked him.

Twan knew the blinking lights meant that someone's life had been ended earlier than God had planned.

"Yo, Meeks, what y'all after this time?" Twan asked the officer standing closest to the curb.

"Another life taken by gunfire," Officer Meeks spoke with caution. Being familiar with Teddy Bear's statutes in the city, Officer Meeks knew Sampson's death had the potential to cause an all-out war among those trying to take his place.

"Who got popped this time?"

"It looks like a friend of yours, Twan," Meeks replied.

"Meeks, you know me—I ain't got no friends. Who got popped?"

"Teddy Bear Sampson," Meeks said. "Some woman just shot and killed ya boy Teddy Bear."

Twan couldn't believe what he had just heard. There had to be some kind of mistake. Teddy Bear Sampson was the biggest supplier in the city. He profited from all drug sales in the area and lived high and mighty.

His stature and personality were in vast contrast to his physical appearance. Teddy Bear was a small man with a baby face. Teddy Bear's father had passed the family drug trade down to him, and Teddy Bear transformed the drug connection into a profitable corporation. He owned a six-bedroom house and a fleet of cars, and wore only tailored suits and custom-made shoes. He had invested his ill-earned money into day spas, clothing stores, and other businesses. Teddy Bear was well liked by everyone because he was what one might call an honest crook. He took care of his people even though he supplied the poison they were dying over and killing themselves with. Now it appeared as though Teddy Bear was his own latest victim.

Twan stood there trying to make sense of the killing. He later learned that Teddy Bear's wife had shot him down after taking one too many beatings from him. Only those close to Teddy Bear knew the real man. He treated his soldiers on the streets better than he treated his wife, who was like property to him that he often disrespected.

For years Teddy Bear had been grooming Twan to take over the south side of the city. Twan was certain of two things: one, the streets would soon become a war zone for those seeking to fill Teddy Bear's shoes, and two, if he kept his head right, he'd be the man to fill those shoes. After all, who was more qualified to take over Teddy Bear's empire than his understudy?

Teddy Bear and Twan's relationship of teacher and student had begun the day after one of Teddy Bear's drug houses on the lower south side was raided by two of Youngstown's worst, Powell and Meeks. At first when the front door of the small house on Plum Street was kicked in, Twan and his best friend, Ant, thought it was a raid. But it became clear that the two officers were not there on official business. Instead of serving the occupants with a warrant, they threw a pillowcase at Ant and demanded that all the money and drugs be placed inside.

Thanks to the snowstorm burying the city under eight inches of ice, business had been light, so there wasn't much cash. The Yo's finest crooked cops left with only a few thousand in cash, a quarter of an ounce of weed, and two ounces of cocaine.

Twan had immediately called Teddy Bear to notify him of what had transpired. Because Twan was responsible for the house and the drugs, even without Teddy Bear suggesting it he took the loss and gave Teddy Bear the money he would have made off of the stolen products. Teddy Bear gained respect for the young man and began giving him more and more responsibilities. After Teddy Bear met with the two officers, he never had another problem with them again.

Twan was more than eager to take on his new responsibilities in the drug game. He had to think fast and map out his plan to take over the streets. With Ant as his right hand and Bossy on his payroll, he knew nothing was standing between him and power.

Three months had passed since Teddy Bear's murder. His death skyrocketed Twan to the head of the drug chain at a pace he had no trouble keeping up with. Besides Bossy, he was the only person aware of how Teddy Bear had run his business.

Spring and summer were good and busy in the life everywhere, but the streets of Youngstown literally lit the hell up with people making moves and flossing things they'd acquired during the winter months. Although Bossy had sat him down and reviewed her rules of street life with him, Twan was still among the flossers. He'd moved his family from their three-bedroom, two-story house on the west side of Youngstown to a four-bedroom ranch in Boardman, a suburb just off the south side of the city. Twan now pushed a 2006 fully loaded pearl-colored Escalade. LaJetia still had the Sienna for when the kids were with her, but she also drove a 2006 silver-gray Lexus.

Twan's age and mind-set were reflective in the ways he recklessly spent his money, throwing it away on designer clothes and jewelry that were bought on a whim. Patrons at Larry's Nightclub and Southern Tavern loved for Twan and Ant to walk through the doors. The two always sprang for bottles of Moët and Alizé for any- and everyone fortunate enough to be sitting at the bar. Hell, on a couple of occasions they even bought the bar out for the night.

Being local celebrities brought the men attention all around the city. Seeing the lifestyle changes the two friends were experiencing caused other men to envy them and women to want them. Ant often took advantage of his new status in the city. He had never been popular with women because of his large frame and hard features. All of his life people had called him ugly. Ant thought it was funny how money could make even a so-called ugly man look good to some women. He had been a virgin until the age of twenty, and even then he had to pay for the experience. Life had changed with money, and he was making every minute worthwhile.

Kayla was inside her apartment chillin' with a glass of brandy and the old-school sounds of Curtis Mayfield. She'd been waiting for Twan to make his regular dropoff and pickup, and as usual, he was running late. Kayla had decided to mellow out more by firing up a joint at the exact minute her doorbell rang.

"This run tomorrow will be the biggest since Teddy Bear died," Twan bragged. "Bossy, are you sure you can handle the weight?"

"How much weight are you talking about, and what type of turnaround time are you looking for, Twan?" Bossy asked.

"I'm looking at twenty pounds of weed to be broken down into twenty- and fifty-dollar bags. They'll be distributed out to six workers. Then I'm looking at fifty kilos of white girl. I know it's time-consuming, but I need half of those keys cut into twenty- and fifty-dollar rocks. Package the other half the same, but keep it in powder form," Twan explained.

"Twan, you want all of that done in the regular turnaround time? Three weeks?" Bossy said. "That ain't gon' work. You know how I feel about rushing my work. Even if I pull Terry and Aisha in to help, it's going to require more than three weeks. Why are you still breakin' down everybody's shit, anyway? That don't make no sense," Bossy vented. She flicked her lighter to the end of the joint while waiting for Twan's response. Bossy wasn't stupid, and such a big order so close to the previous one was telling her that Twan was on some other shit.

"You're the best in town when it comes to this shit. I still have you breakin' down my weight because you don't waste a crumb, and after you put your magic touch to it, the potency is outrageous. Each bag and every rock match my profit in weight," complimented Twan. "It's cool on the time issue. I can stand to wait it out, and you know I don't want you to rush and fuck up my shit."

"See, you trippin'; I ain't never fucked up nobody's shit!" Bossy said defensively. "I gotta sleep at some point, so at least give me six to eight weeks. But I ain't cleaning that weed. Now that's what's up."

"Girl, you know I'm just playing with you. Just think of this shipment as your own personal property. Let's call it Kayla's Keys." Twan caught himself and said, "I know that no one calls you by your government name, so let's go with Bossy's Keys. That will motivate you to complete the assignment in record time. How does three weeks sound to you? I'll pay you and your girls a thousand per day extra for your time."

"Oh, I was chargin' extra for this load no matter what you wanna call it. Bossy's Keys, or whatever, will be completed six, maybe eight weeks after delivery," said Bossy. If Twan was fuckin' with a new supplier it would come out soon enough, and Bossy would call him on it at the appropriate time. Until then she chose to keep things as they'd always been.

Twan had stood to leave when the thought of the block party crossed Bossy's mind. Every year Danny Levy held a big-ass block party on Kenmore Avenue. He had started it about five years ago, and each year it got bigger and better. The affair was nonprofit and allowed the kids around the south-side neighborhood to have some summer fun and see those who'd made something of themselves give back.

"Twan, just one more thing before you leave. Don't forget about that contribution to this year's Kenmore block party. Danny got the entire weekend lined up, and Terry wants KAT69 to be the biggest sponsor for 2006."

"Isn't the annual Kenmore block party the last weekend of July?" Twan questioned.

"No, it's always the first weekend in August," Bossy corrected him. "I know it's two weeks away, but Danny Levy needs the finances to roll in now. Terry got him to let that rapper No-Joke headline the free concert, but throwing a block party costs money—big money."

"What are you talking about?" Twan was puzzled. "Who the fuck is No-Joke?"

"You know, Sirenna Salas's husband, Felix. He's an up-and-coming Y-town rapper. He goes by the stage name of No-Joke. The boy is nasty and going places. After his performance, Ruffus Black takes the stage. The block party gets bigger and better every year."

"Just like my bank account," Twain bragged as he stood up in preparation to leave.

Bossy decided there was no time like the present to speak with Twan about his recklessness.

"Before you leave, have another quick drink with me so I can holler at you about a few things," Bossy insisted.

"Anything for you, Bossy." Twan winked as he made a beeline to the bar. "What's goin' on?" he asked as he cracked open a new bottle of Belvedere.

"Word on the streets is that you and ya boy Ant are flossin' and puttin' ya business out there. Slow down, boy. Everybody ain't ya friend, and we both know there are a lot of haters out there."

"You worry too much," Twan said as he walked back into the living room and refilled their glasses. "But I hear you loud and clear."

"I hope you do, because if you get popped, that affects me and my girls. And let's not forget about that family you got out there in Boardman."

"Bossy, don't worry about nothing. I'm straight, and won't nothing happen to any of us. That's what's up." He nodded before holding his glass in the air in a toast motion and then drinking it down.

"Now that we have that out of the way, I want you to join us the weekend after the block party for a small, informal set. It's going to be here at the crib. You and Ant both are invited. Y'all both are more than welcome to bring a date; just keep in mind one thing—"

"I already know what you about to say," Twan interrupted Bossy, as he could predict the next words that were about to come out of her mouth. " 'Be careful who you and ya boy bring into five thirty-nine.' But you know you ain't even gotta worry about that. You know I don't trust nobody."

"That's what's up. And while we're on the subject of trust . . ." Bossy took a sip of her drink before proceeding. "You need to slow your roll, Twan. I'm hollerin' at you from the heart, baby boy. Be careful," Bossy said with sincerity and concern.

She had never told Twan about the phone call she'd received months ago from LaJetia, so she didn't want to come straight out and talk negatively about his chick. Bossy felt that she was the main person he shouldn't trust. But she didn't even bother to waste her breath on that one. Bossy was experienced enough to know that Twan wouldn't hear anything she had to say about his girl, no way. Young love was blind, hazardous, and volatile. He'd see when he was ready and not a day before.

Bossy saw Twan to the door and then proceeded to package and weigh the product of another longtime associate. It puzzled her as to why Twan and others of his status would take the time to have drugs packaged for street distribution on someone else's behalf. In the end, Bossy decided that it didn't matter why they did it, only that they kept doing it. She preferred dealing with one top-notch person as opposed to six midscale players. So as long as she continued to play her cards right, it didn't matter what hand she was dealt.

3. TIME FOR A CHANGE

"You have to be fuckin' around on me; otherwise you would be home at four in the morning," LaJetia cried into the phone.

"Man, I'm so sick of this shit. Take ya ass to bed and I will see you when I see you," said Twan, hanging up the phone in LaJetia's ear.

As LaJetia lay in bed recalling the argument she and Twan just had, tears began streaming down her face. The tears were flowing from a life of pain and neglect. In her heart she felt the love Twan and her children held for her was genuine and unconditional. But years of feeling neglected by her mother convinced LaJetia that Twan would one day betray her, just as everyone else in her life had done.

LaJetia had felt so alone and insecure her entire life. She always sought attention from strangers in an effort to feel love. Because it was foreign to her, she couldn't recognize the real love that Twan was offering her. Unlike most people, LaJetia didn't allow herself to dream about tomorrow. She kept her focus on today and today only.

She couldn't help but ask herself why now, in her life, she was still so unhappy and angry. To anyone looking at her life things appeared well. Twan had given her and the kids a nice home, clothes, cars, and all of the material necessities. If happiness were measured by material possessions, LaJetia should've been ecstatic. Twan was a great provider, but fell short when it came to giving of himself emotionally.

The more LaJetia recalled the last argument she'd had with her man, the more convinced she became that the late-night hours he kept meant only one thing—the fool was playin' her. LaJetia could come up with a laundry list of reasons for Twan to walk away from her, the number one reason being she did not trust him.

Twan had had enough of LaJetia's insecurities. In the time he'd been in a relationship with LaJetia, he'd given his all. He couldn't understand why his best was never enough. Lately the weight on his shoulders had gotten so heavy that he was becoming physically ill. Twan knew his only option was to walk away from the relationship. He just couldn't figure out how to get LaJetia to understand that his leaving didn't mean he would be walking away from his responsibilities.

Things had gotten so bad that Twan dreaded going home on those nights he could get away and make it to the crib before the a.m. hours. He knew that an argument would greet him the second he walked through the door no matter what time it was. That was just how bad things had gotten. Home was supposed to be the place a man could lay his head and rest. Twan's home was a battleground, and it seemed that his mere breathing could ignite a fight.

Nonetheless, the next night when Twan returned home, he entered with caution and was surprisingly met with quiet and calm. The kids weren't running around ignoring their mother's threats of beatings if they didn't settle down, and LaJetia didn't attack him with a verbal assault, accusing him of sleeping around on her.

After walking farther into his home, Twan heard the sounds of Teedra Moses singing about her man standing her up. LaJetia was sitting in the study with aromatherapy candles lit, and wearing a pair of lilac satin lounging pajamas.

"Hey, baby, what's up with you?" Twan asked cautiously.

"I didn't hear you come in," LaJetia said. "Nothing's up; I'm just taking a minute to myself, since the kids are all asleep." LaJetia turned to face Twan as she spoke. He could see evidence of recent tears on her face.

"Are you okay, LaJetia? Please tell me what I can do to make you happy." Twan felt drained. He had to figure out a way to handle the situation with care, because LaJetia's emotional state seemed fragile. Looking at the mother of his only child, Trayvon, Twan began to rethink his decision to leave the relationship. Anyway, he was the only father her other two children had ever known. Seeing LaJetia like this caused him to fear that she might harm herself—or even worse, harm them.

"If I tell you, will you do it for me?" she asked sadly.

"Yes, what do you need?" Twan said, walking toward her.

"I need you to give me your time and attention. If you're not in the streets, you paying the kids more attention than you do me. I need you, too, Twan. Why can't you understand that?"

"Damn, girl, I'm trying to be as patient as I possibly can. Like I told you countless times before, the streets don't close down. I'm a hustler and I'm my own boss. Shit, I ain't punchin' no time clock. If I'm home, you got ya hand out for money! How can I give it to you if I ain't puttin' time in?"

"See, that's what I'm talking about, Twan," LaJetia snapped, throwing her previous cool, calm demeanor out the window. "You don't listen to me at all. I may as well be a single parent, because you ain't helpin' me raise these kids. You come and go as you please while I do everything around here by myself. You climb into bed and don't even touch me, so you must be touchin' another bitch."

"Come off that shit, girl. How many times I got to tell you I ain't fuckin' around?"

"As many times as it takes!" LaJetia replied as she stood up and exited the study, stomping down the long hallway. Once inside their bedroom, she threw herself across the bed and forced herself to cry. She knew how it affected Twan to see her cry, and she was going to milk the situation until she got what she wanted from him.

Twan refused to run after her, but her crying seemed to echo throughout the house. *Shit, this bitch must think I'm one of those weak-ass niggas from the jets she used to fuck with,* he thought as he remained in the study. *I'll chill at the crib tonight, but if she thinks she gon' keep a nigga on lockdown, she got life fucked-up. And that's my word!*

4. STREET LIFE 101

The private life of Anthonie "Ant" Quarles was in vast contrast to that of his street life. Before Ant went to work each day, he checked in on his mother to ensure that she was safe and wanted for nothing. This particular summer morning was no different from any other.

"Hey, Mama, do you need anything done before I head out to work?" Ant asked between bites of the homemade sausage burrito, sitting at the kitchen table eating, while his mother sipped on a cup of coffee, reading the morning paper.

"No, baby, ya mama is fine," Ant's mother replied. "I keep telling you not to worry about me; the good Lord will keep me safe."

Olivia Quarles was a strong, God-fearing woman who was known for her kind spirit and enduring faith. She had dedicated her life to serving the Lord after the senseless murder of her oldest child, Davis, who was an innocent bystander shot during a bank robbery. That was almost twenty years ago, and her youngest child, Ant, was still trying to come to terms with the loss of his brother.

Ant had been only four years old at the time of the murder, and Davis was the only father figure he had known. As he grew older, Ant began running the streets, dealing drugs, and robbing people for sport.

Every day Ant headed to the only job he'd ever known: slinging dope. After being in the game for seven years and getting away with so many crimes, Ant felt invincible. Any true hustler knew the future held only one of two things: prison or death. Ant wasn't afraid of either, which made him a menace. The streets of Youngstown, Ohio, didn't allot any young black man the option of fearing the unknown.

As Ant drove down Warren Avenue he cracked open his second forty-ounce of White Mountain citrus wine cooler as the clock struck nine a.m. The powerful sounds of Parliament coming from the charcoal-gray deuce-and-a-quarter could be heard coming three blocks before he reached the drug house. Everyone in Youngstown had one thing in common—the hypnotic sounds of funk. George Clinton, Bootsy Collins, and Roger Troutman and Zapp had contributed more to the rearing of young men than their absentee fathers.

"What up wit' ya, dude?" Twan greeted his boy of fourteen years.

"Ah, man, I can't call it. How ya livin, Pimp? Ready to do this?" Ant questioned between sips. The partners in crime were up early to meet with their runners and tally up the week's earnings.

Sitting inside the two-bedroom drug house situated on the corner of Warren Avenue and Overland Street was Ant's southside chick, Shadaisy Davis. She was a high school dropout, dopedealing mother of four, and a money-hungry freak. She kept her dirty brown hair covered with a cheap blond weave and her ass hiked up in leather pants whether it was winter, spring, summer, or fall. Because of her lifestyle and lack of stability, the state had removed all four of her children from her care two years ago. Her mother got custody to keep the children from being lost in the system, and Shadaisy had no plans of getting them back.

"Come on, girl, let's move this shit. You already rollin' and ain't even washed ya ass yet. Shit, you knew I was coming," Ant snapped at his ghetto queen. Shadaisy was tagging along to double-count the money collected and play chauffeur for the day.

"Ah, nigga, fuck you. We got three hours to do this; why you sweatin' me? I just got in a minute ago."

"Ain't nobody tell ya hot ass to close down the after-hours spot. Go wash that ass before I tap that ass," Ant threatened as he finished off his liquid breakfast.

Ant kept his work car, a 1986 Ford Escort, parked at the Warren Avenue drug house. The car needed some bodywork and a paint job, but the engine purred like a kitten. Before making their rounds, the trio headed north to hit up Perkins restaurant for breakfast.

After scarfing down enough food to feed a small country for a week, the trio made their way to the various drug houses Twan kept around the city. After all of the money was collected and bills were paid, Shadaisy was dropped off at home and the partners headed to Sharon, Pennsylvania.

Shortly after Teddy Bear was killed, Ant put the wheels in motion so that one day he would be able to break away from Twan and stand on his own feet. He loved his boy like a brother but Ant was tired of standing in the shadows while Twan received all the glory on the streets. Today was their first meeting with Ant's new contact. The product wasn't as good as what they were getting from their Florida connection, but Ant needed this relationship if he was going to make his move. It took a lot of doing, but he was able to get Twan to go along with the deal. Ant reasoned that Pennsylvania was a lot closer than Florida, and expanding resources was a good thing.

There was only one problem resulting from the new connection—where to house the additional weight.

Twan, what the hell is all of this? I know damn well you're smarter than this. Just like a little kid, you got ya hands in too many cookie jars!" Bossy had tried relentlessly over the past six months to calm Twan down. He was acting like a teenager rebelling against his parents because he thought he knew all of the answers to the world's problems and everyone else was just getting by in life.

"Come on, Bossy, don't trip on ya boy. You like gettin' that paper just as much as me. All I'm doin' is stackin our paper higher and faster."

"Twan, this is already fast money. What type of race are you running?"

"The same one as you and the rest of these hustlers in the streets. You know how it is out here—every baller for himself."

Twan was right. Bossy understood firsthand what it was like on the streets. That was exactly why she'd bent over backward to continue teaching Twan about the streets after Teddy Bear was killed. Frustration grew daily for Bossy, because Twan refused to listen to her teachings, to recognize her experience. It was one thing for Twan to increase the amount of weight he was moving, but he was stepping into an arena he was totally unfamiliar with.

Like a carryout restaurant, Twan's products could now be listed on a menu: powder cocaine, crack cocaine, heroin, weed, Percocet, OxyContin, Valium, meth, and the list grew weekly.

"Listen to me, Twan, because I'm only going to say this once." Bossy paused for effect. "You are making too many trips up and down the highway. You are making too many dropoffs and pickups here. Every day it seems like your name is mentioned at the shop, because the night before you and Ant were out flossin' at the clubs."

"Not this again." Twan sighed.

"I wouldn't be surprised if some wannabe gangsta is measuring you up, looking to take your place. For that matter, I wouldn't be surprised if five-O ain't already on ya trail. And if that's the case, you might have unknowingly led them here to me."

"What you trying to say to me, Bossy?"

"Slow the fuck down or I'm gonna stop fuckin' with you!"

5. BUSINESS IS BUSINESS—PERSONAL AIN'T

Terry walked out of her office to hear two familiar voices engaged in a heated discussion. She had no idea what Aisha could possibly be arguing with Twan about.

"Excuse me, but would the two of you please join me in my office?" Terry's statement was more of a demand than a request.

Aisha sprinted into the office and immediately began pacing the floor. "Terry, do you know Twan has the nerve to want us to keep some of his shit here until Bossy's ready for it?"

Terry couldn't believe what she'd just heard. Twan knew better than to make such a request. In the beginning, KAT69 turned bad money into good money, but since then no illegal activity ever took place in the hair and nail salon.

"Why y'all trippin'? Tryin' to act all brand-new like y'all hands ain't dirty. Shit, it's only this one time," Twan tried to reason.

"You must have lost ya damn mind, Twan. I told you no outside, and I'm telling you no again," fumed Aisha.

"Come on, girl, y'all know I ain't bringing no heat up in here. Just let me stash a couple of keys here till Bossy ready for 'em."

"Terry, you talk to him. The longer I stand here, the more my head hurts." Aisha slammed the door behind her and walked toward the phone to call Bossy. She knew Terry could and would handle Twan and his careless request, but Bossy needed to know what was going on.

Twan stood contemplating his next move. He knew he was wrong for asking this of his friends but he felt he had no choice. He and Ant had made a deal with the new supplier, Clifton "C-Lok" Boyd, without thinking ahead. Ant had made the deal sound so inviting, there was no way Twan could have said no. Now they were stuck.

Before approaching his friends, Twan had contemplated hiding the stash in his basement, or even at Ant's mother's house. His conscience wouldn't allow him to deceive Ms. Quarles, and he didn't want to take the chance that one of his kids would find the drugs at home. He would ride around with the drugs in his trunk before he stored them at home and put his kids in harm's way.

Terry calmly walked around her cherry oak desk and sat down in her black leather high-backed chair.

"Have a seat, Twan. We need to talk about this request of yours," Terry calmly stated.

"Listen, Terry, I'm not trying to disrespect. You know me; we go way back. I wouldn't ask if it weren't an emergency."

"How many times did Teddy Bear say to you, 'No business but hair business takes place at KAT69'?"

"Yeah, but Teddy Bear ain't here no more, and what I need ain't that deep. It's just this one time."

"Twan, I'm all about business, and this place is my livelihood. Teddy Bear set down rules for a reason, and just because he's gone doesn't mean everything changes."

"What you want me to do, beg?" asked Twan.

"No, I don't. But I do want you to think about the possible consequences of your actions."

"Look, I don't need you lecturing me, too. LaJetia and Bossy bitch at me enough. So what's it going to be, Terry? Are you with me or not?"

"Simple—it's going to be no, and I resent you trying to take advantage of our friendship this way."

As Twan stood to leave, he looked into Terry's eyes and said, "Teddy Bear and Bossy were right—ain't no friends in this business." As he walked out the front door, fuming, Twan ran right into LaJetia. She was there for her weekly appointment with Sirenna. Twan explained that he was in a hurry and would see her at home later.

After reminding her man about the promise he had made to the kids for that evening, LaJetia stepped aside and watched as Twan got into his car and sped off down Hillman Street.

LaJetia left KAT69 feeling like a queen. In the two weeks since she'd put on her crying act, Twan had been making her life a little easier. Per her request, Twan had been helping with the kids in the mornings and coming home from the streets by two a.m. Her man had even been attentive and taken time out to join his family for dinner every other day.

Today was Thursday, and Twan had promised the kids he'd be home when Kiara got in from school. It was coming up on eight o'clock and becoming obvious that Twan's promise had been broken.

"Mommy, where's Daddy at? He said he'd be here to watch a movie with us after I did my homework," whined Kiara.

LaJetia's nerves were already on edge, and having to answer questions from her five-year-old daughter was the last thing she wanted to do. LaJetia's disappointment gradually turned into anger. She'd suspected the honeymoon wouldn't last long, but lying to the children was inexcusable. Letting her down was one thing; letting the kids down was something else altogether. LaJetia knew all too well the pain felt when the person who was supposed to love and protect you broke your heart.

Twan turned his key in the lock and braced himself for the impending fight he was about to be party to. The search for a place to store his newly acquired stash had taken much longer than he or Ant could have ever imagined. The last thing he wanted to do was disappoint his kids, but today it just couldn't be helped. It was now three in the morning and all he wanted to do was lie down, but Twan knew LaJetia wouldn't let that happen.

The house was eerily quiet, and that sent a chill up Twan's spine. No voices came from the television, and no soulful sounds were playing in LaJetia's private sitting room. This really took Twan by surprise. LaJetia used that room as her place of refuge. The walls were a soft lilac and housed a state-of-the-art stereo, a plush cream-colored sofa, and two matching wing-backed lounge chairs. The bookshelf matched the end tables, and the scent of aromatherapy candles overtook the room.

LaJetia retreated into her room to read, relax, and escape the responsibilities of motherhood—and to mentally prepare for an argument with Twan.

A plate covered with a paper towel caught Twan's eye as he walked through the kitchen. He took a minute to place his dinner in the fridge and pour himself a glass of water. Twan thought that just maybe he'd dodged a bullet and LaJetia had fallen asleep. The idea allowed him to relax his shoulders and breathe a sigh of relief.

In the bedroom, Twan undressed and slowly got into the custom-made four-poster bed, trying not to wake LaJetia. The second he closed his eyes, LaJetia spoke to him.

"All of my life people have talked about me. They can say anything they want about me, but no one can ever say I'm a bad mother. Even at age fourteen I was a good mother, and I work hard at being there for my children.

"If you ask some people what it is they aspire to be, you might hear a variety of jobs. If someone were to ask me what I aspire to be, I'd answer, 'A good mother.'" LaJetia paused to collect her thoughts.

"You're a very good provider; I can't deny that. From what I hear on the streets, you're even a good hustler, but you fail where it counts, Twan. Kiara, Tyler, and Trayvon worship the ground you walk on. No matter how many times you let them down, all is right in their worlds when Daddy walks in the door." LaJetia's voice cracked as tears streamed down the sides of her face. "A little girl should always be able to count on her daddy, always. He's the only man in her life who will be there no matter what. I say that because Kiara cried herself to sleep tonight because her daddy let her down. It appears to me that you're aspiring to be a sorry-ass father."

Twan lay tense and speechless. He'd never taken the time to measure what type of father he'd become. He felt that providing material things, like shelter and food, and raising another man's child made him a prime candidate for the father-of-the-decade award. LaJetia's words must have held some truth, because no sleep would come for Twan that night. *You're aspiring to be a sorry-ass father.* As the words replayed in Twan's mind, he mumbled to himself, "Damn, that was personal."

6. WE DON'T CALL 911 'ROUND HERE

The air was humid, and all the players were strollin' the strip, trying to be seen. Making his rounds from the south side to the north side up the east side and back south, Twan saw which runners were working and which were missing in action. He made mental notes on who to call into the office on re-up Thursday. Lazy didn't amount to money, and hustlin' wasn't a game for those not willing to put in the sweat, tears, and the risk required to make it. The incompetent would have to find another player to work for, especially since Ant had decided to step the game up.

Two hours later, Twan sat inside his pearl Escalade debating whether to go inside and face the music. He knew word had made its way back to 539 Falls Avenue about what went down between him, Aisha, and Terry three days ago. Before stepping into KAT69 he had known the women were going to have a baby over his request. The confrontation with Terry had actually gone smoother than expected. Knowing things with Bossy wouldn't be as easy, Twan gulped down a few shots of vodka. Bossy was one woman not to be fucked with, and Twan had done just that.

He held his breath when the door slowly opened, permitting him to go inside.

Bossy had seen him sitting outside, but decided to wait for him to make his move. Lately Twan had made so many bad choices that Bossy had begun questioning his loyalty to her and her girls. *I practically raised him and tried to teach him the rules of the game just like Teddy Bear had taught me, and this is how he wants to show his gratitude?* she thought. Bossy looked Twan in his eyes and wondered if she even knew who he was anymore.

"What's up with you, girl? You all right?" questioned Twan.

The minute Twan heard the music Bossy was listening to, he knew the visit wasn't going to be easy. Everyone in the Yo' listened to music as a way to survive, the one thing everyone had in common.

"Yeah, ya shit is over there. Leave my money on the table," Bossy said harshly.

"Look, Bossy, I know your girls told you about me coming into the shop and asking for their help. I know it was wrong, and it won't happen again." Twan apologized without making eye contact, making Bossy question his thinking even more.

"Sit down."

"I know we need to talk, but I got to—"

"Sit down," demanded Bossy. "Don't make me say it again." Twan did as he was told and sat directly across from Bossy. They sat without saying a word while the disk changer switched to Bootsy Collins and his song "Hollywood" began playing.

"Some of the things you do remind me of myself when I was a couple of years younger than you are now. Other things you do are so reckless it pisses me off."

"I know, and—"

"Twan, just listen to what I have to say. Pay close attention, and hopefully when I'm done you'll understand why I'm asking myself if you can be trusted anymore.

"I know you've heard stories about me, how I was back in the day. Some stories good and some bad, but they're probably all true. I've had my fun clubbin' it, robbin' cats out on the streets just for the fun of it, fuckin' with three and four different playas at one time. People used to call me a pimp. I hate that word because it's too generalized these days. What ya generation don't understand is that sometimes pimps gotta ho, too." Bossy paused to let her last statement sink in. "Aisha and Terry hung with me at the clubs, but they never committed any crimes. I love and respect them too much to put them in danger that way. Even today, I only let them get in so deep with what I do, and truth be told, I don't want them involved at all. See, when you love someone, Twan, you protect and look after them." The ice in Bossy's drink had melted, and all she tasted was water as she took her last sip. She stood to pour herself a fresh drink and brought Twan back a beer.

"About ten years ago I was hanging out with my boys Big Black and Poppy. We were real tight. Most people thought they were fuckin' me, but it wasn't even like that. We looked out for one another, and to them I was just one of the boys. Anyway, one day we started drinking around noon and didn't stop until three in the morning. Man, we kicked it that day. I think I won over five thousand dollars from them playing craps, spades, and dominoes. Poppy won half of it back when we hit Corky's and played a few hours of pool.

"That night we rode out to the Sharon line and paid the after-hours spot the Davises' a visit. It was on that night, and we took advantage of every single minute. Just when the spot started jumpin', shots rang out. Me and Big Black were on the dance floor, and Poppy was off in the back smoking with some chick. Shots being fired in that joint was common, so everyone hit the ground and waited for the bouncers to grab hold of the situation. When all was cool, the deejay would start spinning the tunes again and the crowd would return to partying like nothing happened."

Bossy took a sip of her fresh drink before continuing with her story. "Not that night though. When the smoke cleared, three people lay dead, one being Poppy. Big Black and Teddy Bear lost they minds over that shit. By the time we laid our boy to rest, word had hit the streets that some bitch from the Brooks had set him up. That's who was all up in his ear that night. He'd beat her ass a month before, and she wanted payback. I understood the retaliation, but not to the extent of taking my boy's life. Teddy Bear found out who pulled the trigger and plans were in the works to lay them down.

"Big Black took that shit to heart, and it was all he could talk about. We were out one day reminiscing on old times when we spotted them fools that killed Poppy. What happened next was reflex, it seemed so natural. All I could see was my boy lying in a pool of blood with half his face blown the fuck off." Tears began flowing down Bossy's face as she remembered the love she had for Poppy and the sin she'd committed that night. "I grabbed my thirty-eight, Big Black whipped out his nine, and we both started blastin'. When the bullets stopped flyin', a couple of east-side niggas named Eddie 'E-Low' Brown and David 'Slim' Collins were on their way to hell."

Twan was shocked. Never would he have guessed that Bossy had taken someone's life.

"We hauled ass out of there and drove straight to Teddy Bear's. A lot happened that night, including the guns and car we were driving never being seen again. You have no idea how difficult it is to live with the fact that someone is no longer on this earth because of me. I didn't even know their names until I read that shit in the papers. No matter what they did, just like Poppy, they were sons, brothers, maybe even fathers. We all chose this life, and we live it the way these streets demand, but we all deserve respect because we breathe. I tell you this story and say all of this to you just to say this: Do not disrespect the game, the hustle, or my girls' livelihood ever again. And Twan, most important, do not disrespect me. Just because we don't call nine-one-one 'round here don't mean they won't come for you when you slip."

7. CAN I HAVE A MINUTE TO MYSELF, PLEASE?

When Aisha pulled in front of their apartment building, she was happy to see that no one was home. It had been a difficult workday, and she longed for a hot tub. "Good, I can rest before going to have dinner with Mama. Lord knows I need a minute to myself." That idea was short-lived when Aisha spotted Ant's deuce-and-a-quarter parked behind hers. "Now, what does this fool want? I am not in the mood.

"Bossy's not here, Ant, but I'll let her know you're looking for her." Aisha tried to keep him from getting too far out of his car.

"I ain't looking for Bossy. I want to talk to you and Terry," Ant said smugly.

"Why? You don't have anything to speak with us about."

"Yes, I do. Our house on Warren was busted today, and over five hundred thousand dollars' worth of shit is gone. If y'all stuck-up asses had let my boy stash that shipment at ya spot, none of this would have happened. Now somebody gon' pay."

"Ant, I don't have time for your immature bullshit. If you and

Twan can't handle the weight you're digging into, ease up off it. Before that shipment was even picked up, storage for it should have been planned and confirmed. The two of you have been doing shit ass-backward, so you getting busted was bound to happen."

"Look, bitch—"

"No, the hell you didn't come at me sideways! You don't want to get yourself into a name-calling match with me. I understand you being upset, but I am not the one," warned Aisha.

"Fuck that! We ain't got the money to re-up now and have no way to recoup that type of paper. You two bitches better find a way to get us out of this shit or we all gon' be in trouble. If I go down, we all sinkin'."

Ant must have forgotten that she was from the jets herself.

"Are you crazy or stupid?" Aisha screamed back. "When it comes down to it, ain't no partnerships in the streets, and ya ugly ass know that. See, I ain't nobody's bitch, especially not some ugly-ass runner from Smurf Village!" Aisha had had enough. She reached inside her purse, grabbed her .32, and pointed it at Ant. "If you think I won't cap one in ya knees, try me. I dare you— make a move, monkey."

Ant stood still, mouth opened.

"That's what I thought. Now, retreat ya ugly black ass back into ya car and ride the fuck on." Ant did as he was told, and Aisha stood watching as his car disappeared up and over the hill.

"All I wanted was a minute for me; now this fool done drawn me into a place I have no right being."

8. CAN YOU LIVE WITH YOUR MISTAKES?

Ant was pissed as he drove around the city contemplating his next move. His initial plan of intimidating Aisha was a bust. He'd fully expected her to fold like a blanket, but instead she ended up turning into someone totally opposite the Aisha he knew. The woman pointing the gun at him was strong, confident, and straight-up ghetto. In all of the years he'd been around Aisha, she always came off as timid, soft, and ladylike. As the saying went, Never judge a book by its cover.

According to Shadaisy, officers Powell and Meeks stormed the house and left with the stash of drugs but didn't arrest her. Ant couldn't believe how two crooked cops could remain on the force as long as they had. Every hustler in the city had had a run-in with those two so-called officers at one time or another. As Ant pulled up in front of the drug house, he racked his brain to come up with a way to stop their criminal behavior and recover his loss.

Minutes after Ant stepped into the Warren Avenue house, Twan pulled up in LaJetia's silver-gray Lexus. Ant's heart stopped for fear that word had gotten back to Twan about his encounter with Aisha earlier that day. He stepped out onto the porch to greet his boy.

"What up with you, boy; you all right?" Ant asked nervously.

"I'm pissed, man. Someone slashed the tires on my ride!" Twan paused to catch his breath. "What a bitch move."

Inside, Shadaisy overheard the conversation taking place outside and thought how right Twan was. Bitch moves were usually made by bitches, and LaJetia was most likely the culprit.

As soon as Twan stepped through the door, Shadaisy went to

work. "Hey, Twan, did I hear you right? Someone came out to the 'burbs and fucked with ya ride?"

"Yeah, ain't that some shit? Whoever did it better hope I never catch up with 'em." Twan's anger grew as he thought about someone violating the number one rule to a man: Never fuck with his ride.

"Are you sure you don't know who did it? I mean, after the phone call ya girl made to me a little while ago, I'd be looking at home first before trying to look in the streets for who disrespected you like that."

Shadaisy tried to drag out the information as long as possible. She was jealous of the way Twan took care of home, especially since Ant didn't think enough of her to put her in a house of her own. Instead he had her living in a drug house, where at any time her life and freedom could come to an end.

"What the hell are you talking about?" Twan was getting frustrated with Shadaisy.

"Ya girl called me to let me know you have a woman and family and that you ain't going nowhere. She told me to stop fuckin' with you. Apparently she thinks you messing around on her."

"Are you serious? LaJetia did that? How did she get the number?"

"I don't know, but I'm guessing from your cell."

Twan thought back to everything that had taken place at home and realized LaJetia had access to his phone while he was in the shower. She had tried hard to get him to stay home today. He felt bad about breaking his promise to her, but he had to take care of business. Recouping lost money from the drugs that were stolen from them was the priority. Unbeknownst to Ant, it would be no problem for Twan to ante up the five hundred grand they owed C-Lok, but he didn't want anyone knowing he was sitting comfortably like that.

"Man, who the fuck is that?" Shadaisy yelled after hearing the sound of screeching tires outside. Ant knew the shit was about to hit the fan. He'd fucked up big-time, and had to face the music.

When he was a little boy hanging out with the street-corner hustlers, he heard story after story about the boldest bitch in the city. Only those with a death wish crossed Bossy. Ant recalled hearing the story of a drive-by done out on the Sharon line. The way he overheard it, Teddy Bear was caught slippin' at a phone booth one night after the club closed. He was parked down the street from Jitso's Bar, and some young punk rode up on him and robbed him for five hundred dollars. Teddy Bear got a good look at the dope fiend and put the word out about a reward if he was found that night. The description was of a young boy with a boxed high-top cut, light-skinned with a bad complexion, wearing a blue Members Only jacket, jeans, and Adidas kicks.

Finding him was easy, because he bragged about the holdup while chillin' in the Davises' after-hours spot that same night. Big Black, Poppy, and Bossy were chillin' in the parking lot when someone ratted on him. His name was Ali. Bossy went inside and acted like she wanted to spend some time with him. Thinking with the wrong head, Ali fell for it, and he followed Bossy to her car. They took a short ride to a park behind the club. Bossy led Ali away from the car, and Big Black and Poppy snuck up behind them. They had been hiding in the backseat. Ali never knew what hit him. They beat him so bad he was unrecognizable for months. He lay in a coma for eight weeks and awoke unable to remember his own name.

It was said that Bossy shot him in his hands and kneecaps to teach him a lesson. She reasoned that he shouldn't have been so stupid and hit a man with as many resources as Teddy Bear.

Twan walked out on the porch to meet Bossy. She never

showed her face at any spot that might be hot, so Twan knew something was wrong.

"Where's ya boy Ant?" barked Bossy.

"He's right in there. What's going on?" Twan was confused.

"Ant, get your dumb ass out here. Better yet, let's handle this inside so the neighbors don't overhear us and call the police."

Again Twan asked what was going on. Bossy told Ant to explain to Twan what he'd done. Ant remained silent.

"Since his bitch ass won't own up to what he did, I'll let you know." Bossy felt her heart race as she focused on Twan. "He rode up on my spot and made demands on Aisha. He tried to strongarm her into repaying the loss y'all took on the raid."

"Ant, what the fuck you thinking?" Twan demanded.

"You know as well as I do that if we could have stashed that shit in the shop, Powell and Meeks would have come up empty on their illegal raid."

Shadaisy stood in the background listening and realized just how much of a punk Ant was.

"Are you crazy? What kind of logic is that?" Twan asked.

"What I want to know is, how in the hell did they get that much weight from y'all when you always bring it to me first for storage and packaging?" Bossy knew she'd just busted Twan and he'd have to come clean. The Yo' was too small for him to think word hadn't gotten back to her about his deal with C-Lok. Twan dropped his head in contemplation of answering Bossy truthfully.

"Do you think that just because I ain't out here the way I used to be that I'm to be fucked with?" Bossy spoke calmly to Ant.

"Naw it ain't even like that. I just lost my mind for a minute and panicked because ain't no way for us to repay that bill, and soon our connect is gonna come looking for his paper."

Walking closer to her new enemy, Bossy bent over and looked

Ant in the eyes for what seemed like an eternity before she said a word.

"I'm going to say this one time. We are no longer affiliated with each other. I don't fuck with bitch-ass men. If you ever cross paths with me again, it will be the second-biggest mistake of your life. No one has ever fucked with me and gotten away with it, and that includes you." Bossy straightened up and turned to face Twan. "You gon' have to cut this bitch loose, or our relationship is over, too." The room was silent except for the screen door slamming as Bossy left.

Bossy knew she'd have to see—or take care of—Ant before he tried to see her. Bossy had no problem being the last one standing, and she knew just who to call to take care of this problem.

Driving toward her destination, LaJetia was determined to get to the bottom of what was going on with Twan. Her instinct told her that whatever it was had to be serious for Bossy to call their house instead of Twan's cell. Other than that ugly-ass Ant, no one ever called Twan at home. No cars were parked on the corners of Hillman Street and St. Louis Avenue, so that meant all of the employees of KAT69 had left for the day. She decided to head over to the house on Warren.

Waiting for traffic to clear and allow her to make a left-hand turn onto Hillman Street, LaJetia saw Ant's deuce-and-a-quarter speed by. LaJetia sped right past a police car parked in front of New Bethel Baptist Church. The sound of the sirens drew her out of her daydream, frightening her. *Now, what the hell do they want? Shit, I don't have time for this,* she thought. LaJetia pulled her van into Mr. Charles's Used-car Lot and waited for the officers to approach her driver's-side window. To her surprise, they rode past her and stopped Ant.

A block away, Ant made a right onto Myrtle Avenue, and two officers exited the patrol car and approached him. LaJetia parked her van and joined the small crowd watching the traffic stop.

License, registration, and proof of insurance, please," requested Officer Meeks.

"What's the problem, Officer?" replied Ant.

"The problem is we clocked you doing fifty in a thirty-five. Now, please provide your documents." Ant was actually going only five miles over the speed limit, but the crooked officers had no intention of writing him a ticket. That would only provide written proof of their confrontation with the right-hand man of the drug dealer they had been trying to get next to for months now.

"Please turn off the engine and wait here." Officer Meeks turned on his heel and headed back to his patrol car.

After Teddy Bear was killed, the officers lost a good part of their income, because Twan refused to pay them the way his mentor had. Being from New York City and growing up fast and hard, Officer Powell knew how to set a trap and lure in his prey. After months of planning, it was time to get things started.

While off duty one evening, Officer Powell spotted Twan leaving a house on the east side of town. John Powell couldn't let the grand opportunity pass him by, so he carefully followed the unsuspecting drug dealer for miles. At best, Twan would lead him to his home; at worst, he'd lead him to one of his hangouts. Either way, Powell felt he would gain some information on Twan. Twenty minutes after first seeing his prey, Powell watched Twan pull up in front of a ranch-style home in Boardman. Powell later discovered it was the home that Twan shared with his girlfriend and three children.

Officer Robert Meeks returned to the driver's side of Ant's antique car after fifteen minutes and demanded he exit the vehicle.

"I'm sure that everything is up-to-date and the insurance is active, so what's the problem, Officer?" demanded Ant.

"Please get out of the vehicle and keep your hands where I can see them."

Following departmental procedures, Officer Powell frisked his suspect down. Ant prayed that they would write him a ticket and let him go home; at that moment he needed a stiff drink.

Once they were comfortable that Ant was unarmed, they asked for permission to search the vehicle. Wanting the entire scene over with, Ant granted their request. Officer Powell carried out the search while his partner stood in front of the squad car with their nervous suspect.

"We aren't going to find any drugs or weapons inside the vehicle, are we?" questioned Meeks.

"No, I ride around with my children in that car," Ant lied. "Don't you see the car seat in the back?" The car seat was kept in the car to throw off the police.

Returning with a Ziploc bag containing a white powdery substance, Officer Powell asked Ant if he'd like to rethink his answer. Ant stood dumbfounded and nervous, wondering where the drugs could have come from. He was certain he didn't have anything on him when he left the house. The officers must have been setting him up.

Sitting in the back of the patrol car, Ant listened as the officers began to list a variety of charges he'd soon face, including possession, evading arrest, and lying to an officer. Ant shook in his skin at the thought of going to jail, especially after what had happened to him during his last stay in the county.

"Officers, I swear those drugs aren't mine. Someone must have put 'em there. I love my children too much to put them in jeopardy like that. You have to believe me," Ant pleaded.

"We believe you, but we doubt that any judge will even listen to a defense like that," mocked Officer Powell.

"Please, there has to be a way to clear all of this up without taking me to jail."

The partners looked at each other, knowing they had the young punk exactly where they wanted him. Meeks, being the senior officer and knowing how money-hungry drug dealers thought about saving themselves first, got a hard-on at the thought of getting a nice share of Ant's dirty money. The one thing in life he'd always wanted and could never seem to hold on to was money. His life and dreams revolved around it.

The youngest of eight children, he'd known poverty his entire life. His father worked hard at the steel mills to keep food on the table and a roof over his family's heads. His mother broke her back cleaning floors for both white and black families. He and his brothers and sisters would rub their mother's feet and massage her back every night for hours. He promised his parents that when he was able, he'd take care of them. Both of his parents were so proud the day their youngest boy graduated from the police academy. Robert was proud himself, and vowed to provide a better life for the two people who'd sacrificed their lives for him.

Living on a police officer's salary of $35,000 a year was pretty easy in the Youngstown area. The cost of living was low, and Powell could afford to pay his rent and that of his parents with no problem until he got married. After he married and began having children of his own, and his mother moved into a nursing home, his salary could be stretched only so far. He needed fast money. Thus began his life of hustling the hustlers.

"There is a way to get out of this situation, but I'm not sure you can handle it," said Meeks.

"Tell me what it is. I'll do anything. What is it?" Ant begged.

"We know that if the drugs aren't yours, they belong to Antwan 'Twan' Glover."

"How do you know anything about my boy?"

"We know everything about him and you. We know where you both live, what both of you drive, that Twan has three children, and that you visit your dear mother every morning."

"What are you talking about? Have you been watching us?"

"Let's just say we have our sources. We know who Bossy Tucker is, and where she lives, but what we can't figure out is how she falls into the drug ring you and your boy run." Officer Meeks turned to look at Ant and get a feel for which way to take the conversation. The officer noticed Ant had stopped shaking and seemed to be thinking about what they were saying. "We want information on Antwan Glover, Bossy Tucker, and Clifton Boyd. We want to know what their roles are, and how deep this thing goes. Don't start out by lying to us. We know Mr. Boyd is your supplier. We suggest you find a way to get us close to Antwan, Bossy, and Clifton, because if you don't, you will be doing federal time and taking the rap for everyone. That means your dear mother will have to travel a long way to see you, son," warned Meeks.

"Y'all are putting me in a tight spot," Ant whined.

"The prosecutor has enough evidence right now to arrest Antwan and send him away for at least twenty years," Meeks exaggerated. "So what's it going to be? Are we taking you downtown? Before you answer, think about what will happen to your mother if her only living child is behind bars," Officer Powell threatened.

Ant contemplated the deal the officers had placed before him. He knew that Bossy would be looking to punish him for approaching Aisha the way he did. And by the way Twan reacted when he found out what Ant had done, there was a good chance that he was about to cut him loose. That would mean his money would dry up along with his clout around the Yo'. He never thought he'd do it, but Ant reasoned it was better for him to get Twan and Bossy before they got him.

9. DID YOU THINK I WAS BULLSHITTIN'?

August had finally arrived, and the streets of the Yo' were boomin'. It was as if all of the players had added amps, speakers, and TVs to their rides. The strong sounds of bass were everywhere.

The brains behind the annual block party, Danny Levy, added something every year to keep people coming back. Even those who grew up on Kenmore and had moved away always came home for the event. Last year Danny added a car show and parade, and this year he was featuring homegrown artists like rappers No-Joke and Rufus Black and novelist Tysha. He had also booked Toledo native Lyfe Jennings.

Bossy, Aisha, and Terry were each in her own apartment preparing for the block party, all wearing T-shirts with the KAT69 insignia. Being the biggest sponsor this year gave them the perfect opportunity to get word out about the changes KAT69 was in the midst of implementing. By spring KAT69 hair and nail salon would become a full-service day spa offering child care for its clients. They had marketing items like flyers, ink pens, Frisbees, and beer mugs made up, all to be handed out free at the block party.

The women arrived on Kenmore and helped the staff of KAT69 work their table and hand out the marketing items. They held a raffle for free hair services valued at sixty dollars. There would be five lucky winners. Other participating merchants also held raffles to raise money for Danny's nonprofit organization. The money benefited residents of Kenmore Avenue who had hit hard times and the local Little League football and basketball teams, and also went to help beautify the street. The participating artists made donations, although Danny asked them to keep their profits from selling their CDs and books. He said their being there was payment enough.

When the time came for the free concert to begin, the crowd was hyped. First up, novelist Tysha read from her third book, *Young-minded Hustler*, to be released later in the fall. No-Joke went on next and blew the stage up. Rufus Black kept the crowd hyped, and Lyfe Jennings sang his soul out and laid it down.

Twan and LaJetia had brought the kids out to enjoy the clowns, petting zoo, and food vendors. Twan couldn't wait to get his hands on a homemade candy apple and get on one of the rides. Danny had thought of everything, right down to the mini-amusement park.

"I'm going to let the kids ride and have some fun," LaJetia informed Twan.

"Cool, I'm going to buy the CDs from those acts that performed. Do you want that book?" asked Twan.

"Yeah, I do, and see if she'll autograph it for me. But try not to be gone too long."

"No problem, just hold it down with the kids and I'll be right back."

Knowing Bossy was somewhere in the crowd, LaJetia watched Twan disappear into the mix. As the kids went around in circles on the train ride, LaJetia stood looking back and forth between the kids and trying to keep an eye on Twan.

After riding all of the rides, Kiara announced to her mother that she was hungry. LaJetia put Trayvon back into his stroller and led Kiara and Tyler to the line for hot dogs, fries, and drinks. She and the kids found a table to eat at, and again LaJetia eyed her man. He stood laughing and talking to her hairdresser, Sirenna, and her husband, No-Joke, and Bossy. Jealousy instantly rose in LaJetia, and it took all she had not to go the hell off.

Danny returned to the stage and asked the crowd to invite the entertainers back. As everyone made their way around the stage, Bossy kept her eyes on those standing around her. Out of the corner of her eye, she noticed Ant standing off to the side. *What the hell is he doing here?* She scanned the crowd for Aisha and Terry. By the time she looked back in Ant's direction, Bossy couldn't believe what she was seeing. Ant had his hand inside the donation tin. *This nigga must think I'm bullshittin' with him! It's time to lay him the fuck down.*

Bossy and Danny, along with the three hired off-duty police officers, cornered Ant. Powell and Meeks, who pretended to take Ant off to jail, made up two-thirds of the off-duty police security.

When Twan returned to his family two hours later, his kids were worn-out and cranky. Twan and LaJetia made their way to the van and loaded the three children inside. On their way home, Twan told LaJetia what had happened with Ant at the block party.

"That reminds me, the other day I saw the police stop Ant, search his ride, and put him in a patrol car, but he wasn't hand-cuffed. It looked like they found some drugs in his trunk, too."

"Straight up? They were probably writing out a ticket," said Twan.

"I don't think so, because he sat in the police car for at least thirty minutes before he got out empty-handed and walked back to his car."

"How you know how long he was in there?" inquired Twan.

" 'Cause a crowd stood around watching, and I saw someone I knew standing on her porch. So I parked the car at the corner and walked down the street right along with the nosy-ass neighbors," LaJetia lied.

"Do you remember the numbers that were on the squad car?" Twan prayed it wasn't the officers he was thinking of.

"No, but I recognized their faces. It was them cops that be robbin' everybody. Powell and Meeks is they names. My friend told me a couple of stories about them."

Twan remained quiet for the rest of the ride home, his mind ascertaining what Powell's and Meeks's crooked asses could possibly want with Ant. Either they were robbing Ant or they were setting him up to be a snitch, and something was telling him it was probably the latter.

Back at the block party the crowd was thinning out. Bossy grew angrier and angrier thinking about that bitch-ass Ant. She wanted to pop his ass the moment she witnessed him stealing money she knew he didn't need. She had put off making a crucial phone call long enough, but it was now time to return to her roots—some straight-up survival-of-the-fittest type shit.

10. WHERE YOU AT TWAN, WHERE YOU AT?

Bossy finally made the phone call she'd been putting off for too long. Because of Ant's immature ways of thinking, she had given

him the benefit of the doubt after he disrespected Aisha the way
he had. Even after approaching him and warning him not to fuck
with her again, he chose to ignore Bossy's warnings. Trying to steal
the money from the block party was stupid, even for Ant. He
knew who had sponsored the event this year. KAT69 put thou-
sands of dollars into backing the event, so stealing from it was the
same thing as stealing from her.

It took about an hour to drive to the Pittsburgh airport. Bossy
couldn't help but reflect on old times. The night she had taken a
life was something she didn't want to reminisce about, but it was
the one thing that kept coming to mind. After leaving baggage
claim and finding Bossy's 2006 Chrysler 300, Jalil "Big Black"
Perry got right down to business.

It had been about twelve years since they'd seen each other, but
Bossy and Big Black kept in touch with monthly phone calls.
He'd always promised to be there if she needed him and true to
his word, here he was. The only change he'd made in twelve years
was his weight. Bossy didn't think it possible, but Big Black had
actually gotten bigger. He'd always been a big man, at six feet, six
inches and two hundred seventy pounds. He had smooth skin the
color of fudge brownies, and eyelashes that most women would
kill for.

Unbeknownst to Bossy, about two months ago Big Black had
received a call from his lifelong friend C-Lok. In the years that Big
Black lived in Raleigh, North Carolina, the lines of communication had stayed open between the men. They never discussed
business over the phone, so when C-Lok brought the subject of
Bossy up and explained the problems she was having with Ant,
Big Black knew shit was serious. He knew how Bossy was getting
hers, and it sounded as if this young blood Ant was putting her
livelihood in danger.

Big Black knew that if Ant crossed the line, Bossy would need his help, but he'd come only if she reached out to him. So he packed a bag and waited for the call.

"You told me about this punk, but you never said how you, of all people, got mixed up with him."

Bossy filled Big Black in on Twan's relationship with Teddy Bear and his current status in the streets.

"How does his punk-ass boy play into this?" asked Big Black.

"They've been best friends for years, and Ant was in the game, too. So naturally Twan made Ant his right-hand man."

"Let me guess. Ant either got greedy, jealous, or both, right?"

"You know you right. They got bigheaded and started slangin' money around like they were millionaires. I couldn't believe how often Twan was bringing me kilo after kilo to store, chop, mix, and bag. At one point he even got into messing with prescription drugs and that white-boy drug, meth."

"So what changed?"

"Ah, you know me, Black. I let him know he had to slow the fuck down or I wasn't gon' fuck wit' him no more."

"I bet his boy didn't like that." Big Black laughed.

"No, he didn't, and he had the nerve to attempt to threaten Aisha. You know the project girl surfaced in her."

Big Black and Bossy laughed and joked about how Aisha could go from a prissy woman to a ghetto bitch quicker than a crackhead could make a fifty-dollar rock of cooked cocaine disappear on a hot pipe.

"Girl, you still crazy. But back to the matter at hand. I'd like to meet this Twan and get a feel for him. Tell me this—where do you think his head is at?" inquired Big Black.

"I think Twan is a good guy, but still in his twenties—he's impressionable. His loyalty to his best friend made him blind to

Ant's greed and jealousy. In everything that's gone down, Twan has never disrespected me and has never lied to me, even when the truth put him in an unfavorable light."

"We should have a meeting with him once we hit the Yo', right after I get settled in. Besides Aisha and Terry, the fewer people who know I'm in town, the better it will be for all of us. Especially if I end up doing what I think I'll have to do."

11. YOUNG-MINDED GIRL WILL FUCK SHIT UP

Twan stood in line at the liquor store when the barmaid from the Southern Tavern walked up behind him.

"Hey, Twan, I haven't seen you at the bar lately," said Brianna.

"What up wit' you, girl? I just been lying low for a minute. Spending a little time with the family."

"From what I'm told, it's not enough time."

Twan paid the store clerk for the fifth of Absolut and returned his attention to Brianna. "What is that supposed to mean?"

Brianna paid for her purchase and walked outside with Twan. "About two weeks ago I got a phone call from some chick advising me to stay away from you."

Twan wasn't surprised, because he'd heard this same thing from other female friends of his.

"Damn, Twan, I've known you forever, and never knew you could put it down like that. Got that girl acting all ghettofied to keep you?"

"Man, I'm sorry she did that shit and put you all up in my business like that."

"Don't sweat it. We been cool since we met, and you know I got much respect for you. But on the real, you need to check ya girl. She's also called a few other girls we both know, and you're now the topic of gossip because of it."

"Damn, it's like that?" Twan was getting angrier by the minute.

"Yeah, you know how small this city is. Those with nothing to do feed on shit like this. It'll die out soon, though, and another baller will take your place." Brianna tried to make the situation seem like it wasn't so bad.

Twan and Brianna made small talk for a few minutes before he left to sit in his Escalade and gathered himself before driving off. When he left the liquor store parking lot, he made a right onto Southern Boulevard, headed for the lower east side to check on his drug house. Careful to maintain the posted speed limit, Twan coasted down the hill. When he switched lanes, he noticed a familiar ride two cars behind him. Brushing it off as a coincidence, Twan shook his head and put on some classic DJ Quik. Relaxing in his leather seat, he checked the traffic surrounding him and again spotted the familiar car that appeared to be following him. *This has to be some kind of fluke*, thought Twan. He slowed down as he approached a traffic light. As the light changed from green to yellow, he sped through it in an attempt to get away from the Lexus. *If this car runs the light, it's following me.*

Glancing in his rearview mirror, he saw that the Lexus was right behind him. Twan immediately picked up his Nextel and paged LaJetia. She responded immediately.

"Hey, Twan, what's up?" LaJetia asked innocently.

"Nothing, I'm just checking on you and the kids. Where are you?" He hoped she wouldn't lie to him.

"Just chillin' in the park with the kids."

"Liar! I'm looking at you in my mirror. What the fuck you doin' following me?"

"You trippin', Twan. . . ."

"Take ya connivin' ass home and quit following me. You ain't got shit else to do but run up behind my ass?" For weeks now he had felt someone was following him, and he thought it was the police. He never considered that it might be his own woman. Twan hung up his cell, exited the highway, and made a sharp right onto Himrod Avenue while LaJetia turned left to circle back onto the highway.

Her eyes blurred with tears; LaJetia knew she'd been caught and that Twan would demand answers the second he got home. If he came home at all. She may have just lost everything she had.

Deciding to put his rounds on hold, Twan headed home to confront LaJetia. She'd crossed the line by making those junior high school type phone calls, and now she was following him. He didn't know how much more he could take. Ignoring the fact that the babysitter, Auntell, was still there, Twan let LaJetia have it before he got both feet through the doorway.

"So, what is it? Have you lost your mind or are you that damn bored?"

"Twan, calm down, please. Auntell is still here and you're embarrassing me," LaJetia responded calmly.

"I don't give a fuck if ex-President Clinton was sitting up in this bitch with you. You should have thought about that shit before you copied those numbers out of my phone. And you really should have considered the consequences of following my ass like you the fucking police or some shit."

LaJetia had no idea he knew about her making those phone calls. The only way for him to find out was for one of those bitches to run her mouth. "Please calm down; you know the kids don't like to hear us arguing." She was sure that mentioning the kids would make him at least lower his tone.

"Quit talking about every- and anything besides your fucked-up actions. Why, LaJetia? Are you that insecure that you got to put my personal business on the street like that? Do you think that if I was fuckin' one of them bitches she'd tell you the truth? You need to grow the fuck up! I ain't down for this at all."

"When a man don't come home until the wee hours of the morn—"

"How many times do I have to explain to you that the streets never close down?" Twan cut her off. "Don't answer that, because you obviously will never get it. You've fucked with me for the last time, LaJetia. I'm out of here!" Twan marched off to the bedroom to pack a few things with LaJetia on his heels.

"No, Twan, please don't leave me. I'm sorry; just tell me what I can do to make it up to you. I can make this right."

"How can you make this right when you haven't done shit right since I got with ya ass?"

Those words cut her to the bone, but LaJetia was determined not to let Twan leave her. "You can't leave us now, Twan. I'm pregnant!" LaJetia froze as Twan faced her with a look of hatred in his eyes.

"What did you say?"

"I'm pregnant, Twan. I'm going to give you another child, and then we can get married and you'll be able to adopt Kiara and Tyler, like you said. We'll be a real family. So now you know why I did what I did. When I found out I was pregnant, I had to hold on to you."

"You are stupid if you think that lying to me will hold on to me. Did you getting pregnant hold on to any of them other niggas?" Twan reached into the closet and grabbed his duffel bag to throw a couple of outfits into it.

LaJetia sat on the corner of the bed crying and trying to convince Twan of her love and that she'd never lie about being pregnant. Twan walked into the private bathroom and returned with his toothbrush and deodorant. As he walked out of the room, he turned to look at LaJetia and told her, "You should have realized a long time ago that the one and only thing you had to do to hold on to me was just trust me."

The oversize duffel bag landed in the trunk with a thud. His cell phone rang and the caller ID read, KAT69-1. It was Bossy calling.

"Hey, girl, you all right?"

"Yeah, I need for you to get over here to my apartment as soon as you can. We have some things to talk about."

"I'll be there in fifteen," replied Twan.

As he drove away from his lavish house, he wondered if he'd ever call it home again. His Escalade took him away, and he never looked back to see the three kids looking out the bay window, just as their mother had told them to do.

W ell, Bossy brought me up to speed on ya boy," Big Black said to Twan.

"I can't believe he flipped on me the way he did. Money has really changed him," said Twan.

"Correction, young blood: Money didn't change him; it just brought out who he really is."

"Twan, let me ask you a question," interjected Bossy. "Do you trust him?"

"That's an easy question—hell, no! LaJetia told me something that will never allow me to trust Ant's bitch ass ever again."

Twan went on to explain the details of the traffic stop involving Ant and the two dirty officers.

"Did you say officers Powell and Meeks?" Big Black sounded confused.

"Yeah, man, they've been robbin' hustlers all around the city for years. I can't believe they've been getting away with it for this long," complained Twan.

"Neither can I, but the fact that Ant might be fuckin' with dem two bitches makes me worry even more about my girls," Big Black said between gulps of his third forty-ounce. Big Black's physique was intimidating, but his heart was filled with love for Bossy, Aisha, and Terry.

"I wouldn't put it past him to flip on me. He knows my operation from top to bottom." Twan picked up his watered-down Belvedere and orange juice.

"Haven't I always told you there ain't no friends in this business? Seriously, you know I got love for you like a little brother, but you don't know my shit all like that. My girls don't even know everything there is to know, and that's for both their protection and mine," preached Bossy.

"I've heard enough. This fool done stepped to Aisha, stole money, and is layin' down with five-O. That's three strikes, and that lets me know it's time to send Ant on a permanent vacation." Big Black ended the topic of conversation.

Twan rose to leave, but Bossy had one more question for him. If he answered it honestly, she knew she would be able to trust him.

"Twan, before you leave I want to ask you something."

"Come with it."

"Who's your new contact?"

"Clifton 'C-Lok' Boyd," answered Twan.

He'd passed the test.

12. WHAT'S DONE IN THE DARK WILL COME TO LIGHT

With Ant loose on the streets acting like a bitch in heat, lives were in danger, including Bossy's. She knew that with Big Black now involved, once the shit hit the fan, nothing would ever be the same again. Bossy just prayed that the right people were left standing.

She drove more than forty-five minutes to her destination. She hadn't been out this way in years and took a couple wrong turns, making the trip longer than it should have been.

Bossy slowed her car down as she searched for the house number that read 6789. She exited her car as fast as possible so the three young men manning the corner wouldn't mistake her for a customer.

The guarded front door opened wide as Bossy climbed the stairs. C-Lok's frame blocked Kayla from entering his house without first greeting him with a hug.

"Girl, you look good. It's been a long time," said C-Lok.

"I have missed you, too," replied Bossy.

They walked into C-Lok's office, where a couple of his runners waited. There was no need to introduce Bossy, because they had known about her for years. Bossy never knew that C-Lok looked out for her almost as much as Teddy Bear had. The two runners greeted her and exited the room.

"Tell me what brings you this far away from your comfort zone." C-Lok stared into Bossy's eyes.

"I need to talk with you about Ant and Twan," responded Bossy.

"I heard about the rift between those two," C-Lok shared.

"Some things never change. It's never a good idea to mix business and personal. Twan did, and shit has gotten hot."

"That's what I hear. But I take it you think I should know about something more."

"Yeah, I believe ya boy Ant is in bed with dem two bitch-ass po-po, Meeks and Powell. Watch ya back closely, and keep Ant closer." Bossy went on to explain about Ant fucking up three times, and the info about him chillin' with the cops.

C-Lok listened intently to Bossy.

"Good lookin' on comin' to me like this."

"You know what's up," stated Bossy. She had never stopped loving C-Lok, but had long ago accepted that they were not to be.

"How is Devin? That nigga keepin' his head up behind those concrete walls?"

"You know he's straight. If he can keep his nose clean, he can possibly see daylight the next time he comes up for parole. Lord knows between the two of us, we've paid that damn prosecutor enough. By the way, thanks again for helping me."

C-Lok had promised Bossy to take care of her brother, Devin, the day he went up on burglary and murder charges, and had kept his promise. Right before C-Lok moved out of the projects, Devin and Bossy's mother, Linda Tucker, overdosed on a mixture of crack and heroin, leaving Bossy with no family. It was C-Lok who made certain she had a roof over her head that would forever be hers if she wanted it. He'd paid for the apartment building by giving the money to Teddy Bear, and requested that his friend never let Bossy know of his gift to her. He feared she'd feel obligated to work for him. C-Lok and Teddy Bear decided that was not an option.

C-Lok and Bossy visited for another hour, and then Bossy headed back to the Yo'. Big Black was waiting for Bossy in her apartment when she walked in.

"What took you so long? I know C-Lok's ass ain't trip on you."

"Naw, it wasn't nothing like that. He was straight. We got

caught up on a few things. I was telling him about me wanting out." Bossy hadn't told Big Black of her plan to go legit, and waited anxiously for his response.

"It's about time, girl. You just made my fuckin' day. Do you know how much sleep I've lost over the years worried about you? Since that night we lost our boy Poppy, I've wanted you out the game. You just ain't the type of woman to take to somebody telling her what to do," confessed Big Black.

"Well, the time has come, and after this shit is finished, I'm out before some of the things I've done in the dark come to light." Bossy released a sigh of relief.

13. LOVE DON'T LIVE HERE ANYMORE

"Good morning, Ma. You need anything done besides the grass cut?"

"No, son, I'm fine. What I don't have the good Lord will provide," Olivia Quarles solemnly answered her son, Ant.

"Aren't you feeling well today, Ma?"

"Mama hasn't been sleeping too well these last few days. I've been having an unsettling dream that something bad is going to happen to you."

"Ma, ain't nothin' gon' happen to me. You just worry too much."

"I had the same dream right before we lost ya brother. Baby, the Lord speaks to me in my dreams. He's never steered me wrong, and you need to promise me you'll be careful out there."

"I have something in the works, and if everything goes as planned, I'll be able to take care of you the way I want to."

"Anthonie Quarles, you know I'm a simple woman with common sense. I know how you make your money. It's the devil's dirty money, and I'll have no part of it."

Ant wondered how he could have been so dumb as to think his mother didn't know how he made his living.

"It's just temporary, until I save enough to do what I need to do, and I'm almost there."

"I raised you and your brother to know right from wrong, to understand what hard work is all about. I've lost one child, and Lord knows I can't live through the pain of losing another. But you're a grown man and you decide which route you take in life. All I can do is pray for you, son, just pray."

Ant left his mother's house feeling lower than a snake's belly, but he had to do what he had to do. He'd chosen to jump into bed with Meeks and Powell, and he was in too deep to turn back now.

The meeting was set for three in the morning at Volney Rogers Park. It was a dark area that no one frequented after the sun went down. Ant arrived ten minutes early, giving him too much time to wrestle with himself about stabbing his only friend in the back. *Twan was gonna keep me in his shadow, picking up his crumbs. I'm bigger than that. Teddy Bear slept on me, and so did Twan, thanks to Bossy.*

Thinking of Bossy made Ant refocus on his plan. *Getting Bossy out the way will leave Aisha and Terry to fend for themselves. Aisha won't be a Billy Badass no more. I'll show that bitch to pull a gun on me and not use it. Bossy won't be in Twan's ear from behind bars, and then he'll go back to being himself.*

A car turned into the parking lot, making Ant nervous. He wasn't sure he could trust Meeks and Powell. This could be a setup, for all he knew. Ant doubted the two crooked cops even trusted each other.

"I hope you have something for us. You've had plenty of time to get it," Meeks said sternly.

"Slow down, man. Twan's due to make a run to his connection in Florida early next week. You can catch him with a few keys of cocaine on him."

"Prices must be pretty good to travel that far." Hearing about a connection in Florida gave Powell ideas of making trips to the state himself.

"Yeah, they are, and Twan makes the runs like clockwork," explained Ant.

"That'll give us Twan; now what about Bossy and C-Lok?" questioned Meeks.

"Twan takes his stuff to Bossy for packaging and warehousing the same day he gets back in town. We still owe C-Lok money, so Twan is gonna have to see him to give him something to hold on to before C-Lok comes to see us." Ant went on to explain Twan's routine and the complexity of gaining entrance into Bossy's apartment building. Powell and Meeks were already familiar with the difficulty in obtaining access into Bossy's home. But they had a plan to get past the two alarmed steel doors.

"If y'all time things right, Bossy and Twan will have several kilos with them. The rest is up to y'all." Ant allowed himself to believe his assignment was complete.

"Look, Ant, we're going to go with the information you've supplied, but we want you to keep one thing in mind," said Officer Meeks.

"What's that? I've given y'all what you asked for," Ant nervously responded.

"Not quite yet. You've given us a means to get what we want, but if this doesn't pan out the way you said it will, let's just say there will be a price to pay. And you'll be the one doing the paying," warned Meeks.

————

Big Black had just walked upstairs to visit with Aisha and Terry when Bossy's doorbell rang. Bossy pressed the intercom button.

"Who is it?"

"The police. We have a warrant to search the premises."

She buzzed them through the main door and opened her apartment door for Powell and Meeks to walk through. Bossy greeted them with the warmest welcome she could muster.

"Come in, gentlemen. I've been expecting you for some time now."

14. THE BIG PAYBACK

Figuring that his plan to bring down Bossy had worked out, Ant needed to relax. For the first couple of days after meeting with Powell and Meeks, he had been a nervous wreck. He'd only guessed about the information he gave them, and wasn't sure if Twan was even making the runs to Florida anymore.

The longer Ant mulled over the situation he'd put himself in, his mother's dream, and the money he still owed C-Lok, the more stressed he got. Hiding out at his mom's house for two days enabled him to do some chores for her. Ant even painted his mother's bedroom and living room. He hung wallpaper in the kitchen and rearranged furniture in every room of the three-bedroom house. He couldn't remember ever working so hard, and knew he never wanted to work that hard again.

Atlantic City was Ant's next hideout. For three days he gambled, ate, drank, and slept. Ant had ten thousand with him when he left for Atlantic City, and returned to the Yo' with thirty thousand more, thanks to the blackjack tables. To help him relax, Ant didn't carry his cell phone with him. By the time he checked his messages the mailbox was full. He knew instantly that the majority of the messages were from Shadaisy. He dialed her number first.

Shadaisy answered on the first ring. "Yeah."

"What up, girl? How you holdin' it down over there?" Ant had let the drug house on Warren Avenue slip his mind.

"I'm doin' what I do. Where you been that you can't call a bitch back?"

"Just takin' care of some shit. Anybody been lookin' for me?" Ant wanted to be sure that Powell, Meeks, and C-Lok hadn't been tracking him down.

"Naw, ain't nobody come by here lookin' for you. I'm the only person tryin' to get with you, as far as I know. Supplies are low; we gon' have to do something soon."

"I'll be there in a few. You be ready for me; I'm overdue." A huge smile covered Ant's face when he ended the call. He was anticipating seeing Shadaisy laid out on the couch, half-naked, ready to do whatever she had to do to please him.

When Shadaisy hung up from their conversation, she wanted to throw up. She couldn't stand for Ant to touch her, kiss her, or be inside of her. Shadaisy was simply doing what she had to do in order to keep a roof over her head and live rent- and utility-free. To her, she was getting over, and all she had to do was give up some ass and give some head every few months. Even pimps had to ho sometimes, right?

Since seeing for herself how Twan took care of his girl, Shadaisy knew it was time for her to find a baller higher up on the food chain. Ant was in no position to buy her a hooptie, let alone a 2006 Lexus. The house Ant had her living in actually belonged to Twan.

She heard on the street that Ant and Twan had had a rift in their friendship. Shadaisy couldn't have been paid to take from them, but now that Twan had severed ties with Ant's ugly ass, she was going for hers. She had skimmed off some of the drugs and money for herself. To her, life had been hard, cruel, and cold, but the free money and drugs were going to change things, and fast.

After showering and preparing for Ant, it was time to roll a blunt and make a stiff drink. The only way she could stand being intimate with Ant was to be as high as possible. Shadaisy decided to roll a primo for Ant. She also poured him a glass of whiskey laced with crushed Percocets. She was determined to get this date over with as soon as possible, maybe even stop it before it began. Shadaisy decided that tonight would be her last encounter with Ant. After he passed out, she would rob him for whatever he had on him and begin her search for a real hustler.

Ant parked his car behind the house and walked in the back door. As expected, Shadaisy lay on the couch in a matching bra and panty set, two drinks on the table and two blunts in the ashtray.

"You ready to get with this, girl?" Ant sat next to Shadaisy and began running his ashy hand down her leg.

"Of course, but let's enjoy our drinks and smoke a little before we get started," Shadaisy stalled. "You know, to help relax you. It sounds like you've had a stressful week."

"Good idea, let's start this party."

Ant took a toke on the blunt and gulped down the laced drink Shadaisy had prepared for him. As the blunt and drink began to take effect, Ant's body relaxed, and he fought the urge to lie back on the couch and drift off to sleep.

Shadaisy sat watching Ant before slipping out of the room to put on a pair of jeans and a shirt. She walked back into the room and found that Ant was no longer alone.

"What's going on in here? Looks like I'm interrupting a little party." Ant opened his eyes to find Twan standing before him. They hadn't spoken since the block party, and Ant figured he had come by to collect his half of the money they owed C-Lok. Ant attempted to acknowledge Twan but found himself unable to speak.

"What's wrong with you? You send the police after me and you can't even open up ya mouth to speak to me? Ain't that some shit," Twan baited Ant.

"Don't pay him no mind, Twan; he's high as hell and probably don't even know where he is," explained Shadaisy, before asking, "What you mean, Ant sent the police after you? I know damn well he ain't do no foul shit like that."

"Ant ain't tell you that he made a deal with the devil? He sent Powell and Meeks to Bossy's looking for my shit."

"Naw, Ant is capable of a lot of shit, but not that," Shadaisy said.

"He was pulled over on a traffic stop by Powell and Meeks and let go. He was caught trying to rip off the money from the block party, and again Powell and Meeks let his punk ass go. After spending half of her life in the game, Bossy's house is searched out of the blue? It don't take a scientist to figure that shit out. They just happened to show up at her door the same time I would've been droppin' a shipment off from Florida? Something told me to rearrange my schedule until I found out who my enemies were. Ant's a straight-up bitch," fumed Twan.

Shadaisy was shocked at what she was hearing, but it all made sense. "That's why he was missing the last two weeks. He was hiding out." She immediately turned on her heel and began gathering up her shit. Getting out of the house was in her best interest. If what Twan said was true, Powell and Meeks would be looking for Ant, because they had come up empty in their search. Since Twan arrived, Shadaisy had decided to abandon her plan to grab the money and drugs left in the house. She knew that it would be like stealing from Twan. Shadaisy made a beeline for the door, leaving Twan to watch her smoke.

Officers Powell and Meeks were responding to a call of reported gunshots when they discovered the gruesome scene. Minutes later the crime scene unit was lifting prints, taking pictures, and bagging items for evidence.

"Whoever did this guy either hated him, was out for revenge, or was sending a message," said the newest member of the Crime Scene Unit team.

Officer Powell stood in the corner of the room with a full view of the victim. His sergeant walked up beside him.

"What do you think, Powell?"

"Someone was determined to send a message here, sir."

"Do you think this was a professional hit?" inquired Sergeant Collins.

"With him being stripped naked, it does resemble a professional killing. But the single gunshot to each knee isn't the mark of a hired hit. With his tongue being cut out and his testicles placed in his hand, I'd say this was personal, very personal."

"Have we identified him yet?"

"Yes, he's well known by the narcotics division. They have been trying to get him for months now. His name is Anthonie 'Ant' Quarles."

Bossy had already received word of the murder before it ran on the evening news. Things like that flowed through Youngstown like a cascading waterfall. Bossy tried to understand why she had no feelings one way or another about her hand in Ant's death. Years ago, she'd vowed never to be responsible for the death of another human being. As she thought about everything that had taken place, she reasoned that Ant had left her no other choice.

Bossy hadn't heard from Big Black since he left late last night. He said he was headed for the club, but he should have come back by now. *With Ant dead, I can breathe again. When Big Black comes home I'll take a deep breath.*

15. AND FOR MY FINAL ACT: LIFE, DEATH, AND SURVIVAL IN THE YO'

On the backcountry roads from Youngstown to Sharon, Pennsylvania, was a twenty-five-minute ride. Traffic in the small city was always light. Mercer Street was usually booming with activity, but at four in the morning, even the drug dealers were asleep.

C-Lok opened the door and welcomed his visitors.

"Have a seat, gentlemen; you're right on time. Let's get right down to business," directed C-Lok.

"Before we do, don't you want to introduce your friend?" asked Meeks.

"This is my good friend Big Black," said C-Lok. "Big Black, meet two of Youngstown's finest, officers Powell and Meeks. Can you believe they sought me out after Teddy Bear died?" C-Lok and Big Black laughed in unison.

"What they want from you? Protection?" joked Big Black, as if the two cops weren't sitting next to him. The two laughed again before C-Lok replied, "Naw, they wanted me to pay them for protection. Ain't that a bitch?"

Big Black and C-Lok stared blankly at Powell and Meeks, sig-
naling that playtime was over.

"He cool?" Powell wanted to know.

"This is the only person on earth that I trust with my life.
Now, word has gotten back that the job was taken care of. It even
made the news."

"It went very well. When we found Ant he was high as the sky,
but came down fast at the sight of a weapon in his face. He
begged, pleaded, and cried like a bitch in labor before he took his
last breath." Meeks bragged a little too much for Big Black's taste.

"Another job well done. I trust the weapon has been disposed
of properly," C-Lok said.

"Absolutely. This will go unsolved, as usual," Powell guaranteed.

"Here's your fee of a hundred thousand dollars each, plus another fifty grand bonus to split between you. I'll be in touch if
your services are required in the future." Normally, C-Lok would
see his hired hands to the door, but he had other plans for Powell
and Meeks today.

C-Lok had heard from Twan about the problems Bossy was
having with Ant. After Ant disrespected Bossy the second time,
C-Lok's plan to punish him was under way. Ant's jealousy of
Twan made him an easy mark. C-Lok knew it wouldn't take much
on Powell and Meeks's part to persuade Ant to work with them.
The only problem was when Bossy contacted Big Black. C-Lok
knew that he would have to bring his longtime friend in on the
plan he already had in the works. If they ended up stepping on
each other's toes, everything would fall apart.

The day Bossy went to C-Lok about Ant and the police, Big
Black knew that C-Lok would watch his back by not telling Bossy
of their partnership.

Now the two old friends sat together as partners for the first time in almost twelve years. The only difference was the company they were in. C-Lok and Big Black both knew that, given the chance, the two crooked officers would take them out. Shit wasn't going down like that.

When Officer Powell approached C-Lok about providing protection for him, C-Lok had turned him down flat.

"Naw, I'm straight on that, but we may be able to work together," said C-Lok.

Officer Powell was instantly intrigued, and sat down to discuss business with the powerful gangsta.

"Your first assignment is to get this bitch-ass nigga Ant under ya spell. Back him as far into a corner as his dumb ass can fit. Next, get my product back from his ass."

Officer Powell knew better than to ask any questions. Plus, the amount of money C-Lok was offering was far too much to pass up. The deal was made, but officers Powell and Meeks had tried to backstab C-Lok by serving that fake warrant on Bossy.

There was a light tap at C-Lok's office door and the room turned quiet.

"Who else are you expecting?" Officer Powell had started feeling uneasy.

"Chill, nigga," replied Big Black. "We got this."

The door opened to reveal Bossy and Twan standing outside the door. C-Lok had summoned them both to join the meeting. It was time to put the entire episode to an end.

"What's going on here? What are they doing here?" Meeks stammered.

"Just like you, they are here by my invitation."

Bossy and Twan walked in the room and ignored the two officers. Big Black rose from his seat, allowing Bossy to take his place, while Twan stood to the left of C-Lok.

"This room is a bit small for a group of this size. Why don't we go into what I like to call 'the men's room'?"

Powell and Meeks looked at one another, each expecting the other to get them out of the invitation. Finally Powell found his voice.

"No, thanks, man. We have to get back to the station."

C-Lok stepped around his desk, stood over the crooked officers, and replied, "It wasn't a suggestion; it is what we are *all* going to do."

Bossy followed behind C-Lok with that sway in her hips that drove men crazy. With Twan right behind her and Big Black bringing up the rear behind Powell and Meeks, Bossy knew she was safe.

In the soundproof basement, four large-framed employees of C-Lok's waited in the shadows. Hiring the officers was a means to an end for C-Lok and Big Black, but they never figured that the men would double-cross two of the most infamous gangstas in Youngstown's history. Trying to strong-arm Bossy was not part of the plan, and officers Powell and Meeks had finally fucked over the wrong person.

"Bossy, come over here so Big Black and me can clear a few things up with you," requested C-Lok.

Bossy asked no questions and did as she was told. She had no idea what C-Lok had summoned her and Twan for, but upon seeing Powell and Meeks, she pretty much knew the day she was dreading was finally here. She believed it was time to tell C-Lok she was behind Big Black killing Ant.

"Baby, we have something to tell you, and I want you to hear us both out before you say anything," instructed C-Lok.

Bossy remained quiet and nodded her head in agreement.

Big Black went first. "Bossy, back when our boy Poppy was

killed, the retaliation that happened as a result is what brings us here today." Bossy didn't understand where this was going, but she continued to listen. "Me and C-Lok were in charge of taking care of you at the time, and allowing you to pull that trigger meant that we failed. At least, in Devin's eyes we did." Big Black took a deep breath before continuing on. "See, the two of us didn't know what to do in order to protect you, so we paid your brother a visit in prison, and to say he was pissed would be an understatement. Devin wanted to kill us both for allowing you to roll the way we did back then."

"He's right. Devin was pissed, and if he hadn't already been behind bars, he would be now for our murders," explained C-Lok. "When we left the prison that day, Devin demanded that we find a way to protect you. So we did."

"Bossy, twelve years ago when I left here, it wasn't to relocate down South. At least, not the way you think. Based on our plan, I was shipped off to a federal prison to do a ten-year bid for the killings in the park that night."

Bossy couldn't believe what she was hearing. There was no way Big Black had served a dime without her knowing. She'd sent him cards, money, and packages over the years. They had talked on the phone once a month, and his calls never originated from any prison. Bossy stood, bewildered.

"Don't get me wrong. I did do a dime, but it wasn't hard time. With Teddy Bear's help, and a federal prosecutor and a judge willing to receive monthly payments for their services, my time was served in a minimum-security prison. I was allowed to work an outside job as long as I kept my nose clean. That's what I did."

"But how? Why would you do that?" questioned Bossy.

"Baby, I asked you to hear us out," C-Lok reminded Bossy. "Now it's my turn to confess. After we broke up and you refused to accept any help from me, I had to find a way to keep you safe and taken care of. It wasn't Teddy Bear who bought your apartment building and the shop. I gave him the money and had him make the business transaction. It was the only way I could think of that you would accept what was being done for you. I knew that you would feel obligated to me back then if you knew the truth."

"Why are y'all confessing all of this now? I mean, I'm grateful to you both for the sacrifices y'all made for me, but after all this time, why tell me this now?"

Twan took a step forward and knew that was his cue to come clean about his part in what was going down.

"Bossy, when I found out what Ant had done to Aisha, and about him getting in bed with them two bitch-made niggas over in the corner"—Twan pointed at Powell and Meeks—"I felt guilty for introducing Ant into your life. We had just copped a huge shipment from C-Lok, and the only way I could see putting a stop to Ant's stupidity was to come out here and have a sit-down with him. That's when I found out about Big Black and C-Lok's plan to protect you at any cost."

"Yeah, Twan got heart, Bossy. He's a gangsta from the womb," said Big Black.

"So, Big Black, it wasn't you that took care of Ant?" questioned Bossy.

"It's not important who did it. All that matters is that it was handled," barked C-Lok.

"But what about them two over there?" Bossy wanted to put all of the puzzle pieces together.

"Originally they were part of the plan to take care of Ant, but then they made the fatal mistake of coming to your doorstep. For that, they will pay dearly," explained C-Lok.

The bodyguards had since bound and hogtied Powell and Meeks. All that was left to do was put the two men out of their misery. The only dilemma was which one of the three men who'd already sacrificed so much for Bossy would end the life of two police officers.

Bossy looked C-Lok in his eyes and could still see how much he was in love with her. Big Black had always been her protector, but Bossy had had no idea to what extent he had gone to protect her. Bossy was proud of Twan because he had been listening to her teachings. Her day had come, and Bossy felt it deep inside. It was time for her to thank those who'd always protected and loved her.

Reaching behind her back, Bossy gripped her pearl-handled gun and announced, "I got this." As she walked toward the dark corner where her potential victims lay in wait, Bossy felt a strong hand on her right shoulder, stopping her in her tracks.

"No, you don't got this. I'll take care of it. Bossy, you go home," ordered C-Lok.

Bossy put her gun back in place and turned to do as she was told. She knew better than to argue or disagree with the man. Slowly Bossy climbed the stairs and closed the thick door behind her, knowing that no matter what, she would always be protected.

If only Bossy knew how much more lookin' out for her you've done over the years, she would consider being ya wifey," Big Black said about an hour later as he flashed a smile.

"She would never have it. Bossy was reluctant to get off these streets and learn a different way to hustle. She has to be independent, and I need to be a provider. We just aren't meant to be.

"When we left the prison that day, I didn't know what we were going to do." C-Lok turned to look out his bay window and light a stogie to gather his thoughts. "When the apartment came up for sale it was a lifesaver. Bossy and her girls would always have a roof over their heads, and Devin's wishes came true. We protected his sister."

"We can never let it get out that Teddy Bear paid me one million a year for taking that bid for Bossy," confessed Big Black.

"How can one woman have so many men putting their lives down like this? You did a bid for Bossy. Teddy Bear molded his game and lived his life for Bossy. And I . . . well . . ."

"And you love from a distance. What a man won't do for love," stated Big Black.

"Correction," C-Lok said. "What a man won't do for Bossy."

NEXT ON DECK . . .

MEISHA C. HOLMES

GAME FACE

Definition of a broad with a game face: A woman who, like a trained actor, knows how to quickly jump into character and play up to life's camera lens in order to get whatever her heart desires.

1

"What do you mean you can't get me any more credits?" Bobby yelled into the phone.

"Bobby, I got you twenty Gs worth of Gucci credits last week," his boy yelled back into the phone. "That's worth at least eight Gs in the street. I'm hot right now."

"I'm sayin', fly some of your boostin' bitches out to Vegas or L.A. and let them tear up the malls down there! Every fuckin' penny counts, and you owe me, nigga. I need a hundred and fifty thou in less than two weeks, or Oh So Brooklyn Records is going to fold."

"You're broke like that, son? I don't know how you be runnin' through so much paper. Why don't you call Grape and ask that dude for a loan? That nigga is getting mad paper out here on these streets."

"I just finished paying him the hundred grand I borrowed to keep Teesa's ass alive."

"You must really love Teesa, Bobby."

"I must." Bobby sighed.

"Where are you now?"

"Standing outside of the Gucci store on Fifth Avenue waiting on one of my new artists, and the bitch is hot. Her wood game is wack, but her pussy is tight as hell, and she is gorgeous."

"You a muthafucka, boy. You better hope Teesa don't find out. How are you gonna complain about needing money and you out there spending the credits I got you on some trick?"

"How do you think I keep my artists from complaining about pushin' their album releases back? And you know Teesa know the deal." Bobby lowered his voice as he walked into the store and up to a young lady who was trying on a pair of shoes. "I gotta go. Get me some Neiman Marcus credits. We'll talk soon. Bye."

Teesa looked into the mirror and smiled. She scooped up some clear gel, wet her hands, and raked them through her hair, which was tapered closely on the sides and spiked up over the rest of her head. Her dark tan face was smooth, with the exception of the permanent smile lines around her mouth. She painted pale orange lip gloss on her lips and stroked some liquid eyeliner across her eyelids. She was a tarnished dime that had been around the block a couple of times over. Good thing for her northern New Jersey was just as big as the city of New York, because she'd gone through every person she could who had money during her thirty-plus years in the Big Apple.

She threw on a pair of tight-fitting jeans and a cropped stretch white tee that revealed her D-size cleavage, and squeezed into a cropped jean jacket. She slipped into her white Uptowns and placed a huge tube sock over one of them. She grabbed a pair of high-heeled mules, walked out the door, looked at her petite diamond-encrusted Rolex, and sucked her teeth.

"Damn! This nigga hates when I am late. I better hurry my ass up."

She climbed onto her fuchsia-and-purple motorcycle, the crack of her pantiless ass peeking out as she leaned over. With three turns of the throttle she sped off into the hot and humid day. She reached Edge Water, New Jersey, in fifteen minutes flat. She parked her bike in a long, winding paved driveway. Before she could slip into her second shoe, the door swung open and a huge dark-skinned man stood in the doorway wearing long baggy denim shorts, a huge white tee, and slippers. As she adjusted her shoe, she smiled and stared. His teeth were straight and white, his hair was cut close, and waves circled his small head. His skin was dark and shiny, and his arms were almost as big as her thighs. His eyes were deep, dark, and narrow. He stood there, all six feet, three inches and 338 pounds of him. He smirked and waved.

"Damn, Teesa, why you always gotta come up here late?" he asked, breathing heavily and speaking as if he had a mouth filled with marbles. "You know I be wantin' you to rub my ass down right after practice. Come here, mama."

"Hey, baby," Teesa said as she walked up to Trey Wilkinson, the star linebacker for the New York Jets, and gave him a big hug and a steamy kiss. Trey wedged his fat hands down the back of her tight jeans and grabbed a handful of her ass.

"I love when you come here with no drawers on."

He continued to kiss her as he backed into his huge five-bedroom house. Although Teesa frequented his home anywhere from three to four times a week, when she entered his home she never grew tired of staring at the beautiful white columns that stretched all the way up to his superhigh ceilings, or the marble fountain. She slipped off her mules, and the cool feel of the marble floor sent chills throughout her body.

Trey led her to the couch, threw her down, and began to unbuckle his pants as he stared into her eyes. *Damn, she looks good,* he thought. *Teesa is about to get it. I am horny as hell.*

His chef walked into the living room right as Trey began to pull his pants off.

"I'm so sorry for the intrusion, Trey, but your meals for this week are prepared and I am leaving. I will see you next week," the chef said. He looked down to the floor. "Hi, Teesa, how are you?" His face was flushed from embarrassment.

"Fine, thank you." Teesa blushed.

"Your check is on the kitchen counter. Grab that and go out the back door," Trey said.

He barely waited for the chef to exit the room before he pulled his shorts and boxers down and began fondling his dick. Teesa stood up and began taking her shirt off. Trey watched her as she turned her back to him, and rolled her eyes as she unhooked her bra. She inhaled deeply and turned back around. With her prize-winning smile of seduction and her game face tight, she dropped to her knees and began sucking his dick. He palmed the back of her stiff hair and pushed her head down each time it came up. His heavy breathing began to turn her off, but she kept thinking of the big black reward that she held hostage in her mouth.

This fat muthafucka's fuck game is sick, and his dick weighs like his pockets, she thought as she tuned out his heavy breathing and released more saliva on his dick so its massiveness could slide in and out of her mouth with ease. As she came up for air, she stood up and wiggled out of her pants.

"You got condoms, Trey?" she asked.

"Come on, Teesa," Trey said, sucking his teeth. "It's not like you never let me hit it raw before. Just one more time."

He pushed her down, face-first, toward the couch and slid into her wet vagina from behind. She wanted to stop him, but she couldn't. It just felt so good. Once she was fully penetrated he lifted his stomach up and put it on her back as he pumped in and out of her. With each stroke he let out a yell like he was lifting up a heavy weight, and thick beads of sweat dropped off his body onto Teesa's back.

"Trey," she managed to pant out. "Sit down on the couch. You know I can't cum this way," she continued, out of breath.

He turned them both around without missing a stroke and fell back as Teesa stayed seated on his dick. She screamed out in pain as they plopped onto the couch. Once she gained her leverage she rode Trey like he was her motorcycle. Her size-six body looked like a ventriloquist's dummy on his lap in comparison to his huge frame. He cupped her breasts tightly as he pumped into her. On top she was in control. She turned around, faced him, and looked into his eyes.

"Do you love me, Trey?" she whined.

"Yes. You know I do," he moaned.

"How much?"

"Fuck, girl. Let me get my nut off, baby. We can talk that love shit later," he spit out.

She whispered in his ear as she began to twist and grind him harder. "I want to feel this fat dick inside of me every single night. It feels so good inside of me. Damn, you got a big black penis."

She whispered herself into a hard climax. He came seconds after her.

After a game of nude Ping-Pong in his game room followed by

a shower, they retired to his bedroom, where she gave him a massage.

"Baby, can you give me some money? I am short on my bills this month," Teesa said as she rubbed his huge back down with scented oils.

"How much do you need this time?" he said, as if he knew her statement was coming before it even fell off her tongue.

"About five thousand," Teesa answered as her cell phone went off.

"No problem, Teesa. Take what you need," Trey replied, turning over. "Take it out of the stash."

She wiped her hands on his sheets and picked up her cell phone off of the end table.

"Hello?" she answered her phone.

"Hey, Teesa, how are you today?" the caller asked.

"What's up, Delilah? I'm cool. What's going on with you?" Teesa said to her longtime homegirl.

"I'm going to the mall. Can you come with me? I need to pick up some things for my trip next week."

"You didn't tell me you were going away. Where are you off to this time?"

"Guy's boy from Atlanta is having a fifth-anniversary party in Jamaica."

"I'll meet you at the mall in front of the Chanel store in an hour."

"Okay. I'll be there at three o'clock on the nose. See you in a few," Teesa said as she ended the call.

"My girl Delilah and her *husband* are going to Jamaica next week."

"That's the real pretty girl with the long hair, right?" Trey said.

Teesa nodded her head. "Yeah, that's her," she said flatly. She paused for a moment and then asked, "Do you think she looks better than me?"

"Hell, no," Trey lied quickly. "We can take a trip to the Caribbean during my off-season." He sat up in the bed and hugged her lightly. "If I get traded to the Patriots, are you going to come down there with me?"

"If you put a ring on my finger," Tessa said, rolling her eyes. "I ain't going to move out there to be your house whore. We've been seeing each other for two years now, and I ain't gettin' no younger. I want to have kid—"

"Teesa, don't start that shit again," Trey said, cutting her off. "I love you and I'm in this for the long one, mama. I put a fuckin' ring on your finger that you never wear."

Shit, I forgot to put my ring back on after I left Bobby last night, she thought, looking down at her bare finger.

"Trey, you know I don't like wearing it when I'm riding around on my bike. Someone might rob me. Besides, I ain't talking about no friendship ring. I'm talking about an engagement ring and a marriage date."

"Whatever, Teesa. I'm going to sleep. You gonna stay here with me or are you going to go racing out of here like you always do?"

"I'm going to the mall. I'll be back later," she said as she got up out of the bed to get dressed.

"Okay, mama," he said, pulling the sheet over him. "I love you."

"I love you back."

Teesa got dressed, then went into the bottom drawer of Trey's dresser, counted out seventy-five hundred-dollar bills, and shoved them into her inside jean jacket pocket. She kissed him on the cheek, left the house, hopped on her bike, and turned the throttle quickly three times.

Trey rolled over and laughed once he heard her pulling off on her bike. *I think I'm going to ask her to ride across country with me*

next week and marry her. I do want to have some kids. He then
turned back over and fell fast asleep.

2

Teesa watched from inside the Chanel store as Delilah walked to
the storefront and checked her watch. A group of guys walked by
and stared at Delilah.

She is not that cute, Teesa thought. *Why do guys always be trippin' over her? She's fat and has no style and shit. If it wasn't for her
husband, she would be a hot mess.*

Teesa continued to survey Delilah as her friend patiently
waited outside of the store for her. She observed her in her size-
ten pants and shook her head as she silently confessed, *She is thick
in the right places, but she's still fat.*

Delilah was five feet, five inches tall and had bright brown
eyes. Her hair was her most stunning feature. It was long and
healthy to the ends. It was naturally light brown, extremely thick
like a good wig, and cut evenly down her back. Delilah smiled and
spoke very few words to the guys as they walked by. Her smile revealed chiseled cheekbones and a deep cleft in her chin. She swung
her long hair around to the side as she looked for Teesa.

Teesa finally peeked her head out of the store and said, "Hey,
Delilah. I'm inside. I didn't even realize you were standing out
there." Teesa lifted her hand to display the helmet she had hanging off of her wrist by the strap as she spoke. "I drove my bike, so
I got here a little faster than I expected. Tell me what you think
about this bag I'm getting ready to buy," Teesa said, holding up
the purse she had in her other hand.

"Hey, Teesa!" Delilah said in an excited tone. Delilah looked her over as she joined her inside the store. "I love your denim suit. Who is that by? Citizen jeans?"

Teesa nodded.

"That bag is hot to death. Guy came home with the bigger version of that messenger bag about a month ago. But where am I going? I don't have anywhere to wear it. Let me show you the watch and wristband he got me to go with the bag," she said as she pulled her over to a display case.

Why this bitch always got to be showing off? Teesa thought. *Every time that nigga comes back from out of town he always has to bring something for her, something she can't wait to brag about.*

"Teesa," Delilah whispered, "you don't have to buy that bag. You know you can borrow mine whenever you want."

"You know Guy ain't going for that. Besides, Trey just hit me off with some cash, so I'm good," Teesa said as she walked away from Delilah and went to pay for the bag. She dropped her helmet inside the shopping bag that contained her new purse, and the pair walked out of the store and into the mall.

"Teesa, I need your advice on something," Delilah said, and paused for a second. "Guy is going out to the strip club with his boys tonight. Do you think I should let him go?"

Teesa rolled her eyes, but her body tingled with elation. "Why wouldn't you?"

"I don't want my man out there with all of those tight-body hos."

"Girl, please. You don't have anything to worry about. At least he told you and he ain't out there sneakin' around with his dick in the dirt. Aside from business, he hardly ever goes anywhere without you by his side."

"I know, but—"

"But nothing!" Teesa said, cutting her off. "He's a good man, Lilac. Don't be so petty."

Delilah inhaled deeply. "What would I do without your ass? You always give me such solemn advice," she said. "Is there a particular store you want to stop in?"

"Not really. Bobby bought me some credits from Gucci, so I want to go check out what they have. Aside from that, I am your personal shopper."

"After we pick out my wardrobe for next week, I will treat us to something to eat."

The pair walked around Short Hills Mall, laughing and shopping for hours. After a meal in an Italian restaurant, they walked past Tiffany, ready to exit the mall. As Teesa retrieved her helmet out of the bag, a man tugged on it from behind. She turned around and was taken by surprise when she recognized him.

"Frank, how have you been? I haven't seen you in a minute," Teesa said.

"I know," Frank replied, looking Teesa up and down. "You're still lookin' good." He looked at her designer shopping bags and diamond Rolex. "And you're still fly. Are you married yet?"

"Nah, Frank. I'm still waiting for you—that is, if you didn't marry the other girlfriend you had," she said sarcastically.

"Nah, she just wasn't you." Frank smiled, then looked toward a guy standing next to him. "Teesa, this is my cousin Will. Will, this is my ex-girlfriend Teesa."

"Nice to meet you, Teesa. Who is your beautiful friend?" Will said, looking over at Delilah.

"This is my best friend, Delilah," Teesa said.

Delilah blushed and extended her ring hand. "Pleased to meet you," she said.

"You riding motorcycles now?" Frank asked Teesa.

"Yeah. Call me and I'll take you for a ride," Teesa replied.

"Saturday cool? Your number's still the same?"

"Saturday as in tomorrow?" Teesa asked.

"Yep."

"Fine with me."

"I'll call you tomorrow afternoon to confirm," Frank said as he nudged Will to keep it movin'.

"Yeah, you do that," Teesa said as she and Delilah exited the mall.

Frank and Will stared at the two women's behinds as they headed out of the mall.

"Frank, who was that?" Will asked him. "She's a hottie, and her friend, Delilah, is a dime. Too bad she's married."

"I used to fuck with her when I first started playing for the Yankees," Frank said. "A couple of months after I started messing with her my house got robbed, and I flipped on her and everyone else I was fuckin' with. But it turns out that it wasn't Teesa. They caught some young kids who confessed to robbing my house and a couple of others in my development."

"Weren't you engaged when you—"

"Yeah. You see Teesa made it a point to mention that. I'm going to hang out with her tomorrow, though. I don't know, maybe we could rekindle our old flame. And if nothing else, she gives excellent head."

They laughed, gave each other a pound, and continued through the mall.

Now listen to me," Teesa said to Delilah as they exited the mall. "Don't give Guy any lip about going to the club. I'll talk to you tomorrow."

"Okay," Delilah said. "Smooches, girl. Thanks a bunch."

Delilah walked off toward her car and Teesa toward her bike. Teesa cringed as she climbed on.

I can't stand that "smooches" shit. Delilah is so fuckin' corny, she thought.

Teesa squeezed two pairs of shoes under her seat and strapped her Chanel purchase down to the empty seat behind her. She worked her head into her helmet and glanced at her watch before she pulled down the shield.

I better make it to Bobby's before Trey becomes suspicious, Teesa thought. *It's already six o'clock, I don't want to get back there too late.*

She clutched her throttle and revved the bike's engine three times before she sped to Brooklyn. She reached the Park Slope section of Brooklyn in forty-five minutes, and parked her bike right in front of Bobby's exclusive apartment building. She untied her purchase from the backseat of her bike and headed to the door. Teesa placed her key into Bobby's apartment door and opened it, just to have it slammed in her face. She shook her head and exhaled.

"Damn, Bobby," she whispered loud enough for him to hear. "I know you don't have that young bitch in there again."

"Nah, Teesa. It ain't like that," he said, sounding exasperated. "I just don't have no clothes on."

Teesa could hear a woman arguing with Bobby behind the door.

"Whatever, Bobby. I got that money you needed, and I hope you ain't spendin' it on that trick," Teesa said.

Bobby came out of the door with a towel wrapped around his waist and a marijuana-filled blunt hanging between his soft lips. He gently shut the door behind him and stood in front of it.

Tessa looked at his sorry gorgeous ass and, as always, threw her game face on. It was hard and careless, when really she was hurting and cared too much. She went into her pocket and handed him five thousand dollars. As he counted it, the door swung open and he fell backward, colliding with a young woman. Several hundred-dollar bills fell out of his hands as he tried to break his fall.

Teesa stared at the young woman and, to her dismay, saw that she was a different female from the one she'd caught Bobby with a few weeks before. She laughed at Bobby as he tumbled to the ground. The girl couldn't be a day over seventeen, and not only was she young, but she was bold as well. She wore one of Bobby's Oh So Brooklyn Records T-shirts that barely covered her ass.

The young bare-bottomed girl looked down at Bobby and yelled, "Who the fuck is this bitch? And why does she have a key to your apartment?"

Teesa walked over and stared into the young girl's face, stepping on Bobby's hand as he tried to get up. All of a sudden she raised her hand and smacked the girl dead across the cheek with every ounce of strength she had.

For a moment the girl was in shock, but then she raised her hands as if she was going to go after Teesa. Teesa grabbed the girl by her throat and rammed her body into the wall. The girl clawed at her own neck, trying to pry Teesa's fingers from around her throat. Teesa kneed her bare vagina and yelled, "I'm that sorry muthafucka's girl, and I pay the note on that Mercedes he picked you up in, 'cause it's mine! And no, he can't get you no fuckin' record deal because he's over his budget, so you might as well stop fuckin' him."

Bobby quickly got up and pulled the young girl from Teesa's clutches. As he restrained the kicking and screaming girl by her waist, his towel dropped to the floor. His dick was still hard, and Teesa was glad to see that a blue condom clung around it.

"Let her go, Bobby, so I can beat both of your asses!" Teesa yelled right before she backhanded the young girl and then smacked Bobby on the top of the head. Teesa knelt down and started to scoop up the money she had just given him. Neighbors were beginning to open the door to be nosy, so Teesa picked up her pace.

Bobby scooped the girl's hair to the side and whispered into her ear, "She's my ex-girlfriend. Please let me get rid of her. She is just jealous and refuses to let go. Please, baby, give me five minutes."

The bawling girl gave in to Bobby's request. "Five minutes, Bobby, or I am out of here," the young girl wailed. The crying teen went into his apartment, slamming the door behind her, and leaned against it. She cried harder, squeezing her legs tightly together, rubbing her burning cheek and gently stroking her throbbing neck in an effort to alleviate her pain.

On the other side of the door Bobby looked at his neighbors, clutched his penis in one hand, and stuck his middle finger in the air with the other.

"I'll give you a choice—mind your fuckin' business or suck my fuckin' dick," he said to the nosy neighbors. Embarrassed, most of the neighbors went inside, but others kept their doors cracked, trying to get a glimpse of what was to happen next.

"Teesa, I'm sorry, baby, but it is what it is. It's not like you're not out there doing your thing. You know where my heart rests, mama. Now don't do no stupid shit. Give me the fuckin' money," he said as he rewrapped the towel around his body.

Too angry to argue, Teesa threw the money at him and turned away. He counted it quickly and raced behind her.

"There's only five Gs here. I told you I needed ten thousand at least," Bobby said as he looked down at the shopping bag she clutched in her hand and grimaced. "Chanel!" Bobby erupted. His booming voice clogged her eardrums, but she was able to keep her fear at bay and her game face tight as she braced herself for the blow she knew was about to come. She clutched her helmet tightly, ready to counter his blow, but to her surprise, a calm voice and a gentle hand on the wrist that held the bag were all he dealt her.

Bobby inhaled deeply before he spoke. "How much did you spend? Four, five grand on a fuckin' bag, when you know I need cash? You really don't give a fuck about me, do you? How much money have I spent on you over the years on that type of shit? Hermès, more Chanel, Prada. I even took your hood-rat ass to Harrods. Have any of your ballplaying or hustlin'-ass mobster boyfriends done that for you? You would have been on the bottom of the Hudson River sporting a fuckin' pair of cinder-block stilettos with a matching cement clutch if it wasn't for me."

Guilt boomed on her face, and a feeling of triumph overtook his body. He knew he had her. They just stood and stared at each other. Bobby had done a lot for Teesa since they had been together, but the past six months had been hell.

"Take the bag back and bring me the four grand that you spent on it tomorrow," Bobby demanded.

"Bobby, I can't do this anymore," Teesa said as her game face became more difficult to keep up. "What if I told you I had another house for you to rob and that you could get more paper out of the deal than when I set up Frank? I could guarantee you at least one hundred grand, and then we could call it even. Bobby, I am too tired and too old for this relationship."

"You are worth a lot more to me than a hundred grand, Teesa," Bobby said as he pinned her against the wall and gave her a hard and passionate kiss. Her vagina ached for him upon his touch, but when he led her hand between his legs and she stroked his sticky, condom-covered dick, the reality of her present situation forced her to shove him off her.

"What if I promise you a threesome? The one you've always wanted?" Teesa asked.

Bobby stared at her with his eyes open wide. This was the only reason he had stepped to Teesa in the beginning—so he could get closer to Delilah. He tightened his towel and wiped the back of his hand across his mouth.

"I'm listening," Bobby said.

"Bobby, all I want out of the hundred thousand is thirty grand. You can keep the rest, but we're even after this. I love you, but I can't be with you."

She stared at him as he looked at her wildly. His short and thick curly hair was disheveled from his sexual exploits. His dark caramel skin was gleaming, especially around his chiseled forearms and his tight six-pack. When he finally smiled, his thick, dark eyebrows rose, and his beautiful teeth should have sparkled, they were so white.

"All right, if you can produce the cash and set that up, we are even. Come polish me off before you go. That young bitch keeps nickin' my dick with her teeth. You know nobody gives head better than you."

"Fuck you, Bobby," Teesa said as she walked away.

Bobby stood with his mouth ajar. *This bitch is serious. She's never turned me down before,* he thought angrily. "Teesa, have you lost your mind? Get back here," he yelled sternly as he pulled the condom off his limp dick and grabbed her hand. She pulled herself free from his grasp and continued her journey. She took one last glimpse at the love of her life before she made her way through a group of laughing white teenagers and headed for her bike. Bobby's limp dick and sinister look ceased their laughter at once.

He looked at the teenagers and rolled his eyes. "What the fuck you wiggers looking at? Cornball-ass white muthafuckas," he added.

Teesa got on her bike and zoomed off. As she rode back to

New Jersey, she tried to recap her life with Bobby for the three-plus years they had been together. When they first met, he had just acquired a multimillion-dollar record label, and he took good care of Teesa. He pampered her with furs, jewelry, cars, and trips to five-star resorts on several seas. He went as far as paying close to $500,000 to get her out of some serious trouble with the mob to save her life. He moved her out of a small Brooklyn studio apartment into a cozy three-bedroom town house with a pool in Hackensack, New Jersey. Their lovemaking was explosive, especially the makeup sex, which at present she knew would be the bomb.

Bobby's dick ain't no bigger or better than Trey's, and Trey's pockets are bigger. So why can't I just walk away? she thought.

The answer was elementary to all who knew Teesa and Bobby. Not only did she feel she was eternally indebted to him for saving her life, but Bobby had her mind. He had complete control, and he didn't have to spend another dime or lay any more pipe. Teesa knew it. She was surprised she had made it out of there without letting Bobby dick her ass down first. He had her mind tangled, but Teesa was determined to loosen the knots no matter what the cost.

She had left him once before and was free of his mind games for ten months. They had been back together for six months, and at this point in their relationship he had three failing music artists and had run through every penny he had, but his cocky attitude remained. She had to come out of her current situation, and she knew exactly how to do it.

3

Later that same night Entice's phone rang as she sat in front of the mirror applying makeup. "Hello?" Entice said, answering the phone.

"Entice, how have you been? It's been a second," the caller asked.

Entice gently ran her fingers over the tattoo that bore the caller's name a few inches below her bikini line and shut her eyes. *You're a manipulator. I won't give in*, she thought.

"Hey, T, how have you been and what do you want?" she asked.

"Why do I always have to want something?" T asked. "I'm just checkin' up on you. I haven't spoken to you in a minute."

"Yeah, well, that minute hasn't been long enough."

"Are you working tonight? Can I see you before you go to the club?"

"Nah. I'm only in the club two nights a month, and that's every other Friday."

"This your Friday off?"

"Yeah, I have a private session with Merc."

"Merc? You mean the rapper Merciless?"

"Yup, eight-times-platinum rapper Merciless MC. I have been seeing him for the past year. That nigga had a pole built in his master bedroom for me. Not to mention he pays me ten Gs each time I come."

I should never have dumped that bitch, but she was getting too attached. She's gettin' more paper than my ass, T thought.

"Can I see you for a second before you go to work tonight, please?"

"No, T. I don't want you coming near me."

"I have a business opportunity for you."

"Yeah? Well, our business always ends up with us in the bed with you making promises you'll break and me being left alone minus a couple of thousand dollars."

"I can triple that money you're going to make tonight if you just let me come and holla at you. I swear I don't need any money, and I won't touch you if you don't want me to."

Entice thought for a moment before answering. "You can have fifteen minutes of my time. I don't want you in my house either. Meet me downstairs in the lobby. Be here at nine o'clock sharp and not a minute later."

"Thanks, Entice."

Entice hung up the phone and stared at herself in the mirror. *Why can't you just leave that alone? T will never be with you, and you just keep on giving in.*

At nine p.m. promptly, Entice's bell rang, alerting her that someone was in the lobby for her. She didn't answer it right away. She wanted to keep T waiting a minute. Eventually she pressed her intercom button and said, "I'll be down in a minute, T."

After a few seconds, Entice's pointy heels could be heard clunking down the lobby stairs. Once she reached the bottom step, T almost forgot for a minute that she really wasn't gay, and was with Entice only so she could catch her trap. During the ten months the two had been together, Entice would average anywhere from two to four thousand tax-free dollars a night and would spend most of it on Teesa.

Entice was wearing a long sheer brown skirt that was trimmed with copper sequins and a brown wife-beater knotted tightly in the back that hugged her oversize breasts. Her naturally curly hair hung wildly down her back. She was chocolate brown, with slanted eyes and a schoolgirl smile. She folded her arms and looked at her watch.

"Teesa, you have fourteen minutes left. How much do you want, and when are you going to pay me back? Since we haven't been together you have borrowed over—"

"I know, I know," Teesa said, cutting her off. "I don't want any money from you, Entice. I need a favor. This favor can get me the money I need to pay you back. There's a dude going to the club tonight. His name is Guy. All you have to do is work your magic on him and get him to hire you overnight next week sometime so I can get into his crib. He is a good-ass dude with long-ass paper."

"What's in it for me, T?"

"I can promise you twenty thousand out of the deal. Entice, I have to use the bathroom," Teesa said as she jumped around, trying hard to keep her legs pressed together.

Entice removed her keys from a copper-colored satin pouch that hung loosely off of her wrist. "Hurry up. Merc is waiting for me."

Teesa ran up the stairs and let herself into Entice's duplex. She was shocked to see most of Entice's belongings packed in boxes. She inspected most of them and walked into the bedroom. She went directly to Entice's night table drawer, removed some money from it, and placed it into her pocket.

She never counts her tips at the end of the night. She lets them pile up until Monday, then deposits half. I'll give this to Bobby, Teesa thought.

There was a picture lying facedown on the nightstand. Teesa turned it over and wasn't surprised to see a picture of her and Entice. They were standing on a cruise ship with a life preserver that read, U.S. VIRGIN ISLANDS. She put it back down and finally went into the bathroom, where she sat on the toilet fully clothed and in deep thought.

I wonder where this bitch is going? Who gives a fuck? I have to get this plan into motion.

As Teesa heard Entice's heels ascending the stairs, she flushed the toilet, put on the most seductive face she could, and met her at the door. She gently tugged on Entice's skirt and slipped her hand under its waistband. Teesa stroked the neatly cut triangular patch of hair near Entice's tattoo. When Entice neglected to shrink back, Teesa eased her skirt and thong down to the ground. Teesa knelt down and licked the exact spot where the word *Teesa's* was tattooed under Entice's bikini line as she massaged her huge brown cheeks with one hand and spread her legs apart with the other.

"You know this pussy will always be mine," Teesa said. "Why you trying to hide my name?"

Teesa squatted, looked up into Entice's vagina, and began to stroke it with her tongue.

Entice wanted Teesa so badly. She needed it. She missed it. She had to have it. Sex with men bored her. It did nothing for her. But Teesa's touch instantly aroused her, and her moist tongue made her feel loved even though she knew Teesa was bad news.

As Teesa sucked gently on Entice's clitoris, she felt no emotion, no pleasure. She just kissed and sucked as her thoughts kept moving. *This bitch smells like peaches. I hate eating pussy. Entice better come through on this favor.* She stopped her thoughts to spit a hair off her tongue. *What can I say to make this bitch do what I need her to do? Oh, I know—*

"I can't believe I let you go," Teesa moaned seductively. "I was just confused. I didn't know how to manage my feelings for another woman. You turned me out."

As Teesa went to stick her finger in between Entice's big brown cheeks, Entice welcomed it and began to slide her ass against it. Teesa stood up as she worked Entice's asshole with her fingers and gently kissed her lips.

Entice was on cloud nine. Trying to make her feeling of euphoria last longer, she inhaled and encompassed Teesa's kiss, and that was when she thought she smelled the slightest scent of something she knew so well—vagina, and it wasn't her own. Entice began to sob.

"Get off of me, T!" Entice shoved her and walked away from

Teesa. "You smell like pussy! You just finished eating the next bitch's pussy and have the nerve to come over here and try to get up in mine?"

"What are you talking about? I just went down on *you*!" Teesa shouted. She stopped to think for a second. *Unless this bitch smells Bobby's young chick on my lips. Yuck, that means that nigga was probably eating her pussy when I opened the door.*

"Listen, Teesa." She sniffled. "I will do whatever you want me to do tonight if you promise to leave me alone once and for all. As I am sure you noticed, I am moving. Don't look for me. Don't call my family for me either. Just let me be. If I can get this dude to spend one night with me next week, will you promise to leave me alone?"

Momentarily Teesa felt Entice's pain. *She wants to be rid of me like I want to be rid of Bobby. She hates to love me.* "Yeah, I promise."

Entice began to cry harder as she thought to herself, *It's that easy for her to let me go.* She pulled up her skirt and walked into her bathroom.

Teesa watched her walk. She could never understand how her ass was so perfect and so big. It was almost inhuman. She would always tease Entice and say she had silicone in her ass as well as her breasts.

Entice wiped herself down with a cool rag and came back out. "Okay, then I will do it," she said gently as she exited the bathroom.

Teesa went into her wallet, pulled out a photo of Delilah and Guy, handed it to her, and went into the bathroom. She gargled and scrubbed her face. *I can't be smellin' like pussy when I go home to my man. I am going to make this Trey thing work. After this, I am going to turn my life around.* Teesa replied to herself, *You said the same thing when you had Bobby rob Frank's house.*

She looked at herself in the mirror, shook her head, and then exited the bathroom. When she came out, Entice was studying the photograph.

"His name is Guy, and he has a lot of money. So look for the niggas buying the most bottles. Do you need to hold on to the picture?" Teesa asked.

"Nope. I got it."

"Call me later and let me know how it goes. Don't let me down, okay?"

Teesa walked toward the front door.

"I mean it, T. I don't ever want to see you again after I do this," Entice pleaded.

"I heard you the first time. If you pull this off, you have my word," Teesa said, almost feeling sorry for her. "At least let me walk you downstairs."

Entice and Teesa made their way down the steps.

"So, when are you moving?" Teesa asked her.

"Next week," Entice replied.

They walked to the back of the building, and Entice shook her head when she realized Teesa had traded in the 2004 CLK that she purchased for her for a 2006.

"Nice ride, Teesa," Entice said sarcastically.

Teesa smiled as she sat in the car. Before she could reply she realized Entice was pushing a brand-new burgundy Porsche Cayenne S SUV. The temporary dealer plates were still on the back window. Teesa had to prevent her mouth from dropping wide open and drooling.

"It was a gift," Entice called out as she waved and floored the gas petal.

Emotionally destroyed, Entice took off and made her way to the George Washington Bridge. Teesa's actions helped her confirm what she really had to do. When she pulled up in front of Merciless's gated home in Englewood Cliffs, New Jersey, her game face was tight. She entered the home and seductively switched her way into the bedroom, where he was sitting on the end of the bed, fully clothed. She kissed him passionately.

"Sit down, beautiful. I missed you last week. I don't know why you didn't fly down to Brazil with me while I was on the set of my new video," Merciless said as he slid off her stilettos and kissed her perfect toes before he began massaging her feet.

"I didn't want to be out there with all of your whores," Entice replied. "I like being the center of your attention." She stood up and let her skirt drop to the floor. Then she turned around, bent down, and purposely stuck her ass in his face as she picked it up.

"Shit, there ain't one video trick out there that can stand up to you," he said as he looked at her behind. "You the best, and you're mad cool. I don't know why you don't take me up on my offer to fuck with me and me only. Shit, you smart, AIDS free, no kids, and give good head. What more can a nigga ask for?"

"I don't fuck with no one else."

"I'm talking about that strippin' shit. If the right niggas give you the right amount of bread, your ass is fuckin' them, too. Just like you did me. That's your job. But I am willin' to let all of that shit stay in the past so we can build a future together."

Entice got at least three marriage proposals a month from her private clients. She couldn't remember the last time she'd paid a bill using the money she earned. Everything was taken care of by her private clients, from her rent, her tuition, and her car note, right down to her clothes. She took none of them seriously except for Merc. They had a strong relationship that none of his friends could understand. He really loved her.

Naked, she lay on his bed with her ass facing his face. She made her ass cheeks roll seductively one by one, as if they were ripples in water. Merc's throat began to get dry as he watched her ass cheeks slither like snakes. He extended his hands to grab her ass and she opened her legs into a full split and sat up.

"Entice, you gonna get on the pole for me before we—"

"Yes, daddy," she said as she daintily hopped out of his bed and began to climb the pole that sat at the foot of it. His ceilings had to be over twenty feet high.

"Are you going to turn on some music?" she asked.

Merc let a loud moan escape from between his lips as he ferociously stroked his dick. He couldn't answer, so she began her show. Once she made her way to the top of the pole she came down headfirst at top speed with her legs spread-eagled. As she neared the floor she wrapped her legs around the pole and came to a complete stop with her head just a few inches above the ground. She climbed the pole once more and extended her legs open. Then she miraculously swung her lower body back and forth into the pole as if she were fucking it. Then, without notice, Entice swung around the pole, leaving one leg wrapped around it. She spun swiftly and gracefully, with her eyes closed. She felt as if she were airborne and had no worries, because there, with Merciless, she knew she was safe.

When she stopped, Merciless was stark naked, and he motioned with one finger for her to come to him, which she obliged. He grabbed her curly tresses, kissed her forehead, then gave her head a light shove into his groin. She opened wide and contracted her jaws of life around his dick.

He began to sweat profusely in his cool, air-conditioned mansion. He especially loved the raw feeling of her wet vagina on his condomless dick. Six months into their strange relationship, he suggested they both take frequent AIDS tests so he could indulge unprotected. He knew he was gambling with his life, but Entice had him, and he couldn't let go.

He grunted, groaned, and humped her face until he busted off into her mouth. The back of her neck was damp with sweat. He wiped his palms on the sheets, pulled her into him, and stroked her hair.

"Damn, Entice. When are you going to stop playing around and be my wife?" he asked.

Entice just laughed. "Let's see how things work out after we move into our new home. If our relationship stays the same, then we'll do this."

"Let daddy take a nap before we continue. Just watching you climb up and down that pole wore me out."

"Listen, Merc, I have to go to the club tonight."

Merciless released his embrace on her. "Why?"

"I want to pick up my belongings."

"Don't leave—"

Entice kissed his mouth shut. "You have to give me time to tie up some loose ends. Give me one week. We'll be in the new place. I will never go back to the club again, and all three of my private clients will be history." She pulled him out of the bed and gave him a big hug. "Now, come help me get cleaned up."

4

"Lovey, how do I look?" Guy asked.

Delilah looked at Guy and smiled. "You look so good I almost don't want to let you go," she responded. "I think you should take off those dress shoes. Throw on those Louis Vuitton sneakers you have that look like Air Force Ones. You will be upset if you go in there and everyone has on sneakers and you're wearing dress shoes."

Guy changed his shoes, walked into the closet, and opened his safe. From a wooden watch case that contained over one dozen watches, he retrieved a diamond-encrusted Jacob watch with an orange band that matched his orange rugby. He took off his Breitling watch and put it in the case. He put on a thin chain that had diamonds in between each link, grabbed a thick wad of money, and locked the safe.

He walked behind his wife as she sat at her vanity and gave her a tight hug and a wet kiss.

"Never cut your hair, Delilah, or I will leave you," he joked, then grabbed the brush out of her hands.

As he brushed her hair, she thought about how lucky she was. He was good-looking, intelligent, and a street-made millionaire. He had a light brown complexion and was tall and slim with dark brown eyes. He had brown hair and sported a five-o'clock shadow.

Once he was finished brushing her hair, he kissed the top of her head.

"All right, Delilah. I'm out. Don't wait up. I'm going to be in late," he said.

"Behave," she said in a slick tone.

"You don't have to tell me that. I don't even want to go. You know it's Jamaine's birthday."

Delilah watched her husband walk out of their room through the mirror on her vanity and continued brushing her hair. She worked the wig brush against her long mane for fifteen minutes before she wrapped and pinned it up. She pictured her husband standing behind her, as he often did when she was about to wrap her hair at night, running his fingers through it and massaging her shoulders. They were madly in love. She cut off the light and didn't think twice about Guy's night out with the guys.

Twenty minutes later Guy and three of his boys strutted into the smoke-filled club and took a seat at the long bar, which had a huge stage with three poles behind it. The music was extremely loud, with too much bass. But the drunk birthday boy, Jamaine, could be heard over everything, and as the night went on he became more and more obnoxious. Guy and his boys bought bottle after bottle of champagne, even though Guy drank nothing but Heineken.

Jamaine slid a twenty under the bottom of a stripper's shorts and tried to grab her vagina. That was their first warning from security. Any additional behavior that security or the club owners found unacceptable would get them ejected from the club.

"Fuck that. It's my fuckin' birthday!" Jamaine repeated several times that night.

Guy called over a cute petite stripper wearing a SpongeBob bra-and-boy-shorts set that looked like it could fit a five-year-old. The bottom of her round breasts showed from under the small top, and her boy shorts covered only the top half of her ass cheeks.

Guy tapped her lightly and said, "Sweetheart, do you think you could take my boy up into the VIP? It's his birthday."

She smiled and blew a big yellow bubble that popped. "That's seventy-five dollars for a lap dance," she said, then chomped on the wad again, preparing to make another big bubble.

"Here's a hundred and fifty." Guy winked, handing her the money.

The girl grabbed Jamaine by his arm and took him to an open section in the club that was filled with what looked like restaurant booths, but they were each enclosed with half doors. She swung open the door to one of the booths, sat Jamaine down, and began to ride him and whisper into his ear. His boys cheered him on from the sidelines. This was the first time Jamaine had closed his mouth for the entire night. He stared at her as she twisted and turned on his lap. All of her gyrating made him horny and nau-

seous at once. He began to meet her movements with slight hump-
ing motions. The stripper could feel his penis stiffening up, and
blew a bubble that popped in his face.

"Go ahead, birthday boy, you can dance with me. But don't
touch me or my uncle will have to hurt you," she said as she
pointed to the three bouncers who stood outside the booth area.

Just then the MC's voice came over the speaker louder than life
and drowned the music out.

"Make sure you have your paper ready, because we have a
sweet treat coming onto the stage tonight," the emcee said. "This
is her farewell performance. Dig into your pockets and give a
warm welcome and a warmer farewell to Entice."

The regulars in the clubs banged their glasses and bottles
against the bar with excitement. She walked slowly onto the stage
and seductively surveyed her audience, searching for her victim.
R. Kelly's "Seems Like You're Ready" began to pound through the
loudspeakers, and everybody watched as she took the pole. She
climbed it with ease, as if she were simply walking up a hill. Then
Entice worked that pole like she was caught in the *Matrix*. All
conversations stopped. The bartenders stopped making their
drinks and watched in awe as she climbed up the pole and performed seductive acrobatics on it.

Her upper-body strength could be compared to that of a
bodybuilder, but her body still remained as feminine as a balle-
rina's. She hung upside down and held on to the pole with her
hands, letting her head dangle as she opened her legs wide into a
split. She looked around the bar in this overturned position until
she spotted him. She locked her legs around the pole, grabbed her
breasts, and slowly sucked on her nipples. Then she flipped herself
right side up, climbed to the top of the pole, and came down full
speed, at what seemed like forty miles per hour, and landed in a
split.

The entire club went into an uproar. A variety of bills from ones to hundreds were thrown at her upon completion of her dance. She walked and shoved the scattered bills into her copper pouch. She stopped in front of each person at the bar and let them stick their bill of choice into her top. Her last stop was in front of Guy and his crew. She whispered into the bartender's ear and had him help her up on the bar. She walked directly in front of Guy as the bartender used his forearm to shove all of the glasses to the side. He wiped the area clean where she stood and placed a fresh Heineken in front of Guy. She squatted in front of him, directly over his bottle, and looked into his eyes.

Damn, this bitch is fine. Why did she have to bring her fat ass in front of me? he thought nervously. He reached for his drink, but before he could grab it, she quickly squatted farther down, onto the neck of his freshly opened bottle, letting it penetrate her. Security gathered around as she lay on her back and spread her legs in front of Guy's face. She clasped her hands behind her head and eased the Heineken bottle inside of her using nothing but her vaginal muscles. As it slid farther and farther in, the beer inside looked like it was being guzzled by her furry lips. The bottle went down until a quarter of an inch of it could be seen, and suddenly it slowly began to emerge from her insides and rolled down the bar.

She stood up and glided her hips and waistline like an Indian belly dancer. More money was thrown on the stage at her. Once the music stopped she lay back in her spot as Jamaine made his way to the bar. She spread-eagled, and the beer gushed out of her vagina like a waterfall and splattered all over Jamaine and his boys. Men clapped, yelled, and banged on the bar. Jamaine rubbed the vagina-tainted beer all over his face and licked his hands.

Guy was flabbergasted and aroused all at one time. The beer drops that splatted on his chin dripped onto the bar. He cleared his throat and looked away from Entice as she dismounted the bar top, escorted by two big beefy bouncers, and walked all the way around it to collect money once again. Guy's boys yelled and gave one another pounds.

When she reached Guy and his crew she stopped and smiled. He automatically reached into his pocket, pulled out two fifties, and gave them to her.

"Hi," she said. "I heard someone over here is having a birthday."

Jamaine pushed Guy aside and stepped into her face. "That would be me," he slurred.

"Happy birthday." She smiled. Then she moved closer to Guy and whispered in his ear, "I'd rather celebrate with you. Come with me."

"It's my boy's birthday," Guy said. "Why don't you take him? My treat?"

"Let me find out, you pussy. What? Delilah got a LoJack on your dick? Go get your lap dance on," Guy's boy Rome said.

"You gotta live, son; go do it," his other boy Jay said.

"Fuck that! It's my birthday," Jamaine said.

"Come on. It will only be a few minutes," Entice said as she smiled shyly.

Reluctantly Guy got up and followed her. "Why me?" he said in her ear as she led them to the back of the club.

"Because you looked the least intrigued. Entice lives up to her name. You seem like a challenge."

They went into a room. She closed the door and the music became muffled.

"What's your name?" she asked him.

"Guy."

This is him, she confirmed in her head. *He's cute. Seems decent enough. I can't imagine what Teesa has in store for him.*

"Well, I'm Entice, of course. What's a guy like you doing in a place like this, Guy?" she said as she rubbed the imprint his penis made in his jeans and stared into his eyes.

His voice cracked when he talked. He felt like a child on his first day of school. "It's my man's birthday," he replied.

She got up, turned her back to him. Guy grabbed his penis through his pants and squeezed it tightly. Her ass was unreal. Her cheeks were as round as her breasts. Her big chocolate-covered apple gleamed at him. She stood against the wall and spread her arms and legs out like she was being frisked and began to let her cheeks flow. They rippled slowly, like waves in a calm river. As she rolled them, her peach scent floated into his nostrils and tickled his larynx. Guy fought the feeling, but couldn't help but put his hand into his pants and masturbate quick and hard. He called his wife's name softly.

"Stand up and put it on the crack of my ass," Entice ordered him.

Without hesitation, Guy stood up and placed his rock-hard piece on the top of her ass crack. As soon as it touched her, she spread her ass cheeks open and let the bottom portion of his dick rest inside. She clinched her cheeks together, grabbed his hand, placed it onto her clitoris, and humped his fingers. She contracted her ass muscles each time she ran her clitoris over his hand. She called out his name in a faint whisper with each movement.

This shit shouldn't take long at all, she thought. *I could probably be back to Merciless within the hour. I hope he's asleep. His dick is too big, and he can go all night.*

Guy was in a trance. Everything about her enticed him. Her scent made him harder; her ass felt so warm, so soft and good. Not even a minute passed before Guy jumped back and splatted cum all over the wall. Ashamed, he placed his forehead against the wall and looked down at his penis, which was hardening again. She walked over to him and rubbed his back.

"Guy, I am retiring next week, and I want you to take me out. Do you think we could try this somewhere more intimate? There is something about you. I need more. You can choose the place."

Guy looked up at her and couldn't look away. She was gorgeous, exotic, and built like a stallion. She looked like a black Hawaiian. He licked his lips and couldn't believe what he was about to fix his mouth to say.

"I can't. Sorry, but I'm married."

"Well, think about it. That Heineken bottle and your penis are about the same size. I don't want a relationship. I just want to fuck you." She went into her copper satin pouch and pulled out a card. "Call me, please. I really want you to be my last client."

Guy went into his pocket, pulled out four damp hundred-dollar bills, and placed them in her hand.

"Next week. Wednesday. No fee. My last fuck in this game is on me. Clean yourself up, Guy. I'm headed home."

She kissed him on the forehead and, with that, strolled out and had a security guard escort her to the back of the club, where she cleaned out her locker and bade her coworkers farewell. Once the bouncers seated her safely in her truck, she called Teesa, who was in bed next to a sleeping Trey. Her cell phone buzzed on his dresser. She scooped it up and glanced at the number before she answered.

"Hey," Teesa said into the phone.

"Hey, T. He's as good as mine. I hit him with the special, and he is open. I'll call you when he calls me."

"Thanks, girl. I owe you one." She quietly snapped the phone closed and laid it back down. She looked at Trey, who hadn't budged. She snuggled close to him and went back to sleep.

Entice snapped her phone closed, then drove off.

Guy was still back in the private room trying to gather his

thoughts. When he finally made his way back to the bar, his boys wanted to know what took place. Even strangers crowded around him.

"Duke," Rome yelled beyond excited. "What the fuck happened back there, cuz-o?"

Guy didn't know where to begin, but he started nonetheless. "She stood against the wall like I was five-O and spread everything," Guy reminisced. "She ain't have no clothes on."

"She has the ass of life, son," Jay added.

"Yo, shut the fuck up and let the nigga tell it. What happened next?" Jamaine demanded.

"Well, son, she stood against that wall and her ass cheeks looked like they were doing the snake. They weren't clappin'. They were like water in a wave pool. That was fuckin' incredible, yo." At this point in his recounting of events, he became embarrassed and changed his story. "Then she danced for me. I paid her and she left."

"That's it? You ain't get your man buffed, nigga?"

"Nah," Guy said.

His tale was interrupted by the club's emcee, who introduced the next dancer onstage. It was the stripper who wore the fitted SpongeBob underwear, who had given Jamaine his lap dance. As she stepped on the stage he started yelling loudly. He stepped up on his chair and walked on top of the bar in her direction. The club's bouncers thrashed him in the back of the legs and he fell down face-first on the bar and chipped his tooth. They dragged him out the front of the club and left him on the curb, bleeding and cursing. Guy and his boys followed behind, laughing hysterically. They'd all figured this was how the night was going to end, as intoxicated and obnoxious as he became. They all helped to scoop their boy up off the ground, and Jay drove him home.

Guy strolled in at two o'clock in the morning. Without fully undressing, he slid into the bed, grabbed his wife by the ass, and fucked the shit out of her.

Meanwhile, the person responsible for Guy's wanting his wife so badly, Entice, had tiptoed into Merciless's home about an hour earlier. She had showered without waking him, pulled on one of his T-shirts, and fell asleep. By two thirty he was on her back, making passionate love to her.

Entice faked her moans and gritted her teeth through her groans and overdid her orgasms, all three of them. She felt numbness as he pumped his narrow frame in and out of her. Could she withstand this to get out of the game? It wasn't just him who didn't arouse her; it was any man. She played her position until they both fell into a deep sleep in each other's arms.

5

Monday morning came quicker than Entice would have liked. She spent the entire weekend with Merc picking out furniture for their new home, and she escorted him to a concert he had in Massachusetts. The movers came and delivered most of her belongings to her new home. A second set of movers came and removed all of the furniture from her duplex, which she decided to donate to charity. She called her first client, Senator Darrel A. Binton.

"Hey, Darrel. Can you talk?" she said.

"Let me call you right back from my cell phone. We are still on for our two-o'clock, aren't we?" he asked.

"Yes, we are. As a matter of fact, we will speak then."

"Very well."

It was ten thirty in the morning. The senator usually liked for her to be there the night before, so no one could make a connection, but she was tied up with Merc. She arrived at the hotel at eleven fifteen a.m. She arranged for a wake-up call at one forty-five p.m. so she could be ready. Darrel was one of her favorites. He rarely wanted sex, wasn't married, and treated her like royalty. She had gone on countless vacations with him. She sighed as she remembered the vacation where Teesa threatened to leave her if she didn't allow her to come along. So while Darrel was out on business, Entice was spending time with Teesa. They went shopping at Entice's expense, and Teesa stayed in the same hotel. Several nights during their weeklong stay, after Entice would dance for Darrel and he would fall asleep, she went upstairs and made passionate love to Teesa.

After reminiscing for a while about her and Teesa, Entice fell asleep until she received her wake-up call. When the phone rang she got up and unlocked her side of the door. She and Darrel had connecting rooms, as they did every Monday afternoon. He was a $2,500 call, and was responsible for paying her tuition for the two years she had been dancing for him. She closed the curtains over the window, making sure they omitted all light. In the bathroom the light shone brightly as she rubbed herself down with a foamy soap and started a steaming hot bath. By the time she filled it to the top, she could hear the lock to the adjoining room click, and she shut the light in the bathroom off. No sooner had she done so than Darrel walked into the room.

"Entice, sweetie, I am here, and I purchased something really nice for you," he said.

"I'm in the bathroom. Come in here, Darrel."

When Darrel walked into the pitch-black bathroom he was in total shock. He dropped to the floor the jewelry box he carried in his hands and ripped his baseball cap off of his head. Entice seemed to be standing in midair and was glowing bright green from hair to toe. She began to seductively slither from side to side, clasping her hands above her head and rolling her neck like an Indian princess. Darrel nearly tripped as he pulled his jeans off. He looked at her small waist and big thighs rolling around and around and began to lose control.

"Come here, Darrel," she called softly.

He blindly felt his way around the bathroom and bumped into the sink. Using caution, she stepped down off of the bathtub and gave him a peck on the mouth. He gave her a strong embrace and she felt around for the glow-in-the-dark bubble bath on the sink. She poured some into her hands and jerked him off with it. He stood up and out in the darkness like Luke Skywalker's light saber. She led him out of the bathroom into the middle of the dark room, where he could see her fluorescent body and his glowing dick in the mirror, and she sucked him off.

She went with an extra vigor as her way of saying farewell, ignoring the awful soapy taste. He whimpered like a puppy and caressed and stroked her head as she worked. In no more than three minutes he was begging her to move so he could cum. Afterward he stretched her out on the bed and licked her soap-filled vagina until he made a few small suds.

Entice's body was filled with a sensual feeling that usually only a woman could give her. She was overwhelmed. From time to time good oral sex could take her there, no matter what the gender. She felt relieved after she quietly released onto his face.

Leading him back into the bathroom, she sat in the warm bathwater with him. He placed a flawless three-carat ring on her finger and called it a friendship ring.

"I just wanted you to know that I think you are special to me," he said.

"Darrel," Entice said sternly, "this is going to be the last time we see each other. I am not dancing anymore. This is our good-bye. I can't take this ring from you."

Darrel's heart sank. He had made countless offers for her to stop dancing and let him take care of her, but she always refused.

"Entice, why? I mean, I have wanted you to leave that club for years now, but I didn't expect you to leave me as well. I know I pay to see you every week, but I thought we had something special. In my mind you don't perform for anyone else the way you do for me, and I know that holds some weight for you, too. I can tell by the way you look at me. The only reason I haven't tried to form some kind of commitment with you is because you won't allow it."

Entice caressed him from behind and kissed his neck before responding.

"That would not be a good look for your career. Do you know what the press would do to you if they found out your wife was an ex-stripper? I will miss you, but all my numbers will be changed as of Wednesday. Please don't look for me. I want to start a new life, and I expect you to respect my decision."

With that, she stepped out of the tub, dried off, and got dressed. The senator did the same. It was three fifteen in the afternoon, and he knew it would take him at least an hour to reach Connecticut from New Jersey.

"Entice, please keep the ring, and if you ever change your mind, you know where to find me."

Entice watched him walk out of the door that led to his room in his fitted baseball hat, his white tee, and his Armani shades. If it weren't for how tightly his jeans fit, he would look straight out of the hood. He was never recognized when he came into New Jersey for their weekly encounters. She stared at the beautiful

Tiffany diamond that sat on her ring finger as the door slammed behind him. She felt good inside.

One down, two to go, she thought. *I hope Joey's Italian-stallion ass will take it just as easy. I better get ready for school.*

6

The next day Teesa was in a lower-Manhattan neighborhood commonly known as the Village. She entered a huge drugstore on Sixth Avenue and approached a salesclerk.

"Hi! Can you help me?" Teesa asked. "I'm going on vacation. I usually wax, but don't have the time. What brand of hair remover would you recommend? I want one that works fast."

Without answering, the salesclerk walked past several aisles and handed her a tube of Nair. Teesa purchased ten tubes, then left the store. She looked at her watch. It was three forty-five p.m., so she slowed her pace as she made her way to West Fourth Street, where she stopped momentarily to watch a basketball tournament. After ten minutes she walked into one of the dorms at NYU. On the elevator she checked her watch and saw that it was four p.m. She'd made perfect time. She went straight to the fourth floor and tapped the first door to the left of the elevator.

"Who is it?" a female asked.

"Smurfette," Teesa replied.

A young white girl with bleached-blond hair opened the door. "Come in," she said.

Teesa stepped inside and looked around at all of the posters that covered the walls of the room. Although she considered herself a fan of all kinds of music, she didn't recognize any of the groups on the wall.

"Who sent you?" the girl asked Teesa.

"Bobby of Oh So Brooklyn Records."

The girl smiled. "Tell Bob I said howdy. He used to be one of my regulars, but I haven't seen him in a gang of Sundays." She handed Teesa a bag with six small round blue pills.

"Take one of these and you're good, one and a half and you're really good. That's three hundred."

"Damn, why so much?" Teesa asked, twisting up her face.

"Because this Ecstasy is uncut. It's pure."

Teesa stared at the tiny round blue pills in the bag and thought, *Uncut? This ain't no fuckin' coke. Shit, she could tell my ass anything. I don't know shit about no fuckin' X, and she probably knows that, too. Oh, well, I guess I have no choice.*

Later that evening Guy stepped out of his bedroom with a small duffel bag and checked his watch. It was six fifteen p.m. He followed the soulful smell of his wife's cooking down into the kitchen, where she was standing in front of the stove.

"Lilac, I have some out-of-town business to take care of before we leave for our trip this weekend. I will be back tomorrow afternoon," he said, scooping her hair out of the way and planting a kiss on her neck.

"Wednesday?" she questioned.

"Yep."

"Try to be back as early as possible, because I want us to go pick up a few things for the trip before the mall closes tomorrow."

"All right. I love you. I'm out."

"Your ass ain't goin' nowhere until you eat some of this food. It will be done in fifteen minutes."

The couple ate and shared a warm embrace before Guy headed for the door.

"Remember, Guy, please be in here early, at least by three o'clock tomorrow afternoon."

"Don't worry, Lilac, I will," he said.

Three o'clock the next day came and passed and there was no sign of Guy. Delilah was furious.

I don't believe Guy, she thought as she walked around the kitchen slamming pots and pans as she prepared their dinner. *I don't ask for much. He could have at least called to say he was going to be late.*

It was six o'clock in the evening and she hadn't received one call. Delilah decided to call him a third time, and once again his phone rang and went to his voice mail. At this point her anger turned into concern.

Teesa sat in Trey's house and watched television. At six o'clock that evening her cell phone rang. She looked at the caller ID and smiled. Her plan was starting to come together.

"Hey, T. It's Entice," she said. "Your boy just called me. He's meeting up with me tonight at the Marriott Hotel off Route Four at ten o'clock."

"You're the best," Teesa complimented her. "I don't want that nigga back to his house before nine o'clock tomorrow morning. We'll talk about money later."

"You won't owe me jack if you leave me alone."

"That's fine with me. Take care of yourself."

Teesa ended the call and smiled. She was in a state of nervousness and elation all at once. She ran into the bathroom and strained through a bowel movement, thinking it would help calm the nerves that left her stomach in a knot, but it didn't.

Finally, she thought. *Little Mrs. Perfect is going to get dirty.* She smiled to herself as she dialed.

"Bobby, it is going down tonight. Be ready at eight, okay?"
Teesa said.

"Is Delilah going to be there?" he asked.

"Just have your fuckin' ass ready!" she exclaimed, then slammed
the phone down.

At nine o'clock p.m., Teesa and Bobby were parked in a dark
blue rental around the corner from Delilah's luxurious home
in Fort Lee, New Jersey.

"How long do we have to sit out here?" Bobby asked.

"If Delilah doesn't call me, I will call her at ten thirty," Teesa
answered.

Bobby's dick was hard just thinking about finally having Delilah. "Teesa, mama, put your lips on it, baby. I'm about to bust I
am so excited. Come on."

Bobby pulled down the lever next to the driver's seat, which re-
clined him all the way back. The thought of Delilah's demise
made Teesa horny, too. She put Bobby's penis inside her mouth,
and her thoughts drove her to suck fast and hard.

Delilah won't be little Mrs. Perfect after tonight, she thought.
*Bobby won't be so quick to say, "Why don't you grow your hair out
like Delilah's," or "Maybe you should shriek your hair like Delilah's."
Trey won't be able to say, "Baby, you could stand to put on some
weight. What's your friend's name—you know, the pretty one? Yeah,
Delilah, she is a good size."*

The more she thought of her cruel plan, the hotter she became. She hiked up her skirt and hopped on Bobby's dick. She
pounded her narrow frame into his. She used short and forceful
strokes, digging her nails into the seat for leverage.

"That stupid young bitch can't fuck you like this, huh?" Teesa
taunted.

Bobby thrashed up into her with equal force. As he began to climax, he grabbed her ass and slammed it into him harder.

"No, baby. That young stunt ain't got nothing on you. You know you're my number one bitch. I love you, Teesa."

"Delilah ain't going to fuck you like this either. Only I can—say it."

The mention of her name sent a message to his scrotum, and sperm filled his dick.

"Teesa, Teesa, get up quick. I'm cumming."

She turned over to the side and he came all over the driver's window. Teesa was worked up to the point of no return and needed to release. She reached into a plastic bag, grabbed the first thing in it, rammed it inside of her vagina, and humped it. It was a tube of Nair. She continually pulled it in and out of her, and Bobby's dick instantly became hard again. He pulled the Nair bottle out of her hands, licked it, and then threw it on his seat. With his dick hanging out the opening of his pants, he got out of the car and fumbled around to the passenger's side. He yanked Teesa out and slammed her against the car. As he picked her up, his muscles flexed and she nearly lost it. They pounded into each other, and after five minutes of rough strokes, they came together.

Teesa looked around for any spectators, and couldn't remember the last time she was so horny. Out of breath, she entered the car and was embarrassed for herself when she looked at the discarded bottle of Nair in the seat.

I can't front, she thought. *I love makeup sex, though, and that was so intense.* She glanced at her cell phone, and the message indicator on it flashed red. She grabbed it and scrolled through her missed-call list. Delilah's number appeared four times. *This is going to be too easy. I knew she would call. She's such a fuckin' baby. She's probably scared and worried and shit. She is such a fuckin' spoiled brat.*

Teesa calmed down, gathered her composure, put her game face on, and returned her call.

"Hey, Delilah," Teesa said. "What's good?"

"There's something wrong with Guy!" Delilah cried frantically. "I have been calling him all day, and he hasn't returned my calls. I can't believe this shit."

"Why are you crying? It's only ten o'clock at night. He's probably out with his boys."

"He would have called by now. He should have been back."

"Do you want me to come over there and wait with you? You sound really worried, honey."

Delilah put a pause on her emotions and had a moment of clarity in the midst of her tears. *Guy would kill me if he knew I had company over while he wasn't home. But Teesa is like a sister to me, and God forbid something happened to him. I couldn't bear receiving any bad news alone.* "Would you? I really don't feel like being alone right now," Delilah decided.

"I will be there in twenty minutes."

Teesa hung up the phone and nudged Bobby in the side. He was dead asleep. He struggled to keep his eyes open when she woke him and went over the plan for the third time that night.

Thirty minutes later she pulled the car around the corner. She jumped out of the car with a bottle of Hennessy and a bottle of Alizé.

"Make sure you call me in twenty minutes, and don't get out of this car until I come back and give you the okay."

Bobby grunted in reply and drifted off to sleep.

Teesa walked to the door and knocked. Delilah answered it wearing a pair of cutoff jeans shorts and a wife-beater. Her face was red and her eyes were swollen and puffy.

"Hey, girl. I got here as fast as I could, and I brought us some drinks," Teesa said, holding up the bottles.

"I am so worried! I don't know what I would do without him," Delilah sobbed.

Teesa reassured Delilah that Guy was just being a man, and reminded her what a good man he was as they sipped their drinks. She also reminded her what line of business he was in, and that maybe he wasn't able to call. An entire hour passed before Bobby called Teesa on her cell phone.

"Hello," Teesa said, answering the phone. She paused before saying, "You're outside of my condo? You should have called first. I will be home as soon as I can, baby."

Teesa hung up the phone and then turned to Delilah.

"That was my friend. He's waiting for me outside of my place. I have to go," Teesa lied. "Are you going to be okay?"

"I guess," Delilah said with doubt.

"Here, I have something that will help you sleep." Teesa pulled two blue pills out of her bag, went into the kitchen, and poured Delilah a glass of water. She purposely took her keys out of the bag, left the purse on the kitchen counter, and came back into the living room. "Here, girl. Drink these down. I'll call you in a few to make sure they kicked in."

Without hesitation, Delilah swallowed the blue pills with the water and let Teesa out of the house. She was already feeling tipsy from the three glasses of Alizé that she sipped while talking to Teesa. She closed the door behind her friend and retired to the couch.

Within minutes she felt sexually bothered and was warm. She got up and became a little dizzy. She turned up the central air and used the scrunchie on her wrist to pull her hair up. She went into the kitchen to get some more water and noticed Teesa's bag on the counter. She hurried to the phone to call her.

"Teesa," she moaned, then giggled. "You left your bag on my kitchen counter. You gonna come back and get it?"

"Damn." Teesa sighed. "Yeah. I'm not that far away," Teesa lied as she smiled. She was still parked around the corner. She popped a little blue pill herself, and Bobby smiled. She lay back and waited for the effects of the pill to kick in. Within seconds she was hot and bothered.

"I am coming in there in twenty minutes, so don't wear her ass out, you hear me?" Bobby warned.

She walked to the door and rang the bell. When Delilah opened the door Teesa smiled and said, "Are you feeling better, Lilac?" She hugged Delilah tightly. When she released her embrace, she placed a kiss on Delilah's lips. "I hate to see you so worried."

Delilah kissed her back passionately and pulled her into the house. Teesa pulled in the front door behind her but made sure to leave it cracked. She had used and dated several women for money and never felt pleasure from any of their touches. But a mixture of the Ecstasy and the desire for Delilah's demise turned her on. They laid on the couch kissing each other and took turns pleasing each other orally.

Delilah led Teesa to her bedroom and got her vibrator. Teesa blindfolded Delilah. The darkness excited her even more. She heard a click, and a loud buzzing followed directly behind it. Teesa gently maneuvered the buzzing rod in and out of Delilah's wet pussy as she sucked on her perky nipples. The house phone rang and, as Delilah put little effort into reaching for it, Teesa smoothly grabbed her hand and placed it between her own legs. The ringing phone was now the last thing on her mind. If she had answered it, she would have realized that it was Guy on the other end of the call. But he was sexually drained from his escapades with Entice, and figured that his Lilac was fast asleep, so when she didn't answer his call, he hung up the phone and did the same.

Minutes after the phone rang, Delilah jumped when she heard the door slam and a male voice yell, "Teesa? Are you okay, mama?"

"Damn," Teesa whispered. "I forgot my friend was in the car. He is probably worried." She licked Delilah under her navel and slid her tongue between the vibrator and her clitoris. Delilah screamed out in pleasure and Teesa moved to the side. "He has a really big dick and is good in bed. Should I invite him up?"

"Don't stop, Teesa. Keep on lickin' it," Delilah panted.

"I am upstairs to the left," she called as she placed the vibrator inside of Delilah and then began to suck on her clitoris.

Bobby came up the stairs with his dick in his hand. He shoved Teesa out of the way and stroked Delilah's hair.

"Hey, sexy," he whispered. "This isn't going to hurt a bit."

Bobby wasted no time as he eased his dick inside of her, and she welcomed it. It was a lot bigger than Guy's, and Delilah had never felt such pleasure. She moaned and clawed Bobby's back as she pushed up against him. Teesa sucked on her breasts and held her hand but became instantly jealous as she watched how careful Bobby was inside of her. He kissed her face gently and licked and stroked her hairline as he made love to her. Teesa and Bobby always engaged in rough sex. She got up, smacked Bobby in the head, and pouted like a six-year-old. Bobby pointed at the DVD recorder that he had placed on the dresser as he came into the room. Teesa got up and turned it on.

After an hour of sex, the effects of the X started to wear off. Delilah called for Teesa, but she didn't answer. As she begged the stranger inside of her to stop, Teesa got up, turned the DVD recorder off, popped out the disc, and placed it on the bed next to Bobby.

Delilah started to cry. Bobby pulled out his pistol and placed the barrel in her mouth. Teesa became nervous. She got up, stood in the doorway, and watched quietly.

"Delilah, if you listen and cooperate I won't have to use this," Bobby said as he stroked the side of her face with his gun. "What is the combination to the safe?"

"Where's Teesa?" Delilah demanded to know.

"I had to shut that bitch up for good because she was trying to protect your ass. Now, if you don't want to end up like her, you will give me the combination to the safe. . . ."

7

When Entice exited the hotel it was a bright and beautiful Thursday morning. She looked up at the sky and exhaled. She relaxed the muscles in her face and smiled. She was free of false eyelashes, layers of makeup, and imaginary love with real men. No longer would she have to pretend. When she reached Merc's house, the moving truck was pulling off and he stood in front of the house. She smiled and didn't feel the need to look seductive or sexy. She was just herself.

"Hey, Entice. You look really good today," Merc said. "There's something different about you."

"Really?" Entice blushed.

"Yeah, baby," he said, looking her over, trying to figure out what was so different about her. "You have a natural shine. But anyway, we have a flight to catch. Are you ready for Miami, beautiful?"

"The question is, is Miami ready for the new me?"

He hugged her tightly and whispered in her ear, "I know I am ready for you." He really wanted their relationship to work, and

Entice felt it. When they kissed her emotions tingled from her head all the way down to her toes.

Guy reached into his back pocket, ripped up Entice's card, and threw it in the sewer as he approached his house. *That's the only way I won't ever see her again,* he told himself.

"Lilac!" he called, entering their house. "I'm home, lovey, and I'm missing you."

He stopped at the bottom of the steps, covered his face with his hands, and inhaled deeply as he dragged them down to his chin, waiting for her response. *She's probably mad as shit, but that was well worth it. I'll never cheat again. I had to sit in that hotel for an extra day just to drum up enough nerve to call Entice. I'll just tell Lilac that I had to stay out of town longer than I expected and am getting a new phone because I think this one is tapped.*

The walk to his bedroom seemed to take an eternity. He slowly turned the knob and pushed the door open. He walked in to find the bedroom a mess.

"What the fuck?" he whispered as he looked around his room. "Lilac!" he yelled. "Delilah!"

The top and bottom sheets of his bed were on the floor, and empty liquor bottles were littered about. As he walked to the bed he stepped into a pool of vomit, then threw himself onto the bed, unsure what to think. He bowed his head for a moment, then looked up at the television, which was on. The screen was filled with snow, and the lights on the DVD player indicated it was on.

Suddenly an uneasy feeling overtook him and he ran to the safe that was inside his closet.

"They fuckin' got me!" he yelled. "Yo! Delilah!" He grabbed

his cell phone and dialed her cell phone number, but it went straight to voice mail.

Instinct pulled him toward the DVD player. He pushed the play button, only to view his wife listless and blindfolded, with her hands tied to the top of the bed and a black ass ramming inside of her. As disgusted and angry as he was, he couldn't tear his eyes away. He zeroed in on the kinky balls of hair on the man's ass. Angry energy filled his body, and he began to breathe heavily as he made notice of how dark his ass was in comparison to the rest of his body. He played back the DVD several times and listened to his wife's slurring pleas for him to stop over and over again. Then his next thought hit him so hard he was winded.

Entice! He gasped. *They probably sicced her ass on me and my dumb ass fell straight in. But who set me up?*

He savagely ripped through his wallet for her card. "Fuck!" he yelled harshly as he realized he had shredded it mere minutes ago. He fell on the edge of the bed and yelled loud and hard. He scrolled through his call list, searching for her number, but Delilah called him so many times the night before that Entice's number had been bumped. He dialed Delilah's phone again, only to hear her sweet voice on the voice mail. As he ended the call the house phone rang. He picked it up slowly and was quiet.

"One hundred grand, nigga," he heard a male voice say. "You have until a quarter past noon to put that together. There's a white Maxima parked on the corner of St. James Place and Fulton Street in Brooklyn. Place the cash in the trunk. Come alone or your wife is dead. Call the cops and your wife is dead. Bring heat and your wife is dead."

Guy looked at the phone for fifteen minutes after the call had ended. He didn't know where to begin.

Who? Why? Who? What? What the fuck am I going to do? Guy

thought as he let another hour pass, trying to figure out what jealous nigga would do this to him. He looked at the clock on the DVD player and it read 11:15 a.m. He shot up and his head pounded like the police kicking down a door at a drug raid. He dragged his body outside to his car, picked up his cell, and dialed.

"Jay," Guy said into the phone. I need some fuckin' paper. How much you got in the crib, son?"

"Why?" Jay asked.

"They got Delilah, man. Niggas ran up into my crib, fucked her, and kidnapped her ass. I need sixty grand. I got forty grand at my grandmother's house."

Jay was too shocked to respond.

"Dude, did you hear me? They got my muthafuckin' wife!"

"I got about twenty grand here."

"Get that and meet me in a half hour at Jamaine's. Call that nigga and fill him in. I'm running out of time."

Guy frantically scrolled through his call list and placed another call. "Rome? I need forty grand in thirty minutes."

Although Rome could hear the desperation in his voice, his curiosity still prompted him to ask, "For what?"

"I know you got it!" Guy shouted, then paused in an attempt to calm himself down. "Meet me at Jamaine's in thirty minutes with the paper. Call Jay and he will fill you in."

How the fuck am I going to make it by my grandmother's and over to St. James Place? I ain't going to make it, Guy thought. He stomped on the gas pedal and sped through the tolls at the George Washington Bridge. He made it to his grandmother's by twelve on the nose. He got his money and left her house, then sped up, running the red light at the corner of her block.

He picked up his cell phone, dialed, and listened to the phone ring over and over again as he thought of Delilah. He pictured the thick, dark body on top of his wife. He could hear her begging him to stop. He could hear the bed going up and down; then he heard sirens, and that pulled him out of his dreary thoughts. He looked into the rearview mirror, only to see the flashing lights of a police car.

"Fuck!" he exclaimed as he banged the wheel. And then it happened. The first tear came tumbling down his cheek. He pulled over to the curb, nervously went through his wallet, and retrieved his information.

"Driver's license and registration," the officer said as he approached Guy's window.

Guy handed them over without hesitation.

"You are aware of why I pulled you over?" the officer asked.

Guy's throat was extremely dry, and his voice was raspy and hoarse. He was barely audible as the tears poured down his face.

"Using my cell without an earpiece," he answered.

"Yes, and you just ran through two stop signs and a traffic light. Have you been drinking?"

"No."

The officer walked back to his patrol car and Guy started to pray, "Please don't let there be anything wrong with my license."

It seemed as if the cop took a lifetime to come back. Guy turned toward the policeman, his face drenched with a combination of sweat and tears. Guy was issued three tickets and some verbal warnings, and the officer hopped into his patrol car and drove off. Guy checked the time. It was twelve fifteen.

A half hour later he was three blocks away from Jamaine's house when his cell phone rang and pulled him out of his trance. When he flipped his phone he could hear loud yelling and screaming on the phone. The yelling became more and more pronounced, and before the phone reached his ear, he knew who it was.

"Jamaine?" he said hoarsely, trying to talk over Jamaine's hysterical yelling.

"You need to come over here right now, son!" Jamaine yelled. "I don't know what to make of this shit! Get over here!"

"Don't say anything else on this phone. I'll be there in a second," Guy said as he ended the call. *Pull it together, nigga. You have to save Delilah.*

He picked his cell phone up and called Jay again.

"Is everyone there yet?" Guy asked Jay.

Jay replied softly, "Rome and I just got here. Guy, have you spoken to Jamaine? Some foul shit is going down over here. Brace yourself, nigga."

"Yeah, I am on my way over there now. Have all of the paper together."

"No doubt."

Guy pulled up in front of Jamaine's house to find his boys standing outside on the lawn. He got out of the car, not knowing what to expect. He closed the car door behind him and slowly began walking toward the lawn. As he approached the house, Jamaine stopped him and pointed to the mailbox. Guy walked toward it and inhaled deeply.

"Reach inside of it," Jamaine said.

Guy looked back at his longtime friends before he stuck his arm inside, only to feel what he thought was a small and wet furry animal. He yanked his arm out of the mailbox clutching whatever it was in his grasp, and dropped it onto the ground. His eyes opened wide as he viewed a bloody mane on the ground. He didn't know what to make out of it for a few seconds, and then it hit him: It was his beloved Delilah's hair. He could see pieces of scalp and flesh attached to some of it. As he knelt down and scooped up her hair, a DVD disc and a piece of paper fell to the ground. He could smell his Lilac, but her usual Saturday-morning sweet Dominican doobie scent was entwined with a strong-smelling sulfur, which was unfamiliar to him.

He picked the paper up off the ground and read it.

1:30 SAME BAT TIME, SAME BAT CHANNEL OR
YOUR WIFE IS DEAD.

He walked over to his boys holding on to all that he had left of his wife and stopped in front of Jay.

"These niggas have to pay," Jamaine said solemnly.

"I don't give a fuck about that right now! I need my wife, Jay," Guy said as he lifted up her hair and showed it to Jamaine, trying to make a point.

Jay stepped up in front of Guy and gave him a strong bear hug. Guy closed his eyes and prayed silently, *God, please. Don't let her be dead.* Guy went into Jamaine's bedroom, put the disc into his player, and pushed play.

Delilah was seated and bound with twine, and her mouth was covered with duct tape. There was thick white lotion from her forehead down to the ends of her hair. Ten tubes of Nair that looked as if they were squeezed empty surrounded her. Some were on her lap and others dropped to the ground as she made attempts to move her bound body around. He watched the effects of the white cream on her hair. As she violently shook her head, globs of her hair started to fall out. He could feel her muffled screams in his heart. Teary-eyed, Guy clicked off the DVD player. He walked out of the room and fell to the ground.

8

Delilah's body tingled painfully all over. Her head oozed a juicy, pimplelike puss and felt as if it were bubbling over like a boiling stew. She desperately wanted to touch it, but the tightly bound duct tape restricted her movements. She moaned, shifted, and stretched her neck to the side.

She continued to moan loudly as she wallowed in self-pity. *What is my Guy going to think when he sees my hair?* she thought. "Ahhhhh," she moaned. *My body is killing me. Dear Lord, please get me out of this—*

"Shut the fuck up with all that moaning, bitch," Bobby yelled. "Looks like your man doesn't care too much about you after all. He hasn't made that drop yet. I'm going to give him one more chance to come through for you. Why don't you give your hubby a call yourself? If you start yellin' once I take this tape off of your mouth, I will make sure you never see your husband again."

Bobby scrolled through Delilah's call list for Guy's cell phone number and laughed when he saw she had his number saved under "My Guy."

"Your Guy really don't give a fuck about you or he would have had that money in the trunk already. See, if your pretty little ass would have fucked with me in the first place, I would have never had you in this predicament. I would never give niggas a chance to kidnap my piece. But you wanted to play hard to get."

Even thinking became painful for Delilah as she tried to pull together what was going on. *Does he know me or something? Who the fuck is this?* she thought.

Suddenly she felt a rough pain travel across her face as the duct tape was pulled off without prior warning. It tore off a small piece of skin next to her mouth. Now her mouth chimed in with the agonizing pains in her vagina and the excruciating tingling in her head, making a painful drumming throughout her entire body.

Bobby put the phone to her ear. Her eyes were tightly bound with tape, so she waited in complete darkness to hear her husband's voice. She could imagine him whispering sweet nothings in her ear and playing with her hair.

"Delilah?" Guy said. His boys hovered around him and watched him talk.

"Yes, baby," she whispered painfully.

"You're okay? Where are you? Who did this?"

"I love you, honey."

"I love you t—"

Bobby snatched the phone and yelled into it, "No money, no more honey. You're late. I'm giving you a half hour to get my paper together or your wife is dead." With that he snapped the phone shut.

"Do I know you?" Delilah asked timidly.

"We've met a couple of times before," Bobby said as he strapped fresh duct tape to her lips and walked out of the room to answer his own ringing cell phone.

"Yeah," he answered.

"You got that paper yet?" Teesa whispered.

"Nah. Not yet."

"Bobby, I am out of here. I am going out of town to get married," she said in a frightened tone.

"Yeah, yeah, whatever, bitch," Bobby said. "You know you'll be back. But I'm a nigga of my word. As long as I don't get caught for this shit, we are even."

"Teesa, get out of the fuckin' bathroom already! I wanted to get an early start on the road," Trey called from downstairs.

"Bye, Bobby." Teesa hung up her cell and smiled. She strapped onto her wrists the Chanel bracelet and watch that she had removed from Delilah's jewelry box and smiled.

"That bitch won't need them anymore." She laughed as she walked down the steps and kissed Trey.

"What's so funny?" he asked.

Teesa produced a sweet smile as she looked at her huge, sparkling engagement ring. "I'm just happy to be with you. I love you, Trey," she said.

"I love you, too, Teesa," he replied.

"You like my new watch and bracelet? Delilah picked these out for me last week when we went to the mall."

Delilah listened as Bobby's footsteps grew distant and tried to piece her twisted fate together, but she couldn't. She didn't have a clue who had snatched her yesterday, or how she got to where she was now. She didn't have a clue who she had fucked over and over again the previous night, when she felt pleasure only her husband had given her in the past.

If I could only figure out how I got here, she thought, and huffed in frustration. *I barely remember anything that happened after Teesa left. We drank and talked for a couple of hours, and then I got really sleepy. She got a call and left. The next thing I know I am fuckin' some nigga I don't even know. I had to be drugged.*

Oh, my dear Lord, she silently exclaimed after several minutes of thought.

I have something that will help you sleep. I'll call you in a few to make sure they kicked in.

After that, Delilah started having flashes of rolling around in her bed with the mysterious man. She concentrated and thought back to the wild sex she had had, and she broke down in tears as she pictured his face. She faintly remembered him pulling off her blindfold momentarily so he could stare in her eyes as she gave him head, and once again to place a gun into the barrel of her mouth. In her dark silence she went back three years in her thoughts to the mall and placed the face.

"Delilah, girl. Do you see that nigga over there? He is a cutie," Teesa said.

Delilah looked and smiled. "Don't look now, but he is walking in this direction. I think you got his attention, girl," Delilah said, nudging Teesa. Seconds later the guy approached them and gently took Delilah by the hand. She pulled it back and flashed a fake smile. Teesa rolled her eyes and shot Delilah a look of contempt as she sucked her teeth and folded her arms.

"Hi, what's your name, gorgeous?" the guy said to Delilah.

"Delilah, and I'm married," she was quick to say.

He looked into her eyes. "That's not a problem. I can treat you better," he replied.

"This is my friend Teesa. What's your name?"

"Bobby . . ."

The face from last night was the face of her best friend's man. She let her head fall back as she came to the realization, which caused her head to sting.

Oh, my God! Teesa and Bobby set me up. It's him—I remember his face. She thought hard and long, but the previous night's activities were almost a blur. Then faintly she remembered having sex with Teesa, and the mere thought made her sick. The vomit that filled her throat got no release. She regurgitated as visions of her sucking Teesa's pussy went from blurry to being crystal-clear. Again, she needed to vomit. The Alizé and Hennessy came up this time and began to seep from her nose. Delilah could not breathe. She tried to inhale through her nose, but that was clogged with vomit. She continued to gag as she hurled her insides up a third time.

At one twenty in the afternoon Guy pulled up to the designated spot. He saw the empty white Maxima parked on the curb and peered around. The block wasn't overpopulated, but there were enough people walking by. He sat for ten minutes thinking about his wife and who could have set him up. At one thirty sharp he got out of the car with a Nike duffel bag hanging off of his shoulder. He walked over to the Maxima, lifted the trunk, dumped the bag inside, and slammed it shut. He looked around and, of course, as always, the busy people on the Brooklyn streets paid him no mind. He hopped into his car and drove away. He waited for his phone to ring, but nothing happened. He traveled back to Jamaine's house, and hours passed as they waited impatiently for some kind of communication.

"I think we should call the police," Jay said.

"Are you fuckin' nuts?" Guy said. "The only thing that will do is lead back to me and what I do. I just want my wife back safe."

Then an awkward silence invaded the room as Guy began to suspect his own friends.

How the fuck did Jamaine call so fast? It was only minutes after twelve. Did he just go outside and find my wife's scalp in the fuckin' mailbox, and why was that shit still in the mailbox and not on the ground when I got there? Who checks their muthafuckin' mail so early in the afternoon anyway? In the middle of his thoughts he looked at Jay. *Why was this nigga so calm when I told him what happened? He know where everything in the crib is. He has the combination to the safe, and he is the only person Delilah can let in while I am OT.*

As he took his attention off of Jay and looked at Rome his cell phone rang. He answered and heard that same male voice again.

"I got my paper," the voice said. "It's all here, and so is your wife. Go to the Holiday Inn on Route Seventeen. She is in room four twenty-seven, and you better hurry. Your bitch don't look so good. You should take her to the GYN or something."

The voice laughed and then hung up. Guy didn't say a word.

He looked at his friends as he stood up slowly. He was light-headed so he immediately sat back down.

"You all right, nigga? Was that them? What did they say?" Jay questioned.

"They said Delilah is at the Holiday Inn on Route Seventeen in room four twenty-seven, and she needs to see a doctor," Guy answered.

His boys were winded by the news, but stood quietly wrapped up in their own selfish thoughts that involved what they would have done if they were in the same situation. Jay stood and grabbed his boy by the hand, pulling him off of the couch. Guy was weak at the knees and could barely stand, so Jay placed Guy's arm around him and helped him out of the house into his car.

Guy was beside himself the entire ride to New Jersey. His wife was only fifteen minutes away from their lovely home. *Why the fuck didn't I think to look there? I should have searched every damn hotel in this area,* he cursed himself inside.

When they pulled up in front of the hotel, Jay hopped out and Guy remained seated. He didn't know what to expect. Every kidnapping he'd known of in the past ten years left the victim for dead, whether the ransom was made or not. Jay came around to the passenger side of the car and helped his man to his feet.

Onlookers found it odd that a man would be that drunk this early in the day. Naturally, that was what everyone in the Holiday Inn assumed Guy was—drunk. Even the police officer who had pulled him over had mistaken his swollen eyes for alcohol, when it was only a severe case of guilt mixed with grief.

They entered the hotel lobby and took the elevator to the fourth floor. It was a silent ride as each man feared what they might find. As they exited the elevator, they found their way to room 427. The gold slam lock was wedged between the door and its frame, so Jay was able to push it open with ease and literally dragged his man inside. As soon as they walked into the room, sex and sulfur filled their nostrils. They couldn't believe their eyes. Delilah lay there naked on her side, bound and seated in a chair that lay on top of the bed. Brown bile leaked from her nose onto the starched white sheets. Her head was bare and painfully red, with only patches of several long strands of hair sprouting from it. There were pus-filled boils and bumps with dried-up blood and raw flesh in the places where her hair was gone. Her eyes and mouth were covered by duct tape.

Jay turned his back to the bed, and Guy fell at her bedside. He tapped her arm, but she didn't move. He shook her in the chair and she still did not budge. In a panic he checked for her pulse, but it was nowhere to be found. He dropped to the ground at her bedside and cried like a newborn baby as Jay picked up the phone and dialed 911.

As Jay yelled into the phone in panic, Guy suddenly went blank. His emotions ceased as if he had done nothing more than turn off a switch. He stood up and wiped his tears away, but before leaving his wife's side, he bent down and whispered in her ear and then kissed her on the cheek. Someone had made the mistake of thinking that the game was over. They were probably somewhere now enjoying his money and the benefits his tragedy had brought to them. But, in fact, they were sadly mistaken. The game was just beginning, as Guy had just vowed to his dead wife that he would see to it that everyone who had any part in her demise would pay . . . they would pay with their lives.

Guy looked over at Jay, who had just hung up the phone. Jay returned the stare, almost not recognizing the friend who stood before him. Guy almost wasn't recognizable to himself. He had put on his game face, that of a coldhearted man out for revenge, determined not to rest until the death of his wife was avenged.

COVERING ALL THE BASES . . .

JOY

BEYATCH!!!

Definition of a beyatch: A broad who makes the average bitch look like Snow White, markin' her territory by pissin' razor blades on the world.

CHAPTER ONE
MY SISTER'S KEEPER

There was no loving Tahjanaya Cortez, aka, Tahj. When it came to her, grimy, mean-ass muthafuckas either hated her or hated her more. She was that bitch broads made friends with just to keep her close. Besides, it was far better to pretend to be her friend than to for real be her enemy.

Tahj was an in-your-face, I-don't-give-a-fuck type of girl, and she wasn't no backstabbin' broad, that was for sure. She'd put the knife right through a muthafucka's heart. Someone once said, "Why tell the world that you are coming when you can just show the fuck up?" They obviously had never encountered Tahj. When it came to her, a warning was definitely in order.

As a child, Tahj was the sweetest chocolate chip in the bag.

Out of all four of her brothers and sisters she was the most obe-
dient. While the others were acting out in school, stealing money
from their mother's purse, drinking and smoking weed, or fucking in their mother's bed, Tahj was always doing what she was
supposed to do.

She wasn't a genius when it came to school—an average student at best—but she got her work done. In high school most of
her brothers and sisters were known by name by the school ad-
ministrators. This was due to the fact that they were always in the
office being reprimanded for one thing or another. But Tahj, on
the other hand, brought very little attention to herself. Although
no one could mistake the five children for anything but kin, with
each of them being the spitting image of their pretty brown-
skinned mother, Tahj fought not to be compared to them. It was
almost as if she wished she weren't any kin to the badass fuckers.
Unlike her rowdy or fast-ass siblings, Tahj was timid and shy
growing up. She didn't have any boyfriends. It wasn't because she
wasn't pretty. She had straight jet-black hair that almost touched
her shoulders. Her dark brown skin was clear, and her brown eyes
almost looked black, they were so deep. She had a cute set of dim-
ples and perfectly straight white teeth. But growing up in the
loud, out-of-order, three-bedroom, zoolike apartment, Tahj didn't
stand out. She was hardly even noticeable. But by the summer following Tahj's senior year of high school, all of that would change.

After high school there wasn't anywhere for Tahj to go. She had
never thought about it—or life after turning eighteen, for that
matter. The school counselors, even though they had no trouble
out of her, figured she was doomed, due to her living circumstances and the influence of her siblings, so they never even presented her with the idea of college. She was the middle child; her
two oldest siblings had moved out to torment society, her younger
brother had gone to jail, which was where his father was, and her

fourteen-year-old sister, the baby of the family, had just given birth to a baby of her own. So it was Tahj, her baby sister, the new baby, and their work-a-twelve-hour-shift and go-out-and-get-crunked mother left in the apartment. Once she turned eighteen, as far as her mother was concerned, Tahj was officially grown, so she looked for reasons to kick Tahj's ass out of her house. Well, on one particular night, Tahj gave it to her.

It was five months earlier, only four months after Tahj's eighteenth birthday. Tahj, her sister, and the baby were sound asleep on a Monday night when their mother and her company made a noisy entrance into the apartment. In a matter of minutes, loud music shook the house, and the cries of the baby followed.

"What the . . . ?" Tahj said, sitting up in her bed, rubbing her eyes. She looked over at the digital clock on the nightstand that sat in between her and her little sister Lena's bed. "It's two o'clock in the morning."

"Damn," Lena groaned. "I finally just got the baby to go to sleep. All she been doing is staying up crying with the colic, and now she's up again."

"Go on and pick her up. Lay her on your stomach and see if the sound of your heartbeat will soothe her back to sleep. I'll go see what the hell is going on out there."

As Lena proceeded to follow her sister's advice, walking over to the crib that sat in their bedroom, Tahj put on her robe and headed for the living room.

Walking down the hallway to the living room of their one-floor apartment, Tahj could hear voices trying to talk over Beyoncé's and those other two girls in the group. Once she made her way to the living room she saw three black dudes, a white chick, some heavyset red bone, and her mother. They were drinking, talkin' loud, and about to set up for a game of spades. Tahj couldn't believe her eyes. It was two in the morning on a Monday night. Tahj thought that only her mother could work all day at the post office as part of the janitorial crew, head straight to the bar, and still have enough energy for a nightcap. The fact that Tahj's mother ran the streets like a teenager had never really bothered her. Hell, when her mother was home, if she wasn't fussing about nothing, she was lying in bed ordering her around to bring her food, drinks, or just to turn the television up in her room. So Tahj didn't mind at all if her mother ran the streets, but what she did mind was the streets running up in where they had to lay their heads.

"Ma," Tahj said tiredly. Her mother was too busy shaking her ass up on one of the men. Tahj had seen the man before. He had been to the house a couple of times to pick her mother up. This was his first time coming up in the apartment, though. Usually he just pulled up in his heather-gray Lexus and blew the horn for her. He was a nice-looking brotha, a little younger than her mother, but nice-looking all the same. "Ma," Tahj repeated, a little louder. Still getting no response, Tahj decided to walk over to the CD player and turn the volume down.

"What the hell is going on?" her mother said, slurring her words. She then looked up and saw Tahj standing by the CD player. "Turn that back up, girl. That's my song." Her mother started singing the words without the song playing.

"Ma, it's two in the morning. You woke the baby up, and it took Lena all night to get her to sleep. You know the baby got colic. Lena's got school in the morning. I got work. You got work, too. You should be sleep."

A sudden silence that was as sharp as a knife filled the room. Tahj's mother couldn't believe her child was standing in her living room trying to lecture her like she was the child. As hard as she had worked to keep a roof over her family's head and feed them, never mind if she didn't have time to properly tend to her children and give them the love and attention they needed to be productive in life—but she'd be damned if one of 'em was going to stand in her own house and try to tell her what to do in front of her company.

"Who in the fuck do you think you talkin' to?" her mother snapped at her. The dude she had been dancing with tried to grab her arm and calm her down, because he knew she was about to clown.

This stunned Tahj, because her mother had never talked fresh to her. Oh, she had heard her cuss the other kids out plenty of times. She called Lena a ho and a whore throughout her entire pregnancy, but never had her mother talked to Tahj in such a tone. As a matter of fact, her mother never really talked to her at all. Perhaps that was why the other kids did the things they did—to get some attention from her, even if it was negative attention.

"This is my muthafuckin' house," her mother continued in a fierce rage, pulling her arm from the man who was trying to restrain her.

"Teena, baby," the man said in a mellow tone. "Be cool. We can take the party elsewhere. It ain't nothin'. Li'l mama here is right." He then turned to Tahj to speak to her directly. He looked at her, his brown eyes were like two pecans in sugar cookie dough. They were each a perfect oval, inherited from his Asian mother. His hair was a cross between what some black folks referred to as good hair—that wavy, Indian type of hair that curled up—and just regular ol' hair, inherited from his black father. He was very gentlemanly, courtesy of his upbringing. "My bad. We didn't know anybody else was in the house. Our apologies." He then addressed the others. "Come on, y'all. Let's ride out."

"No, Lee!" Teena shouted to him. "This is my house, I said. Let her ass ride out. Y'all stay put. I don't know what everybody so tired for and tryin' to sleep. Y'all's lazy asses don't do shit."

"Ma, we your kids," Tahj said, her feelings now hurt. "You wanna put us out over some company? I was just sayin' that you woke the baby up. And besides, Lena went to school all day. I worked at CVS all day. We cooked dinner and we cleaned the house. We ain't lazy. We doing the best we can do, and we just want some sleep 'fore we gotta get up and do it all over again in the morning. You at least owe us that."

Her mother sighed and looked at her as if Tahj were crazy.

"I don't owe you shit, bitch," her mother said to her. "You eighteen now, so as a matter of fact, you owe me. You all up in my shit tryin' to be grown. Well, grown muthafuckas pay they own way, and since you don't, like I said, you need to ride out."

Tahj was speechless. She didn't know what to say or do. This was the first time she and her mother had ever actually taken five minutes to have a conversation. She'd had no idea her mother would react to her this way. So she just stood there, hoping that the liquor would wear off of her mother's brain, therefore ceasing the lashing out it was forcing her tongue to make. But before she could do anything, her mother was coming at her, yanking her by the arm and pushing her toward the front door.

"You heard me, bitch. Get the fuck out," her mother yelled.

"Ma, stop it!" Lena yelled from down the hall. She was halfway out of the bedroom door, holding the baby in her arms. The baby started yelling even louder. Needless to say, her mother ignored her cry and continued to put Tahj out of the house.

"Ma, stop it." Tahj began to cry. "You know I ain't got nowhere to go. It's the middle of the night."

"Then, bitch, you should have thought about that before you came out here runnin' your mouth," her mother replied. "You should have thought about that warm bed your ass was lying in for free before you talked your ass out onto the cold concrete."

"Please, Ma," Tahj pleaded, twisting and turning her arms, trying to loosen them from her mother's grip.

"No, Ma," Lena screamed over the baby's yelping. "No, Ma, no."

Tahj took her free hand and tried to loosen the grip her mother had on her arm. When she did so, Teena took it as if Tahj were trying to fight her back. Out of nowhere she hauled off and backhanded Tahj with all her might across the face. Tahj was dazed as blood poured from her nose. She just stood there for a minute, trying to maintain her balance, literally seeing stars, little white flashes. She could feel the trickle of the blood reach her lips. She wiped it with her hand, the entire time still dizzy and trying to keep her balance. Her vision was even a little blurred for a moment.

The room seemed dead silent as Tahj just stood there. But the baby's cry soon brought her fully back to the grim reality. She looked down the hall at her sister, who had her hand over her mouth in disbelief. Until now their mother had never laid a hand on any of the children, not even when they stole from her purse, not even when she found condom wrappers in her bedroom. But for reasons unknown to Tahj, she felt the need to strike the child who never, ever gave her any trouble.

"Please don't," Lena said to Tahj softly, shaking her head.

Since the baby, and it being just the two siblings left in the house, Tahj and Lena had started to form a bond. Tahj helped Lena out with the baby and her schoolwork. She was a comfort—a comfort Lena had never had in her mother. "Don't leave me. Please don't leave us." Lena looked down at the baby.

It broke Tahj's heart, but she knew that there was no way in hell she was going to stay in that house. Tears began to run down Tahj's face as she looked at her sister standing there holding her niece. She cried because she pitied her. Tahj didn't see her sister: she saw her mother, the cycle repeating itself. She then looked at her mother, who was waiting impatiently for Tahj to get the fuck out of her house. Her fist was balled and she was huffing and puffing as if she were going to hit Tahj again any minute now. She hated to leave Lena there, where she wouldn't be paid attention to, where she wouldn't get any hugs, kisses, or any sign of love, where she would probably end up having five kids herself and more than likely raise them in that very same apartment.

The last thing she wanted to do was leave her little sister there to become a product of that environment. But if she stayed to watch out for Lena, who would be there to watch out for Tahj? Who would be her keeper? Tahj hated the split-second decision she had to make. Perhaps she should have fought for her spot in that apartment, and maybe her mother would have come to her senses and given in. But deep down inside, Tahj knew that this might be her only chance to get out. She would have to leave sooner or later. She hated to do it, but she knew the sooner, the better. Her mother hadn't wanted her around in the first place. She was sure to make her life a living hell now.

What was a teenage girl to do when not even her own mama would have her back? Tahj didn't think about all of that; she just walked out the door into the arms of her new adoptive mother, the streets. It was then that Tahj realized that no matter who she encountered in life, at the end of the day, all she had was herself. So from that moment on, Tahj was always out for self.

The big fight with Tahj and her mother had taken place five months ago. It was in the past now. Tahj didn't have to think twice about Teena now that she was living in a plushed-out crib in the 'burbs of Cleveland, Ohio. But Lord only knew where she would have ended up if Lee hadn't followed her out of her mother's house that night and taken her in.

CHAPTER TWO
EVERY SUGA DADDY
AIN'T SWEET

"Ain't shit a nigga in this world can do for me," was how Tahj would put it. "A bitch neither, for that matter." And she damn sure wasn't going to do shit for nobody else. How she saw it now was that she was alone in this world. But fuck it! This was her world. Everybody else was simply on a lease agreement.

Tahj was too selfish even to notice when somebody was doing something nice for her. She felt like muthafuckas owed her; therefore, she appreciated very little and took for granted everything, even Lee. She loved him and was glad that he had taken her in and provided her with the finer things life could offer, but she'd say, "Fuck you," to him faster than the speed of light if it came down to it.

Having never met her father perhaps was one reason she lashed out at men the way she did. You could say the same for the lashings she gave bitches, too. Because as far as she was concerned, she might as well have never met her mother either. She couldn't see how knowing her had affected her positively at all. As far as Tahj was concerned, neither her mother nor her father played a beneficial part in her life.

Where the fuck was they at to tell me about the fucked-up hand my life could be dealt? Tahj often thought. *Not one of them warned me about life, about the streets, about all the bullshit I would have to endure just to make it as a young black female.*

Even when Tahj was right underneath her own mother's roof, she never longed for her touch. Hell, she didn't even desire her attention; that was why she'd always stayed to herself. But never in a million years would she have thought her mother would throw her out of the house knowing she had nothing and nowhere to go. Not even once did her mother come for her and try to talk her into coming back home. Perhaps she would have if she hadn't heard about Lee taking in Tahj and making her his PYT.

Teena couldn't take the blow to her ego—her man friend choosing her daughter over her. Her husband, the older children's father, had already left her for another woman—another girl, rather. She was some teenage slut who used to live next door to them. One day, right after Tahj was born, he just up and left Teena and the kids to be with this girl.

Lena hadn't been born yet. Lena's daddy was some white man whose office Teena used to clean. She thought that trappin' him with a baby would put her on easy street. She figured he'd marry her rather than admit he had an illegitimate child. Then she'd have herself a husband with a good job and a well-to-do white daddy for her other kids. In Teena's fucked-up state of mind, she figured a white man could bring far more to the table than a black man ever could. The white man could go from job to job and not worry about the prejudices of not getting hired because of the color of his skin. She knew a white man would always be able to make a way for her and her kids because the country respected his skin more than a black man's. Little did Teena know, but the fool was already married and had three kids of his own. The coward shot himself in the head when Teena showed up at his office with that chocolate baby, threatening to ruin his life if he didn't make good on the situation and be a father to Lena. So Teena had one man who didn't want to be with her and ran off with a girl who hadn't even grown all the hair on her pussy yet, and another man who'd rather be dead than to be with her. Then Lee's choosing Tahj over her destroyed Teena's already damaged ego.

If Teena wasn't a stone-cold drunk out on the streets before, trying to find Mr. Whoever Will Have Me, she certainly was now.

But Tahj could not have cared less about what her mama was doing. It wasn't long before even Lena and her niece weren't on her mind anymore. Her past was just that—her past—and the way she saw it, nothing good could come from any of it. She had no intention of ever turning back or bringing anything from the past into her future, not even Lena. The only thing any of Tahj's life experiences did for her was to make her hard and uncaring.

It may have been safe to say that Lee was a partial exception. Deep, deep down inside, Tahj had love for Lee; she truly did. But she refused to give him all of her love. The way she saw it, he was only human, which still meant that he could turn on her in the blink of an eye and leave her hanging. Using her own mother as an example, it took eighteen years for Teena to eventually turn her back on Tahj, but in the end, that was exactly what she did. Tahj had had a warm place to stay and food to eat and one fall night it was all taken from her. So even with all that Lee had done for her, keeping her laced and iced out with a nice set of wheels, a laid-out home that she shared with him, and a jiggy wardrobe, she still physically and mentally prepared herself for the day he would hurt her, the day he would perhaps throw her away, too. To protect her feelings, Tahj made it up in her head from the beginning that at the end of the day, Lee was nothing more to her than a sugar daddy.

Tahj hadn't been with Lee a month before she started pinching on his personal stash, both money and drugs. Lee never brought weight into the home, but he did keep coke for recreational use here and there. Tahj smoked a little weed, but she didn't do hard drugs like coke. But she'd sure enough flip it for some fast loot in a heartbeat. She had all kinds of ways to put a few extra dollars in her pocket. Whenever Lee was going out of town for a couple of days, she'd ask him for money to go shopping while he was gone. She'd buy him a little something and simply deposit the rest into her bank account. Lee never asked her what she bought, because she would have already distracted him by presenting him with the gift she had bought him.

If shit else didn't motivate Tahj in life, money did. She knew that was what made the world go 'round, and without it you could get dizzy just standing there watching it turn. If she found a quarter lying on the ground, she'd pick it up and deposit it into what she called her "the day will come" account. It wasn't family and it wasn't fake-ass friends that kept Tahj moving through life at a rigidly fast pace. It was money. The last thing she desired was any type of comfort from anybody, even a man.

Now cold and callous, Tahj didn't even long for the man who planted the seed for her to be born. As a matter of fact, she didn't know why her mother had felt the need to give birth to her in the first place. It should be against the law for just any bitch to pop a baby out of her pussy and officially earn the title of mother. That was bullshit, as far as Tahj was concerned. There was too much dirt out in the world to do to get caught up in some ol' emotional bullshit. So Tahj brushed her emotions under the rug like they were broken glass and proceeded to become better acquainted with the streets.

F uck me! Fuck me good, baby!" Tahj shouted as she balled her fist, twisting and turning her body as her arms remained hand-cuffed to the wrought-iron bars of the king-size headboard. Her chocolate, five-foot-seven-inch, 125-pound body lay stretched across the bed.

"You like that shit? You like that?" Lee said, slapping her across the face with each stroke.

"Oh, Lee!" Tahj exclaimed as she raised her hips in order to stay close to Lee's dick, which was feeling all too good to her.

Going 'round and 'round, Lee's dick was hittin' every corner of Tahj's sugar walls. Tahj had been a virgin the first time she ever had sex with Lee, but over the past few months he had taught her shit that porno stars wasn't up on.

"That's right," Lee said, his ass cheeks squeezing tight on the downstroke, sweat dripping off of his body onto Tahj's as he pumped in and out of her as hard as he could. That was his pussy. No other dick had even gotten a peek at it, as far as he knew.

But Tahj knew better. She knew how to make Lee feel like the only one, even though he was one of many. In Lee's eyes, Tahj was the sweet girl he had watched plead with her mother that night for the comfort and security of her and her little sister and niece. She was helpless and dependent upon him. But that was just what Tahj wanted him to think about her. Tahj learned early in the game that the more dependent a man thought she was on him, the more he did for her. Just as soon as a woman let a man know she was independent and could do for herself, the less he felt he needed to do for her ass, and the less he felt he needed her around. So while other women were out getting degrees, trying to climb the corporate ladder and shit to impress a man and get a husband, Tahj played as dumb as a box of rocks with Lee and got more than any bitch with a college degree could have.

Being a hustler, Lee was always out clockin' them ends. New York, B-more, Florida, Chi-town, you name it, and Lee was there. He was away more than he was home. Tahj never saw the logic in all of his hustlin' if he couldn't sit down, relax, and enjoy it. But like most hustlers, he worked hard planning for a comfortable re-tirement, not knowing that his retirement home would probably be a ten-by-nine cell, and that it would be Uncle Sam sippin' on mai tais and enjoying the labor of his years' worth of work.

No sooner would Lee hit the highway to head out of town to handle his business than Tahj would hit the streets to see what was good and who was good. It was like winning the jackpot when Tahj discovered all the sugar daddies in the hood just waiting to take care of a ghetto princess like her. She never worried about Lee hearing things about her on the streets, because Lee wasn't no street cat. He didn't even associate with those lames. He did big thangs. Niggas on the streets more or less had heard of him, versus knowing him, but he didn't know, nor did he care to know, who those lame-ass knuckleheads were. Lee had no desire to fuck with the little paper that knowing muthafuckas on the streets brought. He was interested only in the Donald Trumps and Bill Gateses of the game. Supposedly, Lee kept only one nigga close to him, and that was a dude who went by the name Zon. But no one really knew him either. Not even Tahj had met him. She had heard Lee talk to him a couple of times on the phone before, but Lee was strict about not mixing his personal life with his business life. Cats would lie and shit, saying that they had hung out and kicked it with Lee at his crib or something. But because no one knew anyone who knew Lee, they couldn't verify the stories—but they couldn't discredit them, either. It was safe to say that Lee was something of a hood legend. So what he had seen in her mother, she never knew.

This was what enabled Tahj to get her own hustle on, and she was definitely the true definition of a hustler. Hustlin' was doing whatever the fuck had to be done in order to be on top when the game was over. Tahj never wanted to put out more than half of what she was getting. She never wanted anyone to profit off of her. Even if it meant switching price tags on shit in stores or not telling the clerk that there was soda pop under the cart, or even stealing a retarded man's money. Once the game was over, the hustler was the one who got over, and when someone is over, they sure wasn't under, which means they're on top. It was always Tahj's desire to be on top and stay there. Though Lee spent very little time with Tahj, he always made her feel like she was on top.

"I'm about to cum. I'm about to cum," Tahj moaned as she wildly smacked her pelvis against Lee's. He pushed his back into her. The two looked as if they were having seizures.

"Oh, shit, girl," Lee shouted as he stuck his index finger into Tahj's mouth. She began sucking on it, allowing slobber to drip down the sides of her mouth.

"Oh, umm," she moaned, taking in his finger and taking in his dick.

Lee's toned physique all of a sudden went stiff as he let Tahj do all the work.

"Get that dick, baby," he moaned. "Get it."

"Uh, yeah, uh, yeah. Oh, God," Tahj shouted as she began to cum on Lee's dick. This turned Lee on and he picked up the tempo, putting his hand around her throat and thrusting in and out of her.

"Oh, shit!" Lee yelled as he jerked inside Tahj. "Oh, shit, baby." He then removed his hand from Tahj's throat and grabbed himself as if he wanted to manually shove his dick into Tahj. He wanted to feel her wetness.

"Oh, baby," Tahj cooed as she came down off of her sexual high. "Oh, baby."

"Whew. Damn!" Lee said as he rolled over next to her. He closed his eyes and just lay there, breathing heavily.

Tahj looked over at him, watching his chest go up and down. Her eyes grazed his creamy skin, and a smile covered her face. *He's so beautiful*, Tahj caught herself thinking. *Maybe he really does love me.* She allowed herself to be taken in by the moment, wondering if perhaps she and Lee could have a real, lasting future together. He was older, so he didn't play the games that the dudes she had hooked up with in the streets played. Maybe he was different from all of the men she had known in her short life. But just in case he wasn't, Tahj decided that she wasn't going to take any chances.

Mi-Mi-Mi-Miss Lady," Ray stuttered, galloping behind Tahj, who had just gotten the mail out of the mailbox.

"Not now, Ray," Tahj said, irritated. It never failed. It was like clockwork. Anytime Tahj was outside the house, be it bringing in the mail or the paper, or just watering the grass, trying to be cute in her Daisy Duke shorts, here came Ray the retard to fuck with her. Tahj figured that Ray was just some retarded grown-ass man who lived with his parents because he was too stupid to make it on his own. He couldn't function in society, so she guessed he had nothing better to do than to watch for a neighbor to show their face and then bug the shit out of them.

"Bu-bu-but, Miss Lady," Ray insisted excitedly. "I got somethin', somethin', somethin' to te-te-tell you."

Tahj tried to ignore him by staring down at the mail and walking away from him, but he just kept following her. Finally, Tahj stopped in her tracks and turned to him.

"You know," she said, glaring at him, "you remind me of the black guy in that movie *The Hand That Rocks the Cradle*. You know, the retarded one." Tahj cut Ray a sharp look, then continued walking.

"Tha-tha-tha-thank you, Missssss Lady," Ray said with a smile. "No one, no one's ever sssssssssaid I looked like a ma-ma-movie star before."

Tahj rolled her eyes in disgust. She knew that whatever it was Ray had to tell her, he wasn't going to let her be until she listened.

"All right, Ray," Tahj said. "What do you want to te-te-te-tell me?" Tahj mocked him.

A huge grin came across Ray's face. "I-I-I-I found a dollar!"

"Yippee," Tahj said in a meaningless and dry tone.

"Ain-ain-ain't it purty?" he asked, holding it up.

Tahj looked up at the bill Ray was proudly displaying. "Let me see it," she said, snatching it from Ray's hands.

"Ca-ca-careful," Ray said.

Tahj examined the bill, then said to Ray, "This is a dirty old dollar, Ray. I have a real pretty one inside. You'll like that one much better. I'll go get it for you."

Tahj headed up the porch, and Ray followed.

"You wait right here," Tahj ordered Ray as she opened the door and entered the house.

With the door open, Ray peeked in the house. He could see some guy sitting on the couch with his feet propped on the table. He didn't have on a shirt, and he was sipping on a drink.

Although she did it only on rare occasions, Tahj would occasionally invite one of her tricks over to the house. But they were always from out of town, somebody Tahj would probably never lay eyes on again and who damn sure couldn't find his way back to her spot.

"What' choo doin', ma?" the guy asked Tahj as she walked over to the table and grabbed her purse from underneath it.

"Nothing," she replied. "Just getting a dollar for this retarded dude down the street."

The guy looked over to the door and saw Ray standing out on the porch. Ray was waving and just smiling. The guy waved back. Tahj stood up to head back toward the door.

"Hurry on back in here," the guy said, slappin' Tahj on the ass. "Daddy ready for seconds."

"Yeah, yeah," Tahj said. "You could barely eat your first helping."

"Ho, fuck you," the inadequate trick said, getting an attitude.

Ignoring him, Tahj switched back over to the door and handed Ray a fresh, crisp one-dollar bill, just like she promised him.

"Tha-tha-thank you, Misssss Lady," Ray said, waving the dollar. "This is al-al-allllmost as purty assssssss you."

"You're welcome," Tahj said. "Now get to gettin'." She watched Ray excitedly walk down the street admiring the fresh new dollar. She closed the door, glad she had acquainted Ray with a nice, clean George Washington, but even happier that he had acquainted her with the Benjamin Franklin that he had actually found.

"That was nice of you," the guy said once Tahj rejoined him on the sofa.

"Yeah, well, I try," she bragged.

"So what about them seconds?" he asked as he began to kiss Tahj's neck.

Tahj rolled her eyes up in her head. She had been quite bored with her fill-in sugar daddy, some guy from West Virginia, after only a few minutes of meeting him. She thought he had big bank, but as it turned out, the dude he was rollin' with was the real G. This guy was just his flunky.

Tahj had met him out at some club called the Gate. Every time she asked him to buy her a drink he'd peel off a twenty and hand it to her. She'd go buy a Coke, minus the rum, and pocket the change. By the time Tahj had spit game and had that nigga in the palm of her hands, ready to pay for the pussy, his partner showed up at the club lookin' the part of a big baller. That nigga got to ordering her guy around like he was his bitch or something. Tahj's pussy went dry just witnessing that shit, but fuck it, she had already played up to him half the night. Tahj was sick about it, though. If only she had waited and scoped out the club a little longer before stepping to that lame.

"I can't give you seconds, baby. You know I gotta go to work, and you need to get going. If I'm late, they'll dock my pay," Tahj lied, because she knew the next thing that was going to come out of dude's mouth. She had played this scene out over and over again. Same scene, different nigga.

"Shit, I'll pay you a day's wages. You ain't said shit, ma," he said, pulling out several bills and throwing them on the table.

Oh, well, I guess every suga daddy ain't sweet, Tahj thought. *But it won't hurt to settle for semisweet every once in a while, I suppose.* Tahj smiled and proceeded to put it on him.

CHAPTER THREE
KNOCKED UP

"I know we at your house and it's your bathroom and all, but can a chick piss in peace, goddamn it?" Tahj said to Pooh as she stood in front of the toilet fixin' to pull her pants down.

"As many times as I done ran up in that pussy, I know you ain't worried about me seeing it now," Pooh said, not about to take his eyes off of Tahj for even a second.

She huffed, sucked her teeth, and rolled her eyes. "Nigga, ain't nobody tryin' to trick yo' ass. What the fuck make you think I wanna be carrying your seed in me?"

" 'Cause bitches is scandalous," Pooh answered. "Now piss on that stick so I can see if a plus sign or a minus sign turn up."

"Nigga, this ain't no math test," Tahj said, intentionally stalling. "It's gon' turn pink or stay white. What the fuck you talkin' that arithmetic shit for?"

"Just piss already. Damn!"

In between fighting like cats and dogs, Tahj and Pooh somehow managed to find the time to screw. Pooh was what Tahj referred to as her layover. He was just some nigga whose house she could stay in and get a good lay while Lee was away. The sex was always off the chain with Pooh's exhibitionist ass. That nigga did everything from lick ass to wantin' a bitch to stick they finger up his. But through it all, the last thing Pooh wanted as a result of their off-the-hook sexual escapades was a baby. He already had two babies by two different girls from around the way. On top of that, he had taken care of a third little bastard for two years before finding out that he wasn't even the baby's daddy. Come to find out the baby's mother had both him and some other cat thinkin' they was the father. She was juicin' both them niggas for mad loot every month.

Once Pooh found out the real, he caught that bitch out at a club and fronted like he wanted to get with her. She went out to his Suburban, willing and ready to suck him to sleep. Just as she leaned over to do her thang he grabbed that bitch by her hair and gripped his other hand around her neck like a fuckin' pit bull was locked on it. He told her that he didn't care what she had to do to get it, but she was gon' pay him back every dime he had given her for a kid that wasn't even his. He threatened that the next time she saw the little bastard, he was gon' be on a milk carton.

Knowing that Pooh was a man of his word, not one to waste time talkin' 'bout shit he couldn't make good on, that bitch did everything from raking leaves to hittin' the block sellin' pussy to get that nigga what she owed him. Eventually Pooh let her off the hook before she was able to pay back anything even close to all of the money he had dished out to her for that kid. He just had to let that bitch know what time it was so that the next ho wouldn't get any ideas. Some people said that deep down inside Pooh loved kids and would never have done anything to hers. That just went to show that some people really didn't know Pooh very well.

Every gold-diggin' ho in the city was trying to get at Pooh. He was rough around the edges, but inside he was smooth as a kite sailing on a windy day. If it just happened to be a chick's lucky day to get a taste of Pooh's fine ass, then more than likely she spent that night schemin' and manipulating on ways to try to keep him. Just one taste was never enough for the average broad.

Built like a bronze stallion, Pooh stood an even six feet, with dark brown eyes, dark hair that he kept cut in a low fade, and a dark past. A notorious hustler, slingin' them thangs since he could learn to count, Pooh was known for handling any muthafucka who tried him. It didn't take long for cats to recognize that Pooh just wasn't to be fucked with. Pooh was no hood legend. That nigga was the truth.

Tahj wasn't your average anything either. Wasn't shit gon' keep her from doing her. The hand she had been dealt wasn't holdin' the ace, so what the fuck did she have to lose in this lifetime? Takin' life serious in a world full of muthafuckas who, if they weren't tryin' to get in the game, were tryin' to get out, was lame. Life was a game that needed to be played. The only problem when it came to Tahj was that there were no rules and it was always her turn.

Tahj had already inserted the valve she had gotten from a medical supply store into her pussy before she even walked into Pooh's house. It was one of those tubes they used to fill at the doctor's office when taking a patient's blood. She wore a white doctor's coat she had picked up at the thrift store when she bought it so that the store clerk would assume she was a lobotomist or something. She had actually driven to the hood and found some pregnant girl to piss for her. She had to pay her one hundred dollars, but she knew there was a profit to be made at the end.

Pooh watched as Tahj started to pee.

"Damn!" she yelled. "I got piss all over my hand. Get me a rag." When Pooh turned to get Tahj a rag, she popped the cap on the valve and let the urine pour onto the stick.

Needless to say, when Pooh saw the pink, he forked over a grand to Tahj for her to get an abortion. Tahj had made a $900 profit off some pregnant bitch's piss.

Plus, after faking the abortion, she acted as though it had mentally fucked with her. Pooh started treating her like she was a queen, Nikki Turner or some shit. Tahj played right into it, too. For a minute there, besides Lee, Pooh was the only nigga Tahj would fuck with. Pooh was a big enough player in the game, which was Little League compared to the league Lee played in, that Tahj could get out of him what she couldn't even get out of three or four niggas. So the shit was sort of like a vacation to Tahj.

But when some nigga tried Pooh one night while he was out at the club, Pooh bladed that nigga, slit his throat. Said he talked too much, and now, without his vocals, he couldn't say shit. Believe it or not, the dude he sliced up didn't even die. The doctors said that if the blade had gone just one-tenth of a centimeter deeper, the guy would have lost his life. He may not have lost his life, but Pooh lost his freedom.

Tahj sat in her living room reading a letter out loud to this chick named Shea that Pooh had written her from jail. He had one of his boys bring it up to the shop to her one day while she was getting her hair done. His boys had been schoolin' him on what the word was about Tahj on the street, how she was playin' muthafuckas left and right. Pooh was on fire, to say the least.

" 'You ain't even brought your ass up here to see me once. On top of that, you won't take my calls on your celly,' " Tahj read Pooh's words.

After reading the vicious letter, in which Pooh threatened Tahj's life and called her every chickenhead and stank whore name in the book, Tahj tossed the letter next to the stack of hundred-dollar bills that were sitting on the odd-shaped glass living room table that probably cost more than the average person's entire living room set. She had seen it in a magazine at the spot where she got her massages and facials. She knew nobody's crib would be rockin' nothing like that, so she just had to have it. She had to have it so bad that she had Lee get it shipped all the way from the Mediterranean for her. Fuck wit' dat!

Taking a pull from a blunt and then passing it onto Shea, Tahj said, "Fuck that mark-ass clown." Tahj leaned over and picked up the bottle of red OPI nail polish and started to polish her toes. "I don't know what done crawled up in his ass. He must have dropped the soap again."

The girls burst out laughing. Their laughter floated through the house and echoed off the high cathedral ceilings.

"Girl, you *niggnorant*," Shea said as she finished off the blunt. She stood up from the square retro burnt-orange sofa and placed it in the ashtray. She then walked over to the full bar and helped herself to a glass of Rémy on the rocks.

"Can you believe this muthafucka talkin' all that rah-rah shit?" Tahj said.

"Hell, yeah, I can believe it," Shea answered. "What did you think Pooh was gon' say when he found out how you was out here livin'? He probably feels like Snoop Dogg did in the movie *Baby Boy*. You let Jody take over your life and shit."

"Bitch, you crazy." Tahj chuckled. "That nigga don't know how I'm really livin'."

"No, you da one crazy. He ain't get life, you know. That nigga gettin' out one day, if you haven't forgot," Shea said, sitting back down on the couch.

Tahj wasn't studying Shea's comments. Just as long as she was up under Lee's wing she was untouchable, so Tahj didn't worry about Pooh's jailhouse threats. She finished up her last coat of polish and started to blow on her toes.

"How much time he get, anyway?" Shea asked.

"Muthafucka got something like twenty-five years or some shit," Tahj said, sucking her teeth. "Talking about beatin' my ass when he get out. That nigga gon' be using a walker and shit to get around by the time he hit them bricks again."

"Oooh, you wrong for that," Shea said.

"Get me a glass of orange juice," Tahj ordered Shea, who immediately filled the request.

"Damn, Pooh got twenty-five years and shit?" Shea said with a sigh. "That's like forever. No wonder you sittin' around like Bone Crusher, never scared and shit. He ain't gon' be kickin' yo ass doing twenty-five years. I know dat nigga's mind is all fucked-up."

"Yeah. I'm sure it is," Tahj said as a devilish grin came across her face. "Hand me that notepad in the kitchen by the phone. Bring me the pen, too."

"Damn, ho," Shea huffed. "Do I look like Florence the maid?"

Tahj gave Shea a piercing look. *This raggedy wannabe-me ho sittin' on my shit that cost more than her whole goddamn Section Eight town house,* Tahj thought. *She smokin' my shit and drinkin' my shit. Bitch lucky I don't ask her to come over and blow my muthafuckin' toes like I had Keisha doing last week. I thought these hos recognized that by now.*

"Why you lookin' all serious?" Shea said, hiding the slight fear that was creeping up on her. "Girl, you know I was just playing." Off she went, returning with the notepad and a pen.

"Good girl," Tahj said, taking the contents out of Shea's hand.

"What you 'bout to write?" Shea inquired as she sipped on her drink.

"I'm gonna write his ass a letter right back and take it to his boy to mail to him. I'm 'bout to let his bitch ass have it. I'm gonna be the last bitch he ever sits down to write some ol' fucked-up letter to again." Tahj shot off an evil chuckle.

Shea shook her head. "Don't do that, Tahj," Shea said. "Girl, just ignore him."

"No, fuck that," Tahj snapped, hating the fact that Shea was trying to piss on her parade. "I ain't thinking about him. He old news. That nigga always thought that just because he was holdin' big paper he could treat people any way he wanted to. Look at him now. Fuck that nigga. It's my turn to floss on his ass now. How about that?"

As Tahj started writing, Shea just shrugged her shoulders. *Fuck it.* What did she care if Tahj pissed that nigga off? If that ho didn't know that a nigga with Pooh's status could reach out and touch a ho even from behind bars, that was her own stupidity. Shea didn't really give a fuck about Tahj's letter hurtin' Pooh's feelings or nothing. She didn't really give a fuck about that at all. She just didn't want to see Tahj cut off the coattail she'd been able to ride on. Tahj had been unordinarily quite friendly with the stash Pooh had left behind for her. She didn't want to see her spontaneous shopping sprees, free trips to the spa, and free Coach bags come to an end. Other than that, what did she care?

CHAPTER FOUR
DEFINITION OF HUSTLIN'

"Hustlin' ain't limited to one craft," Tahj said to Shea as the two of them headed for the exit of the Red Lobster restaurant. They had just eaten a seafood feast as well as enjoyed a couple of margaritas. The meal was delicious and on point, but it was the worst meal they had ever eaten, let Tahj tell it. At least, that was what she had the manager convinced of, anyway.

She complained about every little thing that she could think of in order to get free food. She complained that the Cheddar Bay Biscuits were too cold, there was too much salt around the rim of the margarita glass, the meal took too long to be served, and that she had ordered vinaigrette dressing for her salad instead of the Italian dressing that was on it.

By the end of their meal, Tahj demanded to speak with the manager, relaying the complaints she had been making all evening long. When all was said and done, the manager ripped the bill up and gave both Shea and Tahj a free dessert on top of that. This was everything Tahj expected when she had planned her little act before she even entered the restaurant. Of course, Tahj had more than enough money to cover the bill, but she'd rather keep her money in her pocket, where it belonged. Couldn't stack the loot if you were spending it, so finding a way to get what you wanted for free was a hustle in itself.

"I just can't believe your ass hustled a free meal," Shea said with a smile, shaking her head while admiring Tahj's skills.

Tahj stopped in her tracks. "Correction, bitch, two meals," Tahj bragged as she continued her strut.

"Oh, my fault. I mean two meals, bit—" Shea said, catching herself, almost letting the word *bitch* fall off of her tongue.

The last time Shea had called Tahj a bitch, even though it was jokingly, the way Tahj called her one, Tahj mopped up the floor with her ass. Tahj hadn't gotten into many fights as a kid, but she had witnessed a couple of her older siblings beat enough asses to know how it was done.

Even though Tahj always called her girlfriends *bitch* or *ho,* their calling her a bitch was off-limits. The first and only time Tahj had ever been called a bitch was by her own mother, and those words cut like a knife. That night her mother had said plenty of nasty things to her, but that particular word played over and over in Tahj's head, sometimes waking her from her sleep. So Tahj was sensitive when it came to the B-word. She didn't give a fuck who was saying it—Tupac, Ja Rule, Lil' Kim, or whoever. That word was like nails down a chalkboard to her.

"Anyway," Tahj said. "Don't sleep on the hustle game. That's muthafuckas' problems. Everybody wanna label they ass as a hustla but don't wanna do but one goddamn thing to make a come-up. Fuck that . . . lazy bastards. Everything you goddamn do in life should be a hustle. Everything!"

"I hear you," Shea agreed.

"Here," Tahj said, digging down in her Gucci purse and handing Shea the keys to her car. It was a nice li'l Gucci purse that Lee had bought her. Well, actually he had bought her one a size up, but Tahj took it back to the store, traded it for a smaller version, and kept the difference. "Go pull my car around. I'm too stuffed to even walk to it."

Without hesitating Shea followed Tahj's orders, taking the keys, then heading to the rear parking lot, where they had been forced to park due to the Saturday-night crowd.

Tahj walked over and sat on one of the benches while Shea went and got the car. As she sat there rubbing her stomach, a couple walking through the parking lot heading for the door caught her attention. The girl was laughing and saying something to the guy she was with. It was dark, and Tahj didn't want to squint and stare, but she knew she recognized the girl's voice and was trying to figure out who it was.

She turned her head away as the couple made their way up to the door. She didn't want them to think she was muggin' them or anything. The girl stood and waited for the guy she was with to open the door for her, and that was when Tahj decided to get a better look at them.

When Tahj turned around to put a face with the familiar voice, she saw Shondell, a hairstylist she went to sometimes at a shop called Cute Cutz. Shondell was there with a date, a tall, dark, fine-ass brotha with a bald head and a goatee. Tahj recognized him as well. He was Kel, the boyfriend of Lisa, one of the other stylists at Cute Cutz. He had come into the shop a couple of times to drop off some money for Lisa, bring her food, or whatnot. What was even worse was that Shondell was supposed to be Lisa's girl—for real, for real girl.

Tahj couldn't believe her eyes. *Scandalous bitch*, Tahj thought as a smile crept across her face. *I think I like her now more than ever.* Tahj didn't draw attention to herself. That was nothing new, though. If muthafuckas couldn't see her coming, they couldn't prepare for what she was bringin' to the game.

Shondell and Kel went off to enjoy their secret meal together as Shea drove up in the car. A wicked grin formed on Tahj's lips as she stood up, walked over to the car, and got in.

"Why you looking all like the cat who just ate the bird?" Shea said.

"Oh, nothing," Tahj said devilishly. "I was just thinking how I can't wait to go get my hair done Tuesday. Lee will be back in town by then, and I want to get an entire new look. I'm talking perm, sew-in weave, color, cut, eyebrow wax, the works!"

"Girl, that's doing too much," Shea said. "All that gon' cost you an arm and a leg, and here you didn't even want to spend money on shrimp."

Tahj once again grinned. "But, oh, my friend, I got a feeling it ain't gon' cost me a dime."

"Oh, Lord," Shea said with a sigh. "She's at it again."

"You know how I do. Home, James," Tahj said, pointing, ordering Shea to drive home. "By the way, it's canary."

"Huh?" Shea said with a puzzled look on her face.

"It's the cat who swallowed the canary, not bird," Tahj said. "And let's just say that come Tuesday morning, while I'm sitting in the chair at the shop getting my new attitude, I'm going to be coughing up feathers."

The girls giggled as they drove off.

Come Monday, Tahj called Shondell on her cell to set up an appointment for Tuesday. Shondell sounded more than excited to give Tahj a complete makeover. All she could think about when Tahj gave her a list of all the services she wanted done was, *Ching-ching!* Tahj even asked Shondell if she would go get the hair weave for her, because she had never shopped for one before. Shondell agreed, assuming Tahj was going to pay her back for it. Bright and early on Tuesday morning, Tahj showed up at Cute Cutz.

"Hey, girl," Shondell said to Tahj upon her entrance into the shop. Tahj could tell already that Shondell was about to lay out the red carpet for her. Shondell even came over and gave her a hug.

Damn, did this bitch see me spot her at Red Lobster and now she trying to play up to me? Tahj thought. She couldn't quite read Shondell yet. She didn't know if she was excited about the gig or if she was trying to play nice in order for Tahj to keep her mouth shut about her and Kel. *But I know she didn't see me*, Tahj thought. *Fuck it. Let me just play this bitch close and roll wit' it and see how this here plays out.*

"Can I get you something to drink?" Shondell asked. "Coffee, water, soda, or something?"

"I'll take a soda," Tahj said, heading for Shondell's chair. "Hey, Lisa," she said, passing her along the way. "What's up, Tah-Tah?" she said to another stylist.

"Did you have a good weekend?" Lisa asked her, being personable and making conversation. Lisa was genuinely nice, just stupid as hell, in Tahj's opinion. *Hell, you ought to be able to smell your best friend's pussy on your man's breath,* Tahj thought.

"Here you go, ma," Shondell said, handing Tahj a can of soda. Shondell was your typical Shanaynay-lookin' stylist. She had braided extensions in her hair, long-ass acrylic nails, and wore stacks or stilettos to do hair in. Bitch was paid, though. "Now, you know I ain't gon' perm *and* color your hair. Honey child, I'd be sweeping your shit up off the floor. But what I did do was buy you some weave with blond streaks in it."

"Okay," Tahj said, positioning herself in the chair as Shondell started to put a plastic cap on her.

Six hours later, Tahj didn't even look like the same girl who had walked through the shop's door. Shondell had relaxed and deep-conditioned her hair. She clipped her ends and braided strands around her head so that she could sew the weave to it. Lastly, she sewed in the weave, cut it, and styled it.

"Oh, my God," Tahj said, spinning the chair around to look at herself in the mirror. "Shondell. Oh, my God. It looks great."

"Thank you, darling," she said, proud of her skills as she removed the smock from Tahj. "I'm glad you like it. Now you won't mind paying me the three hundred dollars."

Tahj started laughing. "Girl, you so crazy," Tahj said, getting up from the chair. "Remember, I already paid you."

There were no words to describe the look that came across Shondell's face. She put her hands on her hips and was getting ready to say something before Tahj jumped in.

"Remember? I gave you the money Saturday at Red Lobster," Tahj said, just as serious as a heart attack. "Saturday at Red Lobster, when I saw you there with your date."

By now Tahj was giving her the look, and it didn't take long for Shondell to understand the words behind it.

"Oh, yeah," Shondell said in a faded tone. "Saturday." She swallowed. "Red Lobster. Me and my date."

"Yeah, you and your date," Tahj reiterated.

"I almost forgot that I even saw you there," Shondell said, trying to maintain her composure. She damn sure hadn't prepared herself for this.

"Well, I'll never forget," Tahj said, glaring into Shondell's eyes.

"I'm sure you won't," Shondell said, now pissed that she had just laid Tahj's shit out, half doing her other customer's hair in between doing Tahj's, and now wasn't getting paid one red cent. But what could she do? Tahj had her right where she wanted her—on the bottom with her foot on Shondell's neck.

"All right, then, girl," Tahj said as she tapped Shondell on the shoulder. "I'll call you in a couple weeks. I don't know how long I'm going to be able to stand all this hair," Tahj said, running her fingers through her straight, mid-back-length hair. "I might have to have you take it out."

Shondell's eyes watered. She could have spit fire, she was so heated. Instead, she took a deep breath, swallowed, and said, "Okay, then, girl. You have a good one."

Tahj winked at her and headed out of the shop. Once she got into her car, she couldn't help but laugh. After laughing so hard that tears filled her eyes, she started up her engine. As she pulled off, she thought, *That was too damn funny. Bet that ho will think twice before she lets somebody else's man wine and dine her ass.*

But being the true hustla she was, Tahj had already started

thinking up ways to get back at Shondell's accomplice. Kel wasn't getting off that easy. One day Tahj would figure out a way to hustle his ass, too.

In just a matter of months, Tahj was going through men like Jennifer Lopez. Unlike Jennifer, though, who was seeking the fairy-tale, happily-ever-after relationship, Tahj was seeking a nest egg. All she needed to get by was a couple of sugar daddies to cure her sweet tooth. She was young and had her whole life ahead of her. She knew her lifestyle wasn't a moral one and that it wasn't something she could do forever—nor did she want to—but like the stripper who was only going to slide her pussy down the pole just long enough to pay her way through college, it was a profitable one.

"Come on, baby, just let me eat your pussy," Leonard begged Tahj as they parked in front of her house. Lee was out of town. He had been gone for three days and was due back that night. Tahj knew he had probably been craving her while he was gone, so she had to keep it fresh and tight for him.

So when Leonard called her the night before on her cell phone to let her know that he would be in town the next day, she knew it wasn't going to be a big payday, since she wasn't going to fuck him.

Tahj had hooked up with Leonard once before. He lived in Dayton, Ohio, but had people in Cleveland, so he shot through town here and there. A month earlier Tahj had met him at a gas station. He was pushin' a bumblebee-yellow-and-black, tricked-out Hummer H2. The nigga had more gems in his mouth than Mike Jones. Tahj knew off the bat that he wasn't no baller, that he was a man about business who just liked to come out and play every now and then. He didn't have that *it* factor that a baller had. He didn't have the stance or swagger that Tahj could now detect a mile away.

It turned out that Leonard owned a graphics design company. He had started the business by himself right after he graduated college, and now he had a partner and seven permanent full-time employees. He also had three college interns working for him. He was a different class of man, and Tahj liked that about him. She found herself hanging on to his every word. Most niggas only talked about weight they had moved or niggas they had put to sleep, but Leonard actually had interesting conversation. But no matter what a nigga had to say during dinner, at the end of the night they all ending up saying the same thing, begging for some pussy.

Tonight Tahj had enjoyed dinner with Leonard, where she let her mouthpiece get a couple grand out of him. She told him that she was interested in what he did for a living and wanted to start taking classes at the local community college to learn how to do what he did. After several drinks and several bats of Tahj's eyes, he was forking over the money to the girl sitting across the table from him who he thought would become his prodigy.

After dinner Leonard offered to get a suite so that the two of them could chill, but Tahj declined. But that didn't keep him from begging her the entire ride to her house. Once he realized that taking Tahj back to a hotel for a heated night of sexual pleasure wasn't on the menu, he resorted to begging her to allow him to eat her out. He knew he gave good head. He had made many a woman quiver. He felt that getting Tahj all hot and bothered with his tongue action would land him some pussy in the end.

"Come on, baby," Leonard begged one final time as they pulled up in front of Tahj's house. "Just let me taste you."

"No, no, my brotha," Tahj said. "I know how that goes. If I let you eat my pussy, then you gonna expect me to suck your dick or let you fuck me. Thanks, but no thanks. I'm straight on that shit."

Tahj grabbed the handle to open the car door. Leonard snatched her arm.

"Muthafucka, if you don't get your hands off of me . . ." Tahj said through gritted teeth as her heart began to race. She didn't know what this nigga was about to try to do, but damn, he could have his money back. Two thousand dollars wasn't worth getting her pussy stole on.

Leonard apologetically released her arm. "I'm sorry, baby. But I'm serious. Just let me taste you. That's all I want. You won't regret it."

Tahj sat and thought for a minute, trying to come up with a lie. "Naw, it's late, and I gotta go to work tomorrow."

"Fuck work! What they pay you? I got you," Leonard said as he pulled out a wad of cash and started peeling bills off into Tahj's lap. Tahj felt like she was in Vegas and had just hit the jackpot.

This desperate prick, Tahj thought as she stared at Leonard, and couldn't help but laugh at how much he reminded her of the big, black, buff, desperate dude in the movie *White Chicks.*

Tahj contemplated as bills filled her lap. She waited until it looked as though Leonard had reached his spending limit before giving in.

"You really wanna taste me that much?" Tahj said seductively.

"Damn, skippy," he said, leaning in, licking his lips.

Tahj thought for another moment as she collected the money from her lap. "Okay, then," she said, shoving the money down into her Prada bag, which she thought was ugly, but had bought for the name. "Eat up!"

Leonard groaned as he roughly grabbed Tahj's knees and turned her toward him. She leaned her back against the door as Leonard yanked off her hot-pink thong, put her legs over his shoulders, and immediately went to work. Right off the bat Tahj began squirming. Leonard's tongue skills were unbelievable. His tongue felt as long as a dick thrashing in and out of her pussy. After only seconds of Leonard's hot, steamy breath and soft tongue plucking at Tahj's clit, causing her head to fall back against the window, she spurted down his throat. That made Leonard go to work even more. Tahj was all caught up in the feeling until her cell phone started ringing. She reached for her purse.

"Baby, fuck that phone," Leonard pleaded, still licking.

"Umm, I gotta answer it," Tahj moaned. "It might be my dude."

No, this ho didn't, Leonard thought. He wanted to pause and let her words register, but he didn't want her to think he was some rudy-poo Negro sprung over no young chick.

"Hello," Tahj said into the phone, her voice dragging, as she was in complete feel-good mode, high off of Leonard's flickering tongue against her clit.

"What's up, li'l mama?" Lee said into the phone.

"Oh, hey, baby," Tahj said slowly.

Leonard knew that she was talking to a dude, but that only motivated him to go to work even harder.

"Was you asleep?" Lee asked, noticing Tahj's moaning slur.

"No, I'm fine. What's up?"

"I'm heading back to the city," Lee said. "It's gon' be a couple hours, but I wanted to know if you needed anything. You want me to stop and get you something to eat?"

"No, I'm good," Tahj replied. That was just like Lee. He never walked through the door without checking first to see if his woman needed anything. "Yeah, as a matter of fact. Stop and get me some White Castles. I want four cheese Castles, an onion chip, and red pop. Can you do that for me, baby?"

"Anything for you," Lee said sincerely.

"All right then. I'll see you later on," Tahj said, jerking as Leonard hit that spot. "I'll be waiting on you."

Lee smiled, 'cause he knew what time it was. His baby knew how to take care of him. She never made excuses about headaches, that time of the month, or that she was tired. She treated loving from her man as if wasn't nothing better in the world than his lovin'. "I love you," Lee said.

"I love you, too," Tahj said as Leonard sucked on her clit like he was trying to inhale it.

"By the way, why you ain't answer the home phone?"

Tahj's eyes got wide. She had to be quick on her feet. " 'Cause I left the cordless off the charger downstairs and I didn't feel like running down there when I heard it ringing." Quickly changing the subject, Tahj said, "Baby, wait till you see what I bought you when I went shopping. I bought me some of the cutest stuff, too, but you are going to absolutely love what I bought you." Tahj knew damn well she had taken the three thousand dollars Lee had given her to go shopping, spent a hundred on a pair of pajamas for him, and had deposited the rest into her bank account.

"That's my baby," Lee said. "Always looking out for me."

"You know it," Tahj said, thrusting her pussy into Leonard's mouth.

"Well, I'll see you in a bit. Peace out."

"Peace," Tahj said, hanging up the phone and turning her attention back to Leonard, who was looking up at her as he plunged his tongue in and out of her.

"You love that nigga, huh?" he asked. "But do he make you feel like this? Can he do this shit right here?"

Leonard cupped Tahj's ass cheeks in the palm of his hands and pulled her to his face as he went crazy in her stuff. He acted as if he were at a watermelon-eating contest with Tahj's pussy. Tahj couldn't even control herself as she started to explode. She didn't know if she was cummin' or pissin'.

"Oh, shit," Tahj roared. "Oh, shit! Damn."

"Um, hmm. Um, hmm," Leonard said, still eating Tahj, but managing to pull his dick out of his pants and start stroking it. "Oh, yeah, baby. Oh, yeah."

Tahj grabbed Leonard's head and began ramming it into her pussy, making his mouth thrash harder and harder against her clit. "Oh, Leonard," she caught herself yelling. *No, this nigga didn't make me scream out his name*, she thought as she gripped his head and prepared to cum again.

"Ummm. Ummm. Ummm," he moaned as he jacked off while eating her pussy.

"Oh, yeah," Tahj said, closing her eyes. "Oh, yeah. Oh, shit!" she shouted as she exploded once again down Leonard's throat.

"Oh, yeah, baby. Oh, yeah," Leonard said as he threw his head back and proceeded to nut in his hand. He sat there trembling as he jerked.

Tahj was speechless. No one had ever made her feel that good—ever. Neither a tongue nor a dick had pleased her the way Leonard had. It was a feeling she wanted the world to know about.

"Damn, baby," Tahj moaned. "That shit was off the hook."

"Umm, you taste so good," Leonard said, licking his lips. "Just like I knew you would."

"Baby, I hope you don't mind," Tahj said, "but I got to call my girl up and tell her about this."

Leonard smiled at Tahj's cute remark—until she actually got her phone out and started dialing.

"Hey, Keisha," Tahj said into her cell phone. "Girl, you ain't gon' believe the way this nigga just ate my pussy out. This dude you was telling me about ain't got shit on him. Girl, I'm telling you. But I can't just tell you about it; you gotta shoot over my way and come feel it for yourself."

Just then Tahj put her hand over the phone and whispered to Leonard, "You don't mind, do you?"

Leonard's mouth dropped open. He couldn't believe his ears. He just sat there staring at Tahj. He couldn't begin to muster up the words to respond to her query.

Tahj took Leonard's silence as a yes. "Good," she said, turning her attention back to her phone conversation with Keisha. "Girl, we parked out in front of my house in a yellow Hummer. Hurry up," Tahj said excitedly. Tahj hung up her cell phone and turned to Leonard, who was still sitting there in shock. She smiled at him, then said, "Good lookin' out," as she waited for Keisha to show up and get her pussy ate, too.

CHAPTER FIVE
RETARD

It had been four days since Lee had been back in town. He hadn't even talked of heading back out again. This was the longest spell he had stayed home in a while. He normally did that only when there was some serious business he had to take care of at home. This put a halt to Tahj's running the streets and hanging out with her ghetto girls, but she enjoyed being with Lee all the same.

He thought that Tahj was probably tired of sitting in the house, so he gave her money to go to the spa to get her out. Of course, Tahj didn't go to no damn spa. She could think of better ways to use that money someday, so instead she bought a six-pack of Smirnoff Apple Twist and hung out with Shea and Keisha over at Shea's house. After chillin' with them for a couple of hours, she headed back to her house. On her way home she stopped off and bought a bottle of massage oil. She figured she'd tell Lee it was a gift she bought for him at the spa.

"Baby, I'm home," Tahj yelled as she walked in the door. She couldn't help but notice the nice set of Louis Vuitton luggage that was sitting in the foyer.

Lee was on the couch. He had just finished doing a line when Tahj came in the door.

"Baby, I bought you something back from the spa," Tahj said, as if she were singing her words. Lee didn't seem to get excited like he usually did. As a matter of fact, he remained emotionless. "Did you hear what I said? I bought you something."

Lee looked over at Tahj, examining her. Lately he hadn't just sat back and taken in the girl he was sharing his bed with. She was the same girl he had picked up off the curb, but at the same time, he could see where she had very much changed. Unfortunately, it wasn't for the better. "See that right there?" Lee said, pointing to the luggage. "I bought you something, too. I was going to wait and give it to you on your birthday." Lee picked up the mirror that was on the table, snorted a line, then put the mirror back down. "But that was before I found out everything." He paused, sniffing and rubbing his nose.

Tahj stood there, dumbfounded, not knowing what the fuck was going on.

"Lee, baby, what are you tal—"

"I even packed up all the clothes and shit I've bought you," he said, cutting her off. "I ain't trippin'. You can have it all. Ain't gon' fit the next broad nohow. I normally prefer them a little thicker than you. But even so, you can have the shit. I gave it to you, so it's yours. See, I ain't one of them punk-ass niggas you probably be out there fuckin' with that will buy a bitch shit, trickin' and shit. But just as soon as they find out she sucking some other nigga's dick they want her to check that shit in. Naw, I'ma let you have it all, 'cause that's just the type of cool muthafucka I am. Now take all that expensive shit I done bought your stank ass and get the fuck out, beyatch!"

Tahj's heart dropped as her eyes began to water. Suddenly she was experiencing that same feeling again—it was that feeling she remembered all too well, the one that overcame her the night her mother had put her out onto the streets. Tahj thought that her mother calling her a bitch hurt, but for some reason it hurt even more when Lee said it. Her mother had probably let her anger get the best of her when she called her daughter out of her name. But Lee, that nigga said it like he meant that shit.

"I hear you got a slick-ass mouth," Lee said. "They say you can put words together real good. What's the matter? Ain't got shit to say now?"

In all actuality, there was so much that Tahj wanted to say, but she had to collect herself. If she had opened her mouth to talk right then she would probably have burst into tears. So instead, she swallowed, took a deep breath, and then began to speak.

"Baby, I don't know what's going on or who you been talking to, but I lov—"

"Bitch, please," Lee said, holding up his hand to shut her up. "Like that broad Michel'le used to sing back in the day, 'No More Lies.' Take heed to that." Lee threw his head back on the couch and allowed the coke to drip from his nose down his throat.

"Lee, I'm not lying. If you'd just let me—"

"Explain. . . . Is that what you're going to say?" Lee laughed as he stood up off of the couch and started walking toward Tahj. "No need to explain. I know everything. I know about the niggas; hell, I even heard there were a couple of chicks. Wasn't I good enough for you, baby? I mean not the dick, 'cause I ain't jealous over you giving the pussy up. The head, now that's a different story. That's some shit to be jealous of, 'cause you do the damn thang when it comes to that shit, but I ain't even trippin' off of that. I'm talking about wasn't this enough for you? All of this?"

Lee raised his arms in the air and spun around in a circle.

"Baby—" Tahj made yet another futile attempt to speak.

"Shhh, shhh, shhh," Lee said, closing his eyes and putting his index finger over Tahj's lips. "Don't speak." He paused, then opened his eyes. "There wasn't nothing you could have asked for that I wouldn't have given you. Girl, you ain't never asked me for nothing and didn't get it. Hell, half the time your ass didn't even have to ask. That's what's wrong with you young girls. Y'all want everything, but y'all so busy out there trying to get it from every Tom, Dick, and Harry that you don't even realize that you could have gotten it all in the first place from Tom. From just one source." Tahj had tears flowing down her cheeks. Lee rubbed her chin with his finger. "Baby, I was your source."

Lee walked away, and Tahj started behind him. Once again she found herself in a position with nowhere to go, only this time she was going to fight for her warm bed. Lee was right: She was good at using her mouthpiece. She had talked her way in and out of plenty. She had smooth-talked some of the best; now it was time to really put her skills to work. Fuck what Lee heard; she would make her words more convincing than the words of whoever decided to run their mouth about her.

"I'm sorry," Tahj said. "I don't know what you've heard or who you've heard it from, but I'm sure I can explain. It's probably just somebody who's jealous—who's jealous of you, who's jealous of me, hell, who's jealous of us. I know how muthafuckers out there are, Lee."

After the first sentence, Lee paid Tahj not a lick of mind. He allowed her to ramble on as he walked over to the bar and began fixing himself a drink. After taking a sip, Lee picked up a remote that controlled the entertainment center. All of a sudden Tahj's bare ass covered all sixty inches of the big-screen television. Seeing herself on the screen put a halt to Tahj's words. Lee would rewind and fast forward for her. Tahj was either fucking or getting fucked. She was sucking or getting sucked. He even had footage of her and Leonard parked in front of the house.

"You know, when I got all this equipment and shit, I got it to watch out for all those grimy muthafuckas out there who don't want a nigga to have shit. I got it for the police. Hell, I got it just to have peace of mind, you know? A nigga need a little security. But, baby girl, I never thought I'd need it for the woman I share my bed with. Or, I guess I should say the girl I share my bed with." Lee took a deep breath, took a swig of his drink, then continued. "I knew you was young, and that was cool. You wasn't street-bred. You didn't know shit about the streets—evidently not, or else you would have known that a nigga of my stature would have eyes in and around all his shit. But that's what I liked about you. That's what made me think it was cool to take you in and shit. I deal with street bitches all the time, and that's just where they belong—in the street. But you was different. When I brought you into my home, I made it ours, because I felt assured that you were different, that there wasn't nothing street about you. But come to find out, you the muthafuckin' black shit they pave the streets with." Lee chuckled.

"It's not like that, Lee, and you know it," Tahj said. There wasn't too much she could say, though. She had been caught on tape like a fuckin' talk-show guest. She knew she was slick and had used her tongue to hustle a lot of shit, but she didn't know if she could grab hold of her G-string and pull her ass up out of this one. But anything was worth a try. Perhaps she would surprise herself. "I've done some fucked-up shit. I do know that much. But, baby, I love you, and you love me, too. You must, because if you been watching me like that, then why did you allow me to stay around this long? I know why. Because you love me and you know I love you, too, and I'd never intentionally do anything to hurt you."

"You didn't think muthafuckas up in my house, probably in my bed, drinking and eating up my shit while they fuckin' my woman, would hurt me? All of this while I'm out grindin', trying to keep shit tight, and you can't even keep your pussy tight for me. I should have left your ass on the curb where I found you. You ain't no better than your mama."

Tahj immediately charged Lee, swinging on him, scratching and clawing until he was able to restrain her by the wrists.

"Fuck you!" Tahj yelled. "Fuck you! I'm nothing like her. Nothing like my mother."

Lee just shook his head and smiled. "Yeah, you're right. You ain't like your mother." He paused. "You're worse. And I don't know why I didn't put your ass out sooner. I guess I just wanted to give you a chance. I guess I was looking for a reason. But that's the reason right there, 'cause you just like your sorry-ass mama."

Tahj angrily tried to release her hands from Lee's grip, and when that wouldn't work she spit in his face. Again Lee laughed.

"Get out," he said, releasing her arms. "Get the fuck out!" he shouted, his voice now a complete rage. "Zon, help Ms. Cortez with her bags, please."

Just then a man came from out of the kitchen. He was dressed in a nice suit with a pair of gaiters, a hat with a feather on the side, and sunglasses. He looked familiar, but with the sunglasses on Tahj couldn't place him.

"It would be my pleasure," the man said as he pushed up the brim of his hat and removed his sunglasses. Tahj's mouth dropped when she realized that it was Ray, the retard.

"Ray?" Tahj said with a confused look on her face. "Wha . . . what's going on?" she stammered.

Zon and Lee couldn't help but chuckle at the shocked expression on Tahj's face.

"Well, hello, there, Miss Lady," Zon said, speaking as clear as ever. "Oh, and the name is Rayzon, but you can still call me Ray if you'd like. I'll take your bags to your car." Zon winked at Tahj, put his sunglasses back on, and pulled his hat down as he proceeded to carry her luggage out to her car.

Tahj just stood there. She had been caught for sure, and there was no talking her way out of shit. She just looked up at Lee, shook her head, and smirked. Wasn't no use trippin'. What was done was done. The good thing about it, though, was that there was a lesson behind it all. Tahj learned that the next time, like Shannon Holmes's book said, she'd have to *B-More Careful!*

Getting thrown out by Lee hurt Tahj. She'd known that day would eventually come, but she had no idea it would be so soon. For some reason, she'd thought that it would be because of some ol' dirty shit Lee had done to her. For the first time in her life, Tahj didn't feel good about the shit she had done. Never truly giving her and Lee an honest-to-God chance might have been one of her biggest mistakes ever. By her preparing for the worst, the worst came. Perhaps she should have prepared for the best. But it was too late to worry about it now. Her bed had been made. Hell, she didn't do so bad. She had a lot of nice shit, a car, and money in the bank.

With her Louis Vuitton luggage piled up in her car and her "the day will come" account, Tahj put the car in drive and slowly drove off. She didn't have any particular destination in mind, but she knew wherever she ended up, it would be on top.

FINAL INNING . . .

A WORD FROM WAHIDA CLARK

WHEN THE DUST SETTLES

After my girl Nikki and the sistas on her team put it down in this book, are you still thinking about, dreaming about, and grooming yourselves for the game? Before you go putting yourself out there, know this: The game doesn't play fair, and the majority of you players end up *losing*. *Losing* to a busta-ass nigga who leaves you holding the dope, then swears on the Holy Bible in front of a judge that it was all yours. *Losing* to the stripper's fantasy: *I'm hot. I'ma work this body just long enough to get on my feet, save for college, get me a car, blah, blah, blah. . . .* Three to five years later you still gettin' thigh burns from slidin' down the pole. And what? You're no longer hot, and that new young bitch done stole your spot in the VIP room. *Losing* to snaggin' that big balla shot caller or any dude with lonnng dough: He's gonna take care of you for the rest of your life. You chase, you chase, you chase, and chase. You go through one, then another and another, just to discover that you were chasing an illusion. Temporary happiness and satisfaction. *Losing* to gettin' that fast money . . . fast! By any means necessary.

The bottom line is . . . do *you*! Who better than yourself can take care of you? Educate you? Better you? Do *you* and you'll find that everything you're seeking will come to you in abundance! I'm not trying to put any of my sisters down, because I know how it is. I'm doing a ten-year bid as we speak. Some of you get out of the game before the game gets you, but the majority of us don't.

The game sits back and smiles at the sistas who are locked down, the chicks whose bodies are no longer eye candy at the gentlemen's club. The game smiles and lusts after the sista who was determined to snag that balla. But when she looks up, the years have run by and she's still looking, all alone, with nothing to fall back on. The game drools over the sistas chasing that fast money. Running credit card, bank, and checkbook scams. Again, it's all an illusion.

I hope the reader appreciates the message in each of these stories and knows that the game is just that—a game. An illusion that is rarely won by the opponent.

Stay up and focused on reality!

Bis-Mi-Illah.

—Wahida Clark, Queen of Thug Love Fiction
   Author of *Thugs and the Women Who Love Them*
   Every Thug Needs a Lady
   Payback Is a Mutha

ACKNOWLEDGMENTS

LaKesa Cox: First and foremost, I would like to thank God for ALL that he has done and will continue to do for me. Thanks to my hubby, Mike, for all the support and to my three kids who are the motivation behind all that I do. Thanks to my mom and also to my second mom, Patricia and Joan, respectively. Last but not least, to Ms. Nikki Turner, my homegirl who has graciously put her stamp on the world in this street lit game, I appreciate you and sincerely thank you for the opportunity! God bless!

Chunichi: As always, I would like to thank God for blessing me with such a wonderful talent. To my fans, thanks for your support; without you there's no me! To my homegirl, my literary big sis, my agent, Nikki Turner, thanks for giving me so many opportunities to shine. To my parents and my family, you're my inspiration. To my husband, thanks for being my ultimate support. To my friends, keep the drama coming—it makes for great material. To the baby mothers holding it down, do your damn thang! This one's for y'all. And last but not least, thanks to the streets, you made this possible! The streets have given me wisdom that no Ivy League school or college textbook could have ever given. To anybody I forgot . . . blame Nikki Turner for giving me only one paragraph for my acknowledgments!

Meisha Holmes: I'd like to thank God for his countless blessings. Thank you, Nikki Turner, for reaching out to me so I could be a part of this *hot* project! Thanks to Nancy Flowers for her recommendation, my daughter, Kayla Lyric, for keeping me focused, and the rest of my family and friends for encouraging me to keep on writing. Final thanks go out to all the readers who purchased my novel *Brooklyn Jewelry Exchange,* I appreciate you spreading the word—and the prequel will be coming soon!

TYSHA: First and foremost, I give thanks to God for each blessing I receive. I would like to thank my husband, Vincent, for all the love, support, protection, and encouragement he gives me every day. Mommy, thank you for believing in me and being the strong woman you are. To my sister Tracey and brother Jae-Jay, no big sister could love you more than I do. Y'all are in my heart. To the rest of my family, there are far too many to name. I love you all and thank you for supporting my dreams. I give a heartfelt thanks to both Nikki Turner and JOY. I could not have asked for better mentors in this business. Finally, I dedicate this work to my grandparents, John and Ruby Hill. Thanks to your love and guidance, I know for sure that I can do anything I choose in life.

JOY: I would like to acknowledge all of the many readers who have supported my JOY projects, both full-length novels and anthology contributions. What an amazing literary ride it has been. Although I have answered my calling to write stories of a different nature, I do hope you will continue to keep in touch by visiting me at www.joylynnjossel.com. Peace and blessings.

PLAYER STATS

MEISHA C. HOLMES puts it down in *Street Chronicles 2,* earning her crown as the "Countess of Street Lit." But even before her appearance in *SC2,* Meisha proved she was worthy of her title with her stellar novel *Brooklyn Jewelry Exchange.*

CHUNICHI, reigning in Atlanta, Georgia, is the "Diva of Street Lit," putting it down with the most divalicious tales from the infamous *A Gangsta's Girl* and *Married to the Game* to her short story featured in *Girls from Da Hood* and her now blazing contribution to *Street Chronicles 2.*

JOY, also known as Joylynn M. Jossel, is a seasoned vet and known in the industry as the "Empress of All Trades," mastering the different literary genres, from the contemporary drama-filled chick lit she projected in her debut novel, *The Root of All Evil,* to the steamy erotica she pumped out in *An All Night Man,* and the gritty street tale she penned in *If I Ruled the World.*

LAKESA COX has self-published two drama-filled tales titled *After the Storm* and *Water in My Eyes.* In the underground literary world, LaKesa has been crowned the "Countess of Urban Drama." Ready to carry her title mainstream, she is currently seeking a book deal for her next novel.

TYSHA is a new author to the literary game. Early in 2002, a mysterious illness began attacking Tysha's body, forcing her to resign from her job and pick up an old habit of journal writing, which turned into a short story and then into a novel that will be coming to a bookstore soon!

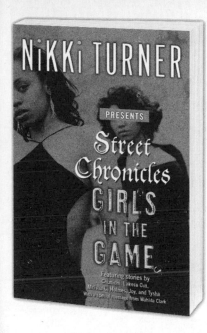
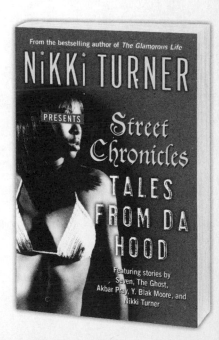

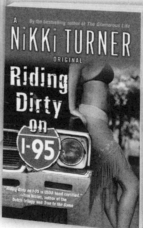
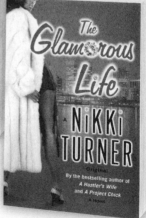